FINE
AGAIN

MICHAEL S. VASSEL

For Angie, Mom, Jason, Rob, Abbey, Jen, Jackie, Derrick, Kristen, and all my other family.

I know it hasn't always been easy; it's been fun for sure, but not always easy.

Diary: October 19

I can't believe it's been a month since I lost you.

In some ways, it feels like you've only been gone moments. In others, it feels more like a year. More like forever.

Forever is a funny word — a ridiculous word. A word we told each other like it was something tangible, something obtainable. Yet, that is what we said we would be to each other.

During these cold winds and rainy days, I sit here without you as I try to remember back to all we had and to all we had shared. And I miss it.

We missed it.

We missed what forever really meant, or what it was supposed to mean. It's the idea that our lives could remain unchanged by environment, unchanged by time. That our lives could continue on forever . . . unchanged by life.

It was a fallacy, you know. To think that environment, time, and life would not change us. Because life is change. Life is experiences, and reaction to those experiences.

And life can be cruel — so, so cruel.

All I know is, as time and life go on, that I miss you.

I miss us.

CHAPTER

1

I remember the first day we met.

And I don't mean the first time we went out. I mean the actual first time we laid our eyes on each other, and the first time we talked. The first time we smiled at each other and gave each other shy responses. I know that maybe I didn't come off as shy at first, but believe me I was.

That day started out like any other ordinary day in my life. I woke up, got ready for work, made sure my kids had what they needed for school, said goodbye to the wife, and went to work. At the time work was my job as a mechanical engineer at a materials handling company named Vector.

It was a Tuesday, just an ordinary Tuesday, and nothing special was happening at work, except for the daily rush to finish old projects and start new ones. That made it a perfect day to call my friend Bill Totes to see if he wanted to go to lunch.

Bill, a fellow engineer, worked for Raster Consulting, a company located just down the street from mine. He and I had previously worked together and had been friends for years.

I called him up around 10:30 a.m. to ask if he could escape the grind for a quick lunch. As in any business, escaping said grind was a crap shoot. Like me, he often got caught up in the minutia of conference calls or working sessions that would mess with the time table for the day.

Normally to get ahold of Bill, I had to call up Raster's main switchboard and ask for him. His company, wanting a more personalized feel, had a receptionist to answer and direct calls. Raster's receptionist, Mary Jane, and I were very familiar with each other's voices, so when I heard your voice for the first time, it threw me off.

"Raster Consulting. This is Amy. How may I help you?"

Hearing your voice, one much different from Mary Jane's sixty-something vibrato, it suddenly hit me that Bill *had* said Mary Jane was leaving for another job. But I didn't recall him saying when.

"Umm . . . Hi. Uh . . . Bill Totes please," I uttered, faltering on my words.

"May I ask who's calling?" you asked.

"Mike Samstag," I said, my voice mildly less shaky.

"One moment, please," you replied, which was followed by the familiar click one hears when being put on hold.

I remember thinking, *Whew! I made it through that,* as sweat starting to roll down my neck. Having never been much of a social type, I've always had problems speaking to others, especially women.

"This is Bill," I heard a moment later, thankfully ending the awful musak that was playing in the background.

"Hey man! The usual?"

"Sure!" Bill replied, recognizing my voice instantly. "12:05?"

"Done, and done," I responded hung up.

When I arrived at Raster, promptly at 12:05 p.m., I parked my car, entered the building, and walked toward the front desk. Again, expecting to see Mary Jane's motherly face, I stopped the moment my eyes fell upon the gorgeous woman now sitting just beyond the window.

"Can I help you?" you asked, very polite and professional.

"Ha . . . hi!" I stuttered. "Bill Totes please."

"Oh! You must be Mike. I'm Amy. It's nice to meet you."

Instantly your familiarity threw me off. I could tell, from recognizing my name and the way you looked at me, that Bill must have spoken about me. This made me way nervous, of course, because I couldn't fathom what he could have, or even would have, said about me. Like an idiot, I stood there for a minute trying to think of something to say or ask.

Before I could utter a word though, Bill appeared from around a back corner and stopped me in my tracks. "Hey Mike! Did you meet Amy?"

"Yes," I replied as I looked momentarily toward Bill.

"Oh, good!" he remarked as he opened the inner door to join me in the waiting area. "Are you ready to go?"

I turned to face you then, and managed a, "It was nice meeting you, Amy."

"It was nice meeting you too, Mike!" you replied as Bill and I turned and walked out the front door.

Once we were in my car, I looked at Bill and asked, "What was that about with Amy? It was like she knew me."

With a wry smile, Bill said, "I mentioned you were coming to pick me up for lunch."

"No," I retorted. "I mean, what did you *say* about me? It was like she *knew* me."

"I may have talked a little bit about you," Bill taunted so he could see how I would respond.

Knowing this, I narrowed my eyes at him. "Do I have to ask? What did you say about me?"

"Not much. We were talking about music, and she mentioned she liked Industrial. I told her you did too, so she wanted to know more about you is all."

"So what else did you say?"

"I just mentioned you were married and had a couple kids, and that you're a great guy, *okay?*" Bill said defensively. I continued to stare at him for a moment before shrugging my shoulders and continuing to drive.

When we got to Mel's, our usual restaurant, we worked our way past the lingering crowd and sat at the bar.

As we did on most days, Bill and I spent our lunchtime talking about work or venting to each other about crappy things others were doing to mess with our calm. But as we talked, my mind kept going back to you.

I mean, I was married and had no intention of leaving or cheating. But there was something about you that made me curious. Industrial music wasn't one of your run-of-the-mill music choices, after all. The fact that you liked it, when most cringed at hearing it, made me wonder how you became interested in it.

When I felt a good amount of time had past — the time I believed mentioning you would sound as an afterthought — I brought you up again. "So, what's Amy's story?"

"She started last week. She has a boyfriend. They've been together for a while. I believe he's a salesman."

"Anything else I should know?"

"Not that I can think of. I've only known her a week," Bill said, and then narrowed his eyes at me. "Why are you so curious?"

"I don't know," I said, in all honesty. "Maybe it's just you two talking about Industrial music. Did she say any more about it?"

"She talked about a few groups I've never heard of, so I dropped the subject," Bill said, and then changed the topic. "Are you ready to order?"

"Yeah, I'm getting the usual," I am, after all, a creature of habit.

We didn't discuss you anymore that day, although I wanted to know more. Speaking to Bill about you just felt awkward. So when we finished up, I dropped Bill off and continued on with my normal life.

The next time I saw you was about two weeks later. That day, when I contacted Bill about lunch, he asked if I would mind if a few others from his office could join us. If I remember, it was because your boss was out of town. After telling him it was fine, and secretly hoped you'd be one of the people joining.

As it happened, I was in luck. When Bill exited the building, he was followed by two fellow engineers, Keith and Dave, with you trailing behind. Bill - being the gentleman that he was - showed you to my front seat while he, Keith, and Dave piled into the back of my car.

We went to Mel's as usual, this time asking for a table for five. As we each sat, I picked the seat opposite yours in hopes that we could talk. But I, being the shy and socially inadequate person that I was, didn't know how to start the conversation. I worked out several possible opening lines in my head, but they all seemed lame. Working up the nerve, I finally just decided to start talking.

"So, Amy, I hear you like Industrial music?" I asked tentatively.

"Oh, Bill mentioned it?"

"Yes, he did. Can I ask who do you listen to?"

At this, you smiled and rattled off a bunch of names I had never heard of. I had always considered myself pretty knowledgeable when it came to different genres of music, but when it came to Industrial, you were the expert.

"Who would you say is your favorite artist?" I inquired.

"I'd say, hands down, Nine Inch Nails."

"Mine too," I said truthfully, having liked NIN since their early days in the Cleveland music scene. "In fact, I met Trent once."

You perked up at this. "You did?"

"Yep. I met him years ago when he was with the Exotic Birds. Nice guy," I added.

"That's cool!" you said with a sparkle in your eye.

The remainder of the lunch was . . . how do I describe it? Nice? But nice seems to understate how much I enjoyed our conversation about music and life. Words seem to fall short on how much I enjoyed the time we shared. The first *time* we shared together. I hated when it had to come to an end.

When we returned to your office, I remember saying goodbye to you, and I remember the cute little wave you gave. *Nice* doesn't even come close to how elated I felt. But, after all, I *was* married, so that's how I had to describe it in my mind.

As I left Raster, I resigned myself to the fact that, no matter how cute you were, or how cool you were for liking Industrial, or how pleasant our lunch had been, I couldn't do anything about it.

And, I didn't.

In the next two years, when I saw you on the occasions I picked up Bill for lunch, I tried to keep you out of my mind. Out of sight, out of mind? After all, you had a boyfriend, and I was married. And that thought process worked.

That was, until things started going downhill in my marriage, and I heard you and your boyfriend broke up.

I remember a certain day in early October, a day I drove over to pick up Bill for lunch. He was running late, so, instead of waiting in the car, I chose to wait for him in the lobby on the off chance I might get a glimpse of you. I know it sounds lame, but I wanted refresh my memory, my thoughts, of you. To have something I could carry around with me on bleak days.

You were sitting at your desk just on the other side of the sliding window, concentrating hard on some paperwork, so I felt bad disturbing you.

"Hi Amy."

"Oh, hi Mike! How are you?" you replied, shifting your focus from the paperwork to me.

"Can't complain, I guess. How are you?"

"Good, actually. I'm glad you stopped in."

When you said *glad you stopped in*, my mind started racing, questioning the meaning behind your statement.

"Oh? Why's that?"

"Because I was wondering if you've ever seen the movie *Dark City*."

I pondered the question for a moment. "No, I don't believe I have. Why do you ask?"

You straightened in your seat a little and folded your hands as if you were about to get serious. "Well, it's a really cool movie, and it's playing at the Cedar Lee Halloween night."

Pausing, your eyes moved and stared at your desk, and I could tell you were trying to build up your nerve. Straightening your composure, you cleared your throat, and then asked, "I was wondering if you had any interest in going to see it with me?"

My only thought, as my vision narrowed, was *Ho-lee-shit! Did I just get asked out on a date*? I considered this for what seemed to be minutes but in all reality was only a few seconds. Snapping out of it, I gave you the only lie I could think of in such short notice.

"I'd like that . . . but I'll have to check my calendar, though . . . I think there's a Halloween party that night I may be going to."

There was no party, of course. The only plan I had was, I was married and couldn't just go out on a date with some woman, no matter how much I was tempted.

"Is it okay if I get back to you?"

"Sure, no problem," you said, smiling. "If not, it's showing other nights too. It'd be nice to go with someone."

I wasn't sure what to think at this remark. Were you just looking for *someone* to go with or looking for a *date*? Luckily for me, I didn't have to think about it too long. Bill appeared from around the corner and signaled he was ready to leave.

"Well, it was nice talking to you!" I said as Bill joined me in the lobby.

"It was nice talking to you too! Don't forget to let me know about the movie!"

I waved in acknowledgment to you as Bill and I went out the door.

As soon as we were on the road, I told him of the conversation.

"Yeah, she broke up with her boyfriend about three months ago. She was asking about you, and I told her you might be available in the near future."

"You did *what*?" I barked.

"I told her you might be available soon," Bill replied with a wry smile. "I mean, you've been telling me for about a year now that as soon as your daughter graduates you were planning on getting a divorce."

"I know I *said* that! But, dude, that's like a year off!"

Shrugging, Bill replied, "I was just trying to do you a favor. I mean, you like her, right?"

"Yes, but . . ." I started, but didn't know what else to say.

"Listen, she's interested. You might want to speed up your timetable," Bill countered.

"Bill, it's not really an option right now. I mean, man, I'm *married*! Heather won't be out of school for another year. I just can't—"

"Okay! Okay! I thought I was doing you a favor!"

I looked at Bill kind of disgusted, really wishing I could change the situation. I knew he was trying to help. He knew the personal hell I was living through at home and was just trying to be a good friend. But I had responsibilities and couldn't just do that to my family.

Happily, we didn't discuss the topic at lunch. As I dropped Bill off, I considered the subject dead.

As Bill was leaving my car, he asked, "Hey, do you want to hang out at my house Friday night?"

"I'll have to check with the wife, but I think it'll be ok. Should I bring anything?"

"Just beer; I've got the food covered. Oh, and I have some micro-brews for you to try."

"Sweet! I'll let you know tomorrow sir!" I said as I waved, put the car in gear, and drove back to work.

On my way home that evening, I rehashed the conversation. It made me feel fantastic that someone as stunning as you liked me. I mean, there I was, an older guy, and this somewhat younger and attractive woman actually thinking about me. I was in heaven.

I stopped on the way home that night to rent *Dark City*. I figured if you liked it, I wanted to see why. I also thought that maybe, just maybe, if there was a future for us, it would be something we could share.

The minute 5:00 p.m. hit on Friday, I shut down my computer and hit the door. After making a quick stop for beer, I drove to Bill's.

When I walked into Bill's kitchen, I noticed something was up. Looking around his kitchen I saw a couple party trays of snacks, and a couple appetizers warming on the stove.

"Oh, are you expecting others tonight? I thought it was just going to be you and me."

"After I asked you the other day, I asked a few others if they wanted to come over."

"So, who's all going to be here tonight?" I asked as he handed me a waiting beer.

"Just a few people from work ... including Amy."

I stopped in mid gulp, looked at Bill, and bellowed, "*You dick! Why the hell didn't you tell me that?*"

"I didn't want you getting cold feet. Just relax and go with it!" Bill laughed.

Although I was initially upset, I took his advice, I did just that.

About an hour later, and a couple beers in, you showed up. Although it seems weird, I was very happy that you didn't change out of your casual Friday work clothes. For some reason, the jeans and blouse made you look more down to earth, and pretty hot, I might add.

When our eyes met for the first time that night, my heart skipped a beat. As you walked over, I didn't know what to do or say. I'm glad you didn't have that same issue.

"Hi Mike! Glad you made it."

"Yeah, they do let me out of work occasionally." I joked.

Even though I thought this was the lamest joke ever, you laughed, which made me feel a little more at ease. After that, talking to you was comfortable. So comfortable, in fact, that we spent the rest of the night talking – just the two of us.

That night we chatted about everything under the sun. We discussed your childhood and mine. We talked at length about our jobs and our futures. And, most enjoyable of all, we talked about music.

Music has always been a central element to my life — a grounding point. Something I could always turn to, to take my mind away from the frustrations of everyday life. Music, to me, has always been the most important thing in the world.

And, unbelievably, you felt the same.

I know we didn't have a lot in common when it came to our likes and dislikes, but it was a starting point. And the passion you showed when discussing music showed me how much you enjoyed and leaned on it as well.

"I can always escape into music," you said and smiled. Again, my heart skipped a beat.

I sat there as you talked, just looking at you, truly looking at you. How your lovely shoulder length brown hair played with the top of your blouse as you moved. How your deep, thoughtful, brown eyes teared just slightly as you talked about music that touched your heart. How your smile pierced my heart every time you spoke. These, and the dozen other things, that made you, you.

The hours flew by, and before we knew it, it was past midnight.

"I have to head home. My mother gets worried if she wakes up in the middle of the night and I'm not home."

"Oh, you live with your parents?"

"Yeah, I've just never had the motivation to get a place of my own," you replied, as if you felt like you needed to justify your actions. "I help pay the bills, and my mom likes me being there."

"I didn't mean it as a derogatory comment! I . . . I just didn't know," I backpedaled.

"It's just me and my mom, and I haven't seen a reason to leave."

"I understand . . . and, seriously, I didn't mean it in a bad way. I lived with my mom up until I got married."

"Well, I better go . . ." you said as you looked down at your wristwatch.

"Me too," I replied, doing the same. Pausing for a moment, I worked up the courage and asked, "Can I walk you out?"

"Sure thing!" you said as your smile grew.

We found Bill a few minutes later and said our goodbyes. As we left him, he grabbed my arm and gave me a wink. I discretely whispered to him, "We will talk about this later."

Walking you to your car, I did the gentleman thing and opened the door for you and closed it after you were safely in. As you pulled away, I walked to my car beaming, a smile that I kept all the way home as I reminisced about our evening together.

The next day, I called Bill to tell him about the fantastic evening I had with you, and to thank him for being so underhanded.

"So?"

"So, what?" I countered.

"So?"

Knowing what he was referring to, I reiterated, "Dude, I'm married. I really like her and wish I wasn't, but I am."

"I understand," Bill said, and then paused when he heard something in the background. "Hey, gotta run. I'll talk to you next week."

"Sure thing," I said, hung up, and went on to my weekend chores.

The next week, when I called your work to talk to Bill, I lied to you again by saying I indeed had plans on Halloween and wouldn't be able to join you at the movie. I remember you saying okay in a matter-of-fact sort of way before transferring me to Bill. And I felt bad because I knew I was spoiling a chance to be with you.

A few more weeks went by, and I didn't see you much. Bill had a habit of waiting at the front door when I picked him up, so I never made it in to see you. Obviously, this gave me mixed feelings. On one hand, I didn't get to see you or talk to you. On the other hand, I wasn't being driven insane from not being able to be with you.

As it happened, Bill invited me to another Friday night party. And, this time, I asked ahead of time if you were invited as well.

That night, much like the previous party, you and I spent that evening drinking and talking with one another. Together, no subject was unapproachable and we discussed everything on our minds. As you prattled on about work or your mom or your brother, I looked deep into your eyes and fell just a little deeper for you. How could I not?

As before, at the end of the evening I walked you to your car, said goodbye, watched you leave, and then drove home with a smile stretching for ear to ear. This time, though, when I parked in my driveway and shut off my car, I sat there for a minute as I reconsidered my timetable.

In the next four months there were two more parties. Each time it was the same: me, seeing you, talking to you, and falling for you more and more. And every time I left you, I smiled until I got home and wondered what the hell I was doing with my life.

It was sometime that next spring that I finally decided enough was enough. My wife and I were arguing constantly when I was home and complaining when I wasn't. Every night I'd go to bed wondering why the hell I was still married.

Then it hit me. Why *was* I staying married, especially given the fact that you were out there, possibly waiting for me?

Don't get me wrong. It wasn't that I was in a loveless marriage. I did love my wife. Not because she was my wife, though. I loved her because she was the mother of my children. And like a lot of other couples out there, the only thing we really had in common was our children. Looking back on it, I came to realize it had almost always been this way. From the time my wife first got pregnant, our relationship became about the kids and not about us. I knew things would have to change eventually; even my wife knew things had to change. And we both knew it had to be sooner than later.

It was at that point I made the decision to leave.

After considering my options, I called Bill and asked him if I could stay with him while I figured out my life. He, of course, said yes. We had previously discussed this option when times had gotten tough before, and he, being the friend that he was, presented an open offer to crash at his place whenever I wanted.

The next day, I said goodbye to my old life in the anticipation of a new life — a new and better life – hopefully with you in it. I sat down with my wife and told her I knew we were both unhappy with the marriage and I felt I should move out.

There was some yelling, and a punched door or two, but in the end we both agreed it was for the best.

The worst part was breaking it to the kids. My son, the older of the two, kind of knew what was happening and was very accepting of the situation. My daughter, on the other hand, didn't want to see me leave.

There's something unique about a father–daughter relationship that can't be expressed in words. It killed me to leave her, but, with all things considered, it really was for the best.

That night, when I went to Bill's house, he was kind enough to make room for me in his basement. It wasn't quite a *finished basement*, but it had a bed and a television — all the comforts of home. We discussed rent, assuming it would be a few weeks before I could afford a place of my own, and came to an agreement.

A week went by before I called you. I didn't want it to seem like I was leaving my wife for you. In all reality, I really wasn't. I really did it for the *potential* of you, or someone like you. Someone that shared common interests, common wants.

That night, a Friday night, I got your number from Bill and called you before I left work.

"Amy . . . hi. It's Mike."

"Hi Mike! How are you?" you responded cheerfully.

"Good. How are you?"

"Good! What's up?"

"Well . . . I . . . um . . . am separated. Finally," I coughed.

"Oh?"

"Yeah. I finally took the step. A much needed step. I moved into Bill's house about a week ago."

"Good for you! I know you said you weren't happy there."

"I really wasn't, and thank you," I replied, waited a moment considering what I was going to say next, and then resolved to go all in. "Well, the reason I'm calling is to . . . umm . . . well . . . to ask if you if you had any interest in going out with me?"

There was a slight pause that, to me, felt like a million years and made me wonder if I made the right move. I mean, was I totally wrong about your feelings for me? Was I wrong about my own feelings? Did I just fuck up my life? All these thoughts came rushing into my head in the second or two before you responded.

"Well, yeah! Duh! I was just waiting on you to leave your wife."

Hearing your words, you could have knocked me over with a feather. I would have laughed if I wasn't so nervous and stunned by your remark.

We talked for a bit about our work week and jobs in general but finished our conversation by making plans to meet up at Bill's house the following Friday night. You mentioned you had a copy of *Dark City* and wondered if I'd like see it, since we never had the chance to see it together. I said I thought that was a fantastic idea and looked forward to finally seeing it with you.

The next week seemed to drag on forever. I couldn't wait to see you and spend time with you alone. I know we talked a few times that week, and texted daily, but the time couldn't go fast enough as far as I was concerned. In fact, in anticipation of our date, I hardly slept that Thursday night. And Friday alone felt like two or three days combined. But, before I knew it, I was on my way to Bill's house to get ready for our time alone.

It was around 6:00 p.m. when I received your text telling me you were on your way. In our chatter, we had agreed to wait until you got there to order pizza so it wouldn't get cold. Not that I cared about food at that point; I was way too nervous to eat. This was, after all, the first date I'd had in many, many years.

When you arrived, I wasted no time in ordering pizza for you. I knew you were hungry, and I aimed to please. While we waited for the pizza to arrive, we stood in the kitchen and drank a beer. I think this is when I first noticed you were nervous, as well.

This, of course, was a huge relief to me, knowing I wasn't the only one stressing about how this evening would go.

After the pizza arrived and we had cracked our second round of beers, we adjourned to the living room to start the movie. I picked the loveseat on one side of the room, while you chose the chair on the other side. I thought it was a little strange that we weren't sitting together, but at least we could eat and kind of face each other while watching the movie.

When we both finished our pizza and were ready for another round, I paused the movie while I took the plates in the kitchen. When I came back into the living room, I was pleasantly surprised to see that you had moved to the loveseat.

"I hope this is okay . . . me moving over here."

"No problem at all," I replied as I sat down, handed you a beer, and restarted the movie.

It was about five minutes later that you spoke up and mentioned your toes were cold.

"There's a blanket over here. Do you want it?" I asked as I started reaching for it.

Before I had a chance to retrieve it, though, you moved closer and wormed your toes under my leg. As you had indicated, those babies were freezing. When I realized this, I reached down and started rubbing your toes to warm them. As I did, you moved even closer and began massaging my thigh.

"So, do you like the movie?" you asked as we caressed one another.

"Well, I haven't actually watched the last five minutes or so," I admitted.

At this you pulled your feet out from underneath me, rose from the couch, and sat in front of me so I could hold you and still see the movie.

"Better?" you asked softly.

"Better, much better." I replied, not referring to my view of the TV.

As the movie played, we hugged and warmed each other. I nuzzled my cold nose against your shirt and neck, laying my lips there to warm your neck with my breath. You, in turn, pressed your lips gently on my arm, gently kissing my skin.

We sat that way for the remainder of the movie, which only felt like a minute. And as the movie ended, we continued to sit there as the opening screen replayed, enjoying each other's warmth and closeness.

It was around midnight when you said you had to leave. After helping you put on your jacket, we exited the house and walked to your car. I remember giving you a long hug before we said goodnight and closed the car door behind you. I pressed my fingers to the window, silently wishing you a safe ride, as you placed the car in reverse to start your journey home.

I watched you pull away, knowing there would be more nights like this, but still wishing the evening had never ended.

Diary: November 19

Two months ago was when I lost you.

I spend my weekdays engrossed in work to try and keep the pain to a minimum. I spend my weekends running errands and visiting new friends, doing anything and everything to divert my mind from the pain and sorrow that seems to envelop me.

And alcohol doesn't help, no matter how many times I go out with those who know what I'm going through. It only leaves me more sad and angry that we didn't have more time together.

When nothing helps, my mind goes back to the time we had together — the many years of joy.

But I also remember the many years you weren't in my life.

It's funny to look back on those days and recall all the fun I had as a preteen and teenager. All the good times I had with my friends and girlfriends.

God how I wish I had known you back then. It seemed like I spent my whole life looking for you, looking for that one person to share my life with.

That person I ultimately found in you.

CHAPTER

2

I was born and raised in Cleveland, a fact that I am very proud of.

Of all the cities I've been to, it's still one of my favorite places. Just like other cities, there are many things that make Cleveland unique. The summers are filled with festivals and art shows, the winters with skiing and indoor activities. All the restaurants, all the bars, all the sports venues — it truly has something for everyone.

But I think the most unique thing, the thing that makes Cleveland *Cleveland* is the music. We are truly the *Home of Rock and Roll.* It shows in all the music clubs, concert halls, and theaters spread throughout the city and suburbs.

Rocky River, the city where I grew up, is situated on Cleveland's west side, not too far from Cleveland proper. Rocky River, known just as River to a lot of westsiders, in most respects is your ordinary suburb. With its twenty thousand or so inhabitants, you could consider it a small community.

I consider it home.

I guess you could say my childhood was like most others'. My family was never rich, but we always had enough. My mom was the typical PTA going, dinner cooking, child rearing, stay-at-home mom. My dad, the breadwinner, left for work every morning by 7:00 a.m. and returned at 6:00 p.m. on the dot. I had one sister Dee, short for Deanna, who was a pain in my ass and beat me up a lot when I was little. The typical older sister, I would say.

The only exception to being like everyone else, if I had to count one, would be that I hardly knew my dad growing up. When I was young, he was hardly ever around. He was always too busy, either at work or working on his hobbies. During the week, I would normally see him for an hour at night, during dinner, before he was off to the pool hall or bowling alley. On weekends, when he wasn't doing yardwork, he'd be in his man cave fixing things or building something new for the house.

Then, one day, he was gone.

That day, while at work, my dad had a massive heart attack. And though they tried, the paramedics just couldn't save him.

I was eight. I remember my mom being silent, and strong. That's just the way she's always been. I remember a few tears, here and there, like at the funeral, but mostly she held it together. She held it together for us.

My mom was always a strong and independent woman, being raised primarily by my grandfather. Her mother had left when she was little, leaving her and her four siblings alone with their dad. She was the second to oldest but was always the more headstrong of the bunch. I guess that's where I get my strength from.

My sister Dee was nine at the time my father passed and took it a lot harder than I did. My dad and sister were a lot closer, and a lot more alike. I guess you'd say she was a daddy's girl. They just clicked. They had the same sense of humor and the same likes in food. They enjoyed the outdoors and fixing things, hobbies I was just never into.

It's hard to say I didn't miss him. I mean, who doesn't miss their dad when he's not around? But I always felt like I didn't miss him as much as someone else would miss their dad. It's not that he was a bad man. It's just that he wasn't an attentive father. We never played baseball or football. He never took me to Boy Scouts. He did teach me how to shoot an air rifle — I remember that — but besides that he was pretty hands off.

I guess you could say my life didn't change that much after my dad's passing. I went to school. I did my homework. I watched TV until my mom came home, and then we watched it together. She was a sucker for all things science fiction and other-worldly.

There was only one major change after my dad died - my mom sold our house. She used to say it was because of the upkeep required on the yard and house in general, but I think deep down it was because it reminded her of my dad. Whenever you're looking for proof on how much you love someone, always look toward the things you'll miss when they're gone. I believe it's the little things, not the grand gestures, that make life what it is.

On the positive side, the sale of the house created a little nest egg for us to lean on when times were tough. I think my mom really thought of it as a vacation fund. In the summer, when my mom wasn't working, we traveled. We went to Hawaii and California. We took car trips from our place in Ohio to Michigan, Pennsylvania, and Indiana. We also went to Cedar Point, the amusement park, a couple times in the summer.

Of course, it wasn't all pleasant.

Just after my dad passed, my grandfather became ill and couldn't manage by himself any longer. After we sold the house, my mom, my sister, and I moved in with my grandfather for a bit. My grandfather was up there in years, having had my mom in his forties. By the time I was born, he was already retired and living on his own. In some respects, this worked out well for all of us. We had someone to come home to after school while my mom looked for a job, and my grandfather had Dee and me to watch him, just in case anything should happen.

My grandfather, like a lot of elderly men, was very crotchety, bordering on mildly cruel. Quite often, if neighborhood kids accidently hit balls into his yard, he'd keep them. By the time we moved in with him, there was a whole assortment of toys squirrelled away in the rafters of his garage.

Although his garage was off limits to us, occasionally he would allow Dee and me to pick out something to play with. But when we were finished, he would collect the toys and store them back in the garage.

Besides the children's toys, my grandfather collected a hodgepodge of various items. Looking through his cupboards was like looking through forty years of history. Crystal goblets, brass cooking instruments, fast food restaurant stir sticks and napkins — piles and piles of items, hoarded away for some future apocalypse, we guessed. We never had a clue.

My mom eventually found a job as an accountant for a restaurant. A job she kept for many years. A place that didn't mind that she had kids whom she could bring in at night or on the weekend, if needed.

After a few months, my grandfather's health got a lot better, and my mom, on much prodding by my sister and I, figured it was time for us to move out and be on our own. I think it was after being out of the nest for so many years that she wanted someplace that she could call her own. I also think it was because she wanted to start dating again. My mom was never one to rest too long on her laurels.

By the time I was nine, we had our own apartment. Close enough to the elementary school that Dee and I could walk to, but not too far away from my grandfather's house in case there was an emergency.

There we were, just the three of us against the world.

The apartment's superintendent, Mrs. Rousch, lived next door to us. I don't know how my mom managed it, but somehow, she talked Mrs. Rousch into being our after-school watchdog. I guess you could call us latchkey kids, especially in the summer, but somehow we were never too far from someone that could yell at us or call our mom.

The summers were fantastic, probably the best times of my entire life. They were all about making new friends, having the freedom to run around with other kids living in the apartments — all with just a wee bit of supervision.

I have to admit, it was kind of weird being the only male in the household. Not like I had to perform maintenance on anything, or scare off a robber. But it was weird in the respect of not having male guidance or a role model. My grandfather was ok and all, but he wasn't really the role model type at his age. He did take my sister and me fishing occasionally, and to restaurants, but that was about it. All the *male* things like shaving, deodorant and cologne, and general body maintenance I had to learn on my own. For the other non-hygiene items, I had to rely on my mom and sister.

I know this sounds weird, but my favorite summer was the summer when I broke my arm.

Somehow, during what is considered a normal bike ride with my sister, she turned into me causing my front wheel to lock. Needless to say, we both wiped out, hard. She was the lucky one. Dee somehow flew off her bike and hit the grass. Me, well I happened to hit the curb at such an angle that my weight, albeit eighty pounds, snapped a bone in my forearm. Luckily, we were close to home and Dee was able to get Mrs. Rousch to take me to the hospital. Three hours and a ton of money later, I was all patched up and ready to head home.

This, of course, is not why I call it my favorite summer. I call it my favorite summer because that was the summer that I met Heather.

Heather was a friend of Dee's from sixth grade, who just happened to live in the same apartment complex we lived in. And she was beautiful. She had long, brown, wavy hair that flowed down just over her shoulders and lovely blue eyes the color of a clear evening's sky. And she was just starting to fill out her sweater, if you know what I mean. Everything a pre-teen boy would fantasize about. And I did — Lord knows I did.

For some odd reason, Heather took pity on me when she saw my broken arm. Maybe it was the Florence Nightingale effect, or maybe she just liked doting on her best friend's brother — I don't know. I do know that I was smitten from the first time she said, "Hey, do you want to ride on the back of my bike?"

"Okay, sure" was the only response I could make. And frankly, when asked by a hot girl to do anything, one should take it upon himself to say yes to said hot girl.

That summer, there were six of us *apartment kids* that hung out almost every day. There was Heather, of course; me and Dee; Greg and Brad, two brothers that lived in the building next to ours; and Tom, who lived across the street. We were all about the same age and knew each other from school, so our parents didn't mind us hanging out.

The group of us would go to the park, or to the skating rink, or to the school playground to get into trouble. There were also the woods behind the apartments where we'd set up forts and hang out for hours. But, at the end of the day, I always had Heather there to give me a ride home, with or without my sister around.

And there was the occasion where Heather and I would hang out in her apartment. She, too, was a latchkey kid. Her mom and dad were divorced and her mom often worked late, so I'd keep her company until either of our parents would come home.

One such day, around the beginning of August, Heather and I had been playing with the other kids at the park until we figured it was too hot and needed to find some air conditioning. As usual, we went to her house to flip on the AC and watch some TV until her mom got home.

As we sat there and the air became cooler, my cast arm started to itch. Within a few minutes it started to drive me crazy. I looked around for some way to relieve my pain but couldn't see anything that would help. It wasn't long before Heather noticed what I was trying to do. Standing, she left the room, returning a minute later with a modified wire hanger. She proceeded to turn me to my right and, with little effort, stuck the hanger down my cast and started to scratch. It was cold, but as she moved it back and forth the itch started to go away.

"Ahhhh . . ." I exclaimed. "Thank you!"

To this day, I'm not sure why she did it, but she moved behind me, straddling me, continuing to use the hanger to soothe my itch. Though it was a warm night, her bare thighs against mine felt good. It was a closeness I had never felt before.

"I thought you might like that," she whispered in my ear, her warm breath trailing down my neck giving me goosebumps in the process. Shuttering from the sensation, I turned slightly and felt her lips touch my cheek. I wasn't sure, never having experienced this before, but my instincts were telling me she wanted to kiss me.

I was only ten years old and had never shared a kiss with a girl before. Well, there was the time when I was six and had two girls corner me on the playground — but I digress.

As Heather backed away, I leaned in to kiss her, only to have her push me back.

"What are you doing?" she exclaimed, sounding offended.

"I-I thought you wanted me to kiss you! Sorry! Sorry!"

She rose from behind me and moved to the opposite side of the couch, putting as much distance between the two of us as she could. We sat like that for a few minutes, until she looked my way and asked, "Want to watch something else?"

"Sure," I said, feverishly nodding.

I stayed there, seated in the same place, pretty much in silence for about another half hour until Heather's mom came home. Knowing there wasn't much more to say, I said my goodbyes and headed for the door.

When I got home, I went straight to my room and sat there alone for a while, feeling completely idiotic and entirely humiliated.

The next day, Saturday, was pretty much business as usual. The group of us got together right after lunch and headed for the woods. Although it felt funny, I hopped on the back of Heather's bike, and she drove me there like nothing had happened.

The group of us played there for a couple hours, running around in a mock battle around a tree fort. We pretended to fall down dead when shot, only to rise again and shoot someone else. The whole time though I avoided talking to Heather, still too embarrassed from the day before.

Around 4:00 p.m., we ended the melee. When she dropped me off, I went into my apartment, still feeling off. But with the afternoon's fun and Heather acting like the day before never happened, I was able to put it mostly out of my mind.

After dinner, Dee went to her room, so Mom and I sat around watching TV for a bit. Somewhere around 8:00 p.m., she turned toward me and asked if she could talk to me for a couple minutes.

"Sure Mom, what's up?" I replied

Standing, she walked over and turned off the TV. Turning toward me, she said, "Mike, I wanted to talk to you about Heather."

Having put the night before out of my mind, I gave her a blank look and asked, "What about her?"

"Heather told Dee that you tried to kiss her last night," she said. "And I wanted you to know that it upset her. She considers you a good friend and doesn't think of you in that way."

Shocked that she knew what had occurred, my vision narrowed and my face went white as the blood drained. I looked at her for a minute, wordless, not knowing exactly how to respond. With the lack of anything remotely good to say to explain my actions, I simply responded, "Yeah, I know."

It was almost like my mom was expecting that response. After giving me a quick but serious look, she smiled and said "Okay, as long as you know."

Turning, she walked toward the kitchen, stopping just inside the doorway to ask, "Do you want some popcorn?"

I guess you could say this was my mom's way of handling *the birds and the bees* talk. I really don't remember any other *sex talks* after this one. Well, maybe getting yelled at for having sex in my mom's bed counts as one; but that's another story.

The only other sex talk that I received — hell, which most of us received — was in seventh grade Health class. There we learned all about sex organs. This included where they were, what happened when you had unprotected sex, and what even happened sometimes when you have protected sex. But that was it, as far as I remember.

Getting back to Heather, my relationship with her was never quite the same after that fateful night. I'm not sure if it was because she realized that I was attracted to her or if it was the talk with my mom, but neither she nor I could really look or talk to each other the same again.

The next week, when I got my cast off, the bike rides ended. The week after, when the new school year started, also brought a lot of changes. Dee and Heather started at the middle school, so I didn't see her a bunch. Also, right after the school year commenced, Heather started *going steady* with a guy few years older than her; I think he was a high school freshman.

Sometime before the end of high school, I heard her family moved out of state. I felt sorry for Dee because this was her first real friend, and they didn't really keep in touch after the move. Some things just aren't meant to last, I guess.

In hindsight, living with my mom and sister taught me a lot about respect for women. It showed me how some men don't treat women as equals. It showed me how some men are dishonest and untrusting of women. I'm not sure who I'd be today without their influence.

It also makes me wonder what kind of man I'd be today if I had had a male figure dominating my life. Would I be a womanizer? Would I be as chivalrous? I'm not sure, and I'm glad I don't know.

I must admit, the next two or three years really helped shape me into whom I wanted to be. These were the years that my mom started dating again, and my sister started noticing boys.

Although I love my mom and respect the hell out of her, she made some *really* bad choices when it came to dating men. It always seemed that if they weren't married, they were emotionally unavailable. And a lot of them were just down and out scumbags. As a pre-teen boy, this was difficult to see my mom go through. She always acted like it didn't affect her, but I knew it did.

I believe part of her bad choices stemmed from not really being over my dad. I can only imagine the anger and hurt she felt when he passed. Even though he was a hands-off dad to me, he was an attentive husband to her — her *Mr. Right*.

The first of Mom's boyfriends that I met was a guy named Sam. And I've got to admit, as her choices went, Sam was the best. He was a great guy who was always there for my mom during the two years that they dated, and I know she loved him. But there was one problem with Sam that the relationship couldn't weather.

Sam was a married man.

Even though he was married, Sam was around when he could be. Some weekends he'd tell his wife he was going out of town on business, and he would spend the weekends with us. When he was around, we did normal family type things. We went to dinner. We played board games. He even came over once to help paint the house.

I'm not sure exactly why the two of them up broke up. I just remember that one day he just stopped coming over.

To me, Sam embodied everything a dad should be and could be, except for the cheating thing, of course, and I think that his influence made me be a better father to my kids.

After Sam, my mom's next few boyfriends were just a compilation of shit. One was an alcoholic who hit me once. One was a guy that almost got us killed when his newly separated ex-wife showed up at his place with a gun. And yet another stranded her at a bar at 3:00 a.m.

All these shittastic choices lead to my mom's last real boyfriend, Jim.

Jim was the alcoholic son of Mrs. Rousch, our next-door neighbor. He wasn't a bad guy, but his fits of alcoholic rage often left him jobless, penniless, and homeless. But even with all this going against him, he still ended up dating my mom for a year-and-half.

I'm not sure if she found all of his issues endearing qualities, or if she just felt sorry for him, or if she liked the fact that he was ten years younger than her. I'm guessing it was a combination, though.

As far as fatherly pick though, he was horrible. Unlike Sam, who had kids and knew how to be a dad, Jim just didn't know how to act around Dee and me. This was probably a good thing though, because knowing this, my mom kept him away from us a lot.

Somewhere around the sixteenth month into their relationship, Jim asked her to marry him. This came as a total shock to me and Dee. I think I was twelve years old at the time, and although I wanted my mom to be happy, I just couldn't see him as husband material.

About a week or so after the two got engaged, they started looking for a place for the four of us to live. Although the logical next step, this presented a problem because there wasn't much they could afford.

The first house they looked at was in a horrible neighborhood, and she nixed the idea at the onset. The second, and final, house they looked at was in a better neighborhood, but the rooms were small. The room that they picked out for me was a glorified closet, and the one meant for Dee wasn't much better. Needless to say, we complained at length.

Ah, the pre-teen years — all the rage and fighting the system.

I'm not positive of everything that happened after we got home that night, but I found out the next day that the two had called off the engagement. I felt really bad that all that happened. I *did* want my mom to be happy. But I think that also includes being happy with someone that doesn't bolt at the first sign of adversity.

After that, my mom really didn't date much. And the ones she did go on were mostly dinner dates and one-night stands.

I feel bad that she never found another Mr. Right.

This brings me to my sister Dee.

Dee was not the most attractive girl in the school. In fact, as far as cute girls go, she was probably low on the list. She was a little pudgy, had thick glasses, and long straight hair that she didn't know what to do with. You could say she was a little frumpy.

Middle school, the time most of us started feeling infatuation, didn't bring her a lot of luck in the boy department. There were a couple guys that showed interest in her, but they were real dorks. And the ones she did find attractive had no interest in her.

How do I know all of this? Well, Dee and I were actually really close.

After my dad passed and my mom started working, Dee and I only had each other to lean on. And with her loss of a best friend, I became the person she talked to about — you guessed it — boys.

We talked about what she thought about this guy and that, what she thought about my friends, what she thought about other girls and their boyfriends, who had a boyfriend and who didn't, and, of course, *why* they did or didn't have one.

Not all of this information came from Dee, though. Some of this was relayed from the normal gossip chain in middle school.

Dee's love life was pretty non-existent up until around her junior year in high school, the year she really came into her own. She lost some weight, ditched her nerdy glasses for contacts, curled her hair, and started wearing cute clothing.

Believe it or not, within no time of her transformation, the boys she *did* like started to actually notice her! It's amazing what a little *polish* will do for both the outer self, as well as the inner.

I was so happy for her the first time she got asked out by a guy she liked. She came home beaming, and her life was never the same again.

I know you're asking: what exactly did all this teach me?

For starters, it taught me that being happy is more than being with someone and that a true partner sticks with you through thick and thin, for better or for worse, as the vows say.

It also taught me loyalty and that you should be with one person at a time, and *only* one person at a time. You can't build trust in a house of cards. You just can't. One lie usually leads to another, and another, and before you know it, all you have are lies. Also listening to the one you love and being a *couple*, just the two of you against the world, that's what it's really all about.

Differences are what make us unique, but too many leads to separation, So one should always show interest in what your partner likes. It doesn't mean you have to like it; just don't act like you hate it.

Last, but not least, Mom and Dee's experiences taught me that I should date around in high school. They showed me there probably is a perfect-for-you person out there if you take the time to look, and not just to settle for Mrs. Right Now.

Diary: December 19

It's been three months now, and although I've have had opportunities to date, I can't bring myself to do it. Lord knows I've tried. Friends of friends setting me up with someone they think I'll click with. But it just doesn't work. The memories of us, and what we had, still haunt my every thought and my every dream.

Just last night, I had a dream that we were still together. We were kissing and holding each other. We were making love like we did for so many years. And as I held you, I asked you to marry me. And you said yes.

I woke to the echo of your acceptance.

Oh, how I wanted to spend the rest of my life with you, to be with you, holding hands with each other throughout our lives.

I regret the things we never had. All the things we could have had, and could have been, haunt me every waking moment.

How can I date someone when all I think about is you? How can I date someone that isn't you?

CHAPTER

3

I remember the first time I told you I loved you.

The first four months we dated were like something out of a dream. We started out seeing each other two or three times a week, mostly weekends, taking in dinner or occasional outings to art shows or concerts. But as summer approached and the days grew longer and warmer, we were together almost every day.

Those days, depending on the weather, we'd go hiking or just find someplace outdoors to be alone. We would meet right after work and drive to a park or find some trails, anyplace we could think of, as long as it wasn't too far from our offices or your house. Sometimes, we'd even meet at the local Metro Parks to go hiking or biking, just walking or riding, so we could enjoy the sunshine and nature, as well as each other's company of course.

It was sometime in mid-July, if memory serves, that went hiking in the Metro Park. The weather was perfect, with the sun still two or three hours away from setting. The sky had just started to turn the distant clouds a reddish hue.

As usual, I waited for you to finish up your last bits of work so you'd feel comfortable leaving for the evening. I stood in your office lobby and watched as you shuffled papers from stack to stack, circling this or lining out that. I really did love watching you work. You were so focused and professional.

"Ready?" you said as you started shutting off the office lights.

"As always!" I replied.

After exiting the building, I waited by your driver's side door, ready to open it for you upon your arrival. A minute later you were there, and after making sure you were safely in the car, we were off.

We drove down to our usual starting point near the pavilions and parked side by side. As usual, I waited outside your car as you changed into your tennis shoes. Standing there, I couldn't help but smile thinking how cute you were to wait until we reached the park to change into your tennis shoes. Like changing any time before that felt unprofessional or undignified.

It really was a beautiful evening, a romantic evening, the combination of the setting sun and the tree cover over the trails making the air not too hot, but not too cold. A light breeze was blowing through the trees making the leaves rustle ever so slightly, adding a musical arrangement to our evening walk.

I believe we both were feeling the romance in the atmosphere, holding hands as we walked together talking about the day's events. I listened intently while you talked, and enjoyed every utterance, every syllable, no matter what it was about. Even if your words were complaints about *this person* or *that job,* it didn't matter to me. It was just a delight to have you near me. Walking side by side with you was heavenly. And part of me was still in shock that a woman as gorgeous as you could find me attractive, even in workout attire.

The trail we normally hiked was a dirt path that traversed alongside the road that ran through the park. The path curved back and forth through the woods, veering at a few points here and there, plunging deeper into the woods and returning. Occasionally, it would spill back out onto a paved path in order to pass a creek or ravine but would eventually dive back into the woods after the obstacle was avoided.

The route from the parking lot to our normal turnaround point was about a mile-and-half and usually took just over an hour to walk there and back. Along the path, every half mile or so, were various pieces of workout equipment that included metal bars, inclined benches, and iron rings to add some diversity into a workout.

I sometimes stopped and performed back flipping dismounts from the metal rings just to make you laugh.

Oh, how I loved to hear you laugh.

That night, hearing you laugh, it hit me: I truly did love everything about you. Your laugh, your smile, your little quirks — all those things, and hundreds more, made me love you.

For whatever reason, be it the time, or place, or laugh, something inside told me that this time was the perfect time to broach the subject of my feelings for you. In fact, I felt that if I didn't get it off my chest, I was going to explode.

So, when we reached a lull in our conversation, I decided to just blurt it out.

"Amy, I love you . . ."

Relief washed over me as the words, words that had been weighing on my mind for a week or so, left my lips. As soon as I said it though, you slowed down your pace to wrap your head around what I just revealed.

Doubt of my timing entered my mind, so I expanded on the thought. "I think I've known since I first met you . . . and I felt it needed to be said."

You continued to walk in silence, and I wasn't sure if you were in shock or if you thought the admission would just go away if you didn't respond. It didn't matter to me either way. To me, it truly was something I needed to say.

"Amy, you know it's okay if you don't say it back," I continued. "I know you love me too . . . I can see it in your eyes and in your smile . . . and I know that, when you're ready, you'll say it back."

We continued to walk in silence. And although I could tell that you were still digesting what I confessed, I thought to myself that it couldn't be all bad because we were still holding hands. I looked over to you once or twice, trying to see if I could tell what was on your mind. I couldn't determine if you were confused or mad at me. I suppose I can understand why. It was an admission from my heart, which was an easy thing for me. I knew it was more difficult for you, but I did truly know you felt the same.

"You can't just drop something like that on somebody!" you snapped after a few minutes had passed.

"I didn't just drop it on *somebody*! I shared it with you! This is something that I've felt for a while. And I wanted to let you know how I felt."

This did not seem to lighten your mood in the least, so I added, "Like I said, you don't have to say it back. I already know you love me. I just wanted you to know."

As we made our turn and started the uphill hike to our cars, you finally spoke up.

"Dammit Mike . . . I love you too," you replied, almost angrily. Still refusing to look at me, you asked, "Can we drop this now?"

I looked at you, smiled, and squeezed your hand. This appeared to help your mood.

It was getting late as we finished the mostly silent walk back to our cars. I knew you were probably hungry, so I suggested we go to Charley's for dinner. Charley's, a local bar/restaurant, was one of our hangouts after work. They had a decent menu and a great beer selection, so we usually stopped there when we had time.

"That sounds good. Do you think they'll care that we're in sweats?"

I jokingly leaned my head down to take a whiff of my arm pit, and said, "Well, I don't know about you, but I don't smell. I think we're good."

You smiled at that, the first time you had smiled since I dropped the bomb on you, so I took that as a yes. "Okay, do you want to leave your car here and we can pick it up on the way back?"

You perked up and said, "Sure!"

As I opened the door for you, you turned toward me and kissed me. I'm not sure if this was because you were putting the last hour out of your head or if you were truly starting to accept our feeling for each other. Personally, I didn't know, and I didn't care. I was just happy that we were together and in love.

Our dinner at Charley's was good, and no, no one cared that we had sweats on. I remember we each ordered a beer and ended up splitting two appetizers. And the conversation was pleasant, not broaching anything about love. After we ate, we got in my car and started to drive. No real destination in mind, just driving to spend more time with each other.

I think we were about twenty minutes into the drive when you asked, "So, do you want to stop at your work?"

Generally, this was code for "Hey, do you want to go behind your work and fool around before you drop me off?" With your mom having retired and almost always at home and my apartment being too far away from our offices to make it convenient time-wise, this was the best solution.

"That sounds good to me!" I said and turned the car around to go back toward my office.

When we reached my office, we turned in the driveway and headed for the back parking lot. Well hidden from the street and covered with trees, it was a great spot to be alone. As soon as we parked, I shut off the car and extinguished the dome light.

We spent the next hour in each other's arms kissing each other, holding each other, trying to hold back from going too far. And it was not easy. I was totally lost in you, lost in my feelings for you.

Knowing it was getting late, we exchanged our last kisses and then adjusted our clothes in preparation to leave. After turning on the dome light, I started the car and drove you back to yours. Once back at your car, I gave you one final kiss before I helped you into your car. That night, like all the other nights before, I followed you home to make sure you were safe and then waved goodnight as we parted ways.

As I drove away, I couldn't help but float on air. You had said you loved me, and I knew that was no small thing for you to admit. I knew that you were reluctant to reveal in words what you showed me in your emotions and actions, so I didn't take it lightly.

I knew that this night was the real start of our relationship together.

For the next few weeks, our schedule was pretty much the same as that evening. I'd pick you up, we'd go for a walk, have some dinner, try to restrain ourselves, and then I'd drop you off and miss you like hell until I got to see you again.

It was routine, and I was good at *routine*, after all. Part of what made me a good soldier, part of what made me a good husband was following routine. Not to say *routine* was ordinary or boring, it was actually far from it. It was just a great sequence that repeated itself. And I loved it. I loved you. I was learning *you*, learning your likes and dislikes, learning your wants and needs. Learning everything that made you the woman I fell in love with.

My life outside of my time with you was also a routine, the less exciting routine of work and family. Heather and Brian were doing well, and I saw them every other weekend. I would pick a day that we didn't have something planned, and I'd take Heather and/or Brian to lunch or dinner to catch up on who they were dating or how school and work were going.

Dee and Mom were also doing well. Mom was still working and serial dating — she would never change. Dee, on the other hand, was dating and living with a guy named Bob Mason. He seemed like a decent enough guy, and I could see how much he cared for her. So much so they were even talking about marriage. I was so happy for the both of them.

Everyone was happy, which made it an opportune time for life to throw in a twist. The twist came in the form of a phone call from my mom one Tuesday afternoon.

"Hi honey. Sorry to call you at work, but I got a call from your Aunt Ruth a few minutes ago. She told me Uncle Joe passed away this morning."

Uncle Joe was my Godfather and was the closest thing I had to a male role model in my family. He was my dad's only brother and about five years his senior. We hadn't been close in years. I only saw him nowadays on holidays and big family functions, but he was a decent, hardworking man that loved his family, and I respected him. More so, I loved him.

"Oh my God, what happened?" I inquired after I recovered slightly.

"Aunt Ruth told me she thinks he had a stroke."

The news shook me to the core and brought up a lot of the feelings I had buried away from when my dad passed. Feelings I had pushed deep down so I could be the strong one for my family, for my mom. In some ways, it even felt like my dad passing away all over again.

"Okay," I replied, not knowing what else to say.

"Aunt Ruth said when she has info, like the details about the funeral, she'll call," Mom said. After about ten seconds of me not responding, she added, "Are you okay honey?"

"Yeah Mom . . . I'm okay. I'm just a little shocked."

"I know honey. I feel the same. It is really hard to believe," Mom said, paused, and then added, "If you need to talk, I'm here."

"I know Mom, and thanks. I guess I should get back to work."

"Okay sweetie. I love you!"

"I love you too, Mom," I replied and hung up the phone.

I sat there for a few minutes thinking about my dad and the times spent with him and Uncle Joe. Mostly thinking about my dad and how much, even now, I missed him. My thoughts were interrupted a minute later by someone entering my office. It really was time to get back to work.

Later that night, you and I met for dinner, and I talked about my Uncle Joe's passing. You and I had only been together a short while so I never really brought up my extended family. I told you about Uncle Joe and Aunt Ruth and how he had really been there for me, Mom, and Dee right after my dad passed.

"In some ways, he was really like another Dad," I said as we sat waiting for our meals to arrive. "I mean, he wasn't around a lot . . . he had his own family to deal with, but the time I did spend with him was great. Watching him with his own family made me want to be like him someday."

I paused or a minute, took a sip of my drink, and then continued, "There was this one time, probably about a month or two after Dad's death, that Uncle Joe picked me up and we went fishing. We had a great time."

"Oh, really? I thought you hated fishing."

"I do, normally . . . but this was different. Uncle Joe picked me up around 6:00 a.m. Way too early for my liking, but he told me that's the best time to fish. He took me down to the valley near the Rocky River, and we fished off the side of the boat docks. He even bought me a pole — my own fishing pole! We just sat there, mostly in silence as to not disturb the fish, with our poles in the water, just the two of us enjoying the early morning peace and quiet."

"That sounds nice."

"It was. Not only because it was a beautiful morning, but because it was just me and him. It's something my dad and I never did. It kind of made it . . . special, you know?"

At that you hugged me. Something I didn't know I sorely needed. We stood there for a few minutes, just hugging, me feeling your warmth and love. Something I will always remember and cherish about you. After a minute, we separated as our dinner arrived. As we started eating, I finished the thought that was heavy on my mind.

"I feel bad, though," I said as I set down my fork and looked toward you. "When I became a teenager, I kind of stopped talking to Uncle Joe."

"Why's that?"

"I guess maybe it was me trying to do my own thing. Or maybe it was I knew that Uncle Joe had his own *rebellious teen* to worry about and he didn't need one more. I really don't know why. I just know that after that our relationship had changed, and I didn't know how to get it back to the way it was."

I picked up my fork and forced myself to eat a few more bites, and then I was done. My stomach, filled with grief and regret, didn't want to accept any more food. So, I just sat there and watched you eat, enjoying your company, and being thankful that I had someone I could talk to, someone to be with during this time.

The next day, my mom called and told me they had scheduled the wake and funeral for the next Friday and Saturday, and that they would both take place on the far west side at Saint James Cemetery.

I was very familiar with Saint James, since it was the place a lot of the Samstags were buried, including my dad. And I couldn't say I was overly enthused about heading back there to attend another funeral. But, it was what it was.

After I hung up with her, I started making my plans for the weekend. The church was about a forty-five minute drive from Rocky River, but it was closer to a ninety minute drive from where I was now living. After considering it for a bit, I opted to rent a hotel room close to the church to limit the drive time.

My next thought was of you. I really wanted you to go with me but wondered how you'd react to my hotel plan, considering that, up until that point, we had never spent the night together.

We had been *fooling around* for several months and were comfortable with each other in bed, but that was a far cry from waking up together. Also, up until that point, we hadn't actual had sex. We had been abstaining until the time was right.

After some hemming and hawing, I asked you to join me. "You don't have to. I mean, you never met Uncle Joe or any of my extended family, so I totally understand if you don't want to join me."

"Of course I'll go with you. I want to be there for you," you replied, and I couldn't help but fall in love with you just a little more.

We discussed our options for Friday, trying to fit in dinner, the wake, and hotel and worked out a tentative plan. Since we were both busy at work

- and taking a vacation day didn't look like a viable option for either of us, we decided to leave directly from work as soon as we could get away. After we left, we would find someplace to eat along the way, attend the wake, and then check into the hotel.

"Sounds like a good plan."

"Plan the work, then work the plan, I always say."

The next couple days seemed to drag on, partly in anticipation of spending a night with you, but mostly in dread of going to the wake. It's not that I didn't want to see family or that I was afraid to see Uncle Joe in the casket. In some odd way, it just felt more like putting my dad in the ground a second time. And I was afraid of how I would react around my family and you. I just kept telling myself that I could, and would, make it through.

When I was finished with work on Friday, I changed into my suit, then called you at work, and let you know I was on my way. When you walked out the front door of your office to meet me, I couldn't believe how stunning you looked. You had on a black dress that made you look even more gorgeous than normal — like that was even possible. I didn't — couldn't — say a word as you approached the car, bag in tow. I just stood there, jaw agape, as you handed me your bag, gave me a kiss, and got into the car.

We had a quick dinner along the way as planned; I couldn't even tell you where. I was still in shock from how amazing you looked and how privileged I felt to be with you, both physically and emotionally. The last few days had been rough on me, and I was so happy to have you there supporting me. As we walked toward the front door of the funeral home, you took my hand and guided me through that evening.

Once inside, I quickly scanned the room for Dee and Mom. Not seeing them right away, we walked around and said hi to seldom seen relatives as I introduced you to my extended family.

We finally saw Dee and Mom standing off to the side. After we chatted for a bit, you and I walked around for a while so I could say hi to other relatives. Occasionally, we circled back to where Mom and Dee were to talk or just be near immediate family. Eventually, we made our way around to Aunt Ruth to offer our condolences.

"Mike, thank you for being here today," Aunt Ruth said as she gave me a hug.

"Aunt Ruth, this is my girlfriend Amy," I said, gesturing toward you.

"So, you're the Amy that Laura and Dee mentioned. It's so nice to finally meet you," Aunt Ruth said as she took your hand.

"It's nice to meet you too! I'm sorry for your loss."

"Thank you, honey," Aunt Ruth replied. "And I'm glad you two could make it. Uncle Joe thought very highly of you."

"And I did of him as well," I said, tears starting to well in my eyes.

"He always thought of you as another son . . . you know that, right?"

I was a little surprised by this. I knew he cared about me and was always there when I needed another man's opinion, but I had no idea he cared that much. I had no idea how to reply to this, or if I should at all. I finally said something that came from my heart.

"I didn't, but I've always felt that if I had a choice of a dad, he would be it. He was always there for me," I said, choking up.

Aunt Ruth gave me another hug as I tried to stop my weeping. And I felt bad because this was her husband. Who was I to be *getting* hugs and support from her, when I should be *giving* the same? Then I realized I was doing just that. I was there, sharing in her grief. This thought helped to alleviate the tears a bit and allowed me to leave her embrace. As I did, you were there to take my hand.

"Thank you, Aunt Ruth," I said as I wiped my eyes. "By the way, where's Joey?"

"He couldn't make it tonight. He called and said he was having car troubles," Aunt Ruth replied, and I noticed a little apprehension in her voice. "I'm sure he'll be at the service tomorrow. Will you be there?"

"We will," I replied as I squeezed your hand. Knowing there were others waiting, I said, "Well, we should go. We'll see you in the morning, Aunt Ruth. Take care."

"You too, sweetie," she replied, shifting her attention to the line waiting to offer their condolences.

"Car troubles . . ." I said aloud to myself as we walked across the room toward the casket.

"What's that?" you asked.

I just shook my head and kissed your hand to avoid telling you what I was thinking. I knew that Uncle Joe and Joey had been on the outs for several years, but to not show up? Wild horses wouldn't have kept me from being at my dad's wake. And I highly doubted it was actually car problems. Taking a deep breath, I let it go, knowing I'd hear the scuttlebutt at some point.

When we got to the casket, we both knelt and said a little prayer. As we finished, I looked in at Uncle Joe. He truly did look at peace. This, of course, was just a representation of the man I knew for so many years; his soul and life were gone from this world. But I understand how it did offer some closure to me and others.

After, we walked back toward Mom and Dee to say goodbye. As we turned to leave, Mom stopped me.

"Honey, Aunt Ruth came up to me earlier before you got here and gave me this," she said as she handed me a box. "She wanted to give it to you herself, but thought it'd be better if I did."

I stared at the box for a few seconds, pondering what it could be and why she just didn't give it to me herself. I looked up at Mom and asked, "Should I open it?"

"Aunt Ruth asked that you wait until after you get home tomorrow."

"Oh?"

"She said it was something Uncle Joe wanted you to have. But she didn't want you opening it in front of Joey, in case he showed up today or tomorrow."

Ignoring the box while I hugged Mom one more time, I told both that I loved them before heading for the door.

When we arrived at the hotel, we checked in, grabbed our bags, and walked to the room. As we made our way through the corridors that led to our room, my nervousness about this night started up again. And, even though I was exhausted by the night's event, I wondered in the back of my mind whether this would be the night we first made love.

As we got into the room, we went about our separate tasks to prepare for the next day. We unpacked, readied our morning outfits, and set out our toiletries. It took me way less time than it took you, so I sat on the bed and turned on the TV while I waited for you to change. While you were in there, I took the opportunity to throw on my pajamas. These consisted mostly of sweat bottoms and a concert t-shirt; I was not into high fashion, in case you didn't know.

A minute later, I heard the water running in the bathtub and remembered you had told me that taking a bath was part of your nightly routine. As I just started getting comfortable watching TV again, you spoke up.

"Mike, do you want to take a bath with me?" Without a reply, I turned down the TV and stripped. I didn't need to be asked twice.

I may be slow at times, but I'm not stupid.

As I entered the bathroom, you were already in the tub. You had added bubbles to the bath water, and they covered your lower body. As I looked you up and down, taking in all your attributes, I saw you were doing the same to me. When I stepped into the bathtub, you moved back against the far side of the tub so I could sit in between your legs. The water was hot and soothing, and as I positioned myself and leaned against you, you proceeded to splash little bits of water on my legs and chest. I started to feel your soft wet kisses on my upper back and neck. These I returned kissing your upper arm and shoulder.

I pivoted my head and torso enough so I could kiss you on your lips and neck. Before I knew it, we were lying beside each other, our hands moving up and down each other's bodies, caressing and playing with each other. As I looked into your eyes, I could see you wanted more, and so did I. I don't know how, but I found the strength to resist entering you. It felt like my entire body went numb from needing to be one with you.

After a few minutes, the water coming from the faucet started to run cold, so we left the icy tub for the expectation of a warm bed. As we pulled down the covers, I realized I still needed something from the car.

"Amy, I need to run out to the car for a minute."

You looked at me quizzically, as if I had lost my mind. I had a beautiful, naked woman in my bed, I had an erection, and I was soaked.

"I have condoms in the glove compartment."

You smiled, almost laughing at what I was prepared to do, but I knew you wanted to be with me as much as I wanted to be with you.

"Okay. Please put on pants though!"

I did as you asked, along with my shirt and shoes. Again, slow, not stupid. I grabbed the room key card and hurried out the door.

It was a little chilly that night as I literally ran out to my car to get the package. When I got back inside the room, you were already under the covers and all the lights were off except for the one in the bathroom. I quickly shed my clothing and crawled into bed with you. I tried to warm my hands the best I could by placing them under my buttocks. After a few seconds, you saw what I was doing and you slowly grabbed my hands and started to rub them.

We started kissing each other, and as soon as my hands were warm enough to be considered bearable, I placed them on your thighs. I slowly moved them up your body to caress your breasts. You, in turn, moved your hands from my upper body to my erection, holding me and fondling me until I was rock hard.

We made love twice that night, and even though we could have probably gone for a third time, we refrained so we could get some rest for the next day. As we separated, I kept my body turned toward you and watched you get comfortable. My last sight, before exhaustion won out over my eyelids, was of your beautifully content face.

The next day, I woke before you and meandered through clothing and pillows to the bathroom to brush my teeth. When I came out of the bathroom, you were already awake and making coffee to start our day. I came over and kissed you, but I could feel you shy away slightly.

"I haven't brushed my teeth yet," you scowled.

"I don't care," I replied, and it was the only reply I made as I kissed you deeper, pressing my body against yours, not wanting to let you go. Not wanting to ever let you go.

Within an hour-and-half or so, we were both showered and dressed and checked out of the hotel. We were both silent as we drove to the church where they were holding the funeral service. You, I think, were silent because of the incredible time we had the previous night. I was silent because, the closer we got to the church, the more I remembered my dad's funeral and the more I dreaded seeing my uncle lowered into the ground.

You must have seen my expression or felt my unease, because you turned toward me and asked, "Are you ok?"

"Yeah . . . I guess. Why do you ask?"

"You're just very quiet. I wanted to make sure you were ok."

"I will be . . . when all this is over."

At that, you took my hand and squeezed it, and, believe it or not, it did help. I squeezed back to let you know just that.

When we arrived at the church for the service, we sat with Mom and Dee in the second row right behind Aunt Ruth. Like the previous day, there was a pretty good turnout of family and what I'm guessing were Uncle Joe's friends. One never knows, going to one of these things, who half the people are; well, I never do.

Sitting next to Aunt Ruth was my cousin Joey. I was glad he made an appearance, but it meant I'd have to see and talk to him at some point. And I hated talking to him because he was kind of a dick.

Growing up, I really didn't see Joey that much. He was only a year or two older than me, but he always made me feel like he was the much-older cousin, always trying to tell me what to do and where to go. And if we got into trouble by going into the basement or somewhere else where we shouldn't or playing with something we were told not to, it always became my fault.

The more I thought about Joey's attitude and him not showing up at the wake last night, the more I fumed. I tried to put all this out of my mind during the service and told myself that this was about Uncle Joe, not about my feelings or about Joey, but it still chapped my ass.

At the end of the service, Aunt Ruth crossed the room toward us from where she was standing with Joey and the pastor that gave the service. After she gave us all hugs, she asked if she could talk to me privately.

"I know it's kind of last moment, but I was wondering if you could be a pallbearer?" she asked hesitantly.

I took a moment to answer, not because the request shocked me, but because I was surprised she felt shy about asking me. I'm not sure if it was because she felt bad laying the burden on me or if she thought there was a chance I would say no. Either way, I felt like it was something that didn't need asking.

"Of course . . ." was all I could muster. I wanted to say more, like I would do anything for her or Uncle Joe, but the words just wouldn't come.

"Thank you, Michael," she replied motioning toward where she had been previously standing. "Please talk to Father Paschal. He will tell you what needs to be done."

I nodded, hugged Aunt Ruth one more time, and turned toward you.

"It's okay," you said and, after seeing Mom and Dee acknowledge my thoughts of staying with you, I walked over to join the Father and Joey.

When I got there, I said hi to Joey and introduced myself to Father Paschal and the few other pallbearers. The Father, and one of the gentlemen that I was guessing was from the funeral home, gave us some quick instructions and asked us to wait there while they went off to finish some last minute preparations.

"Are you doing okay, Joey?" I asked, trying to break the ice ever present between us.

"Okay . . . I guess. You?" Joey said, sounding more like a knee-jerk response than actual concern.

"I'm okay," I replied, ignoring his apathy. "I'm sorry about your dad . . . about your loss. He was a great guy."

At that Joey just nodded. There was definitely something upsetting him besides his dad's passing, but I let it slide. Again, we were here about Uncle Joe, not Joey and me. I really did want to bury the hatchet with him, at some point. But I guess that *some point* would not be here or today. A minute later, Father Paschal and the funeral director motioned to us to come toward and positioned us around the casket.

We escorted the casket out to the waiting hearse, and after helping place Uncle Joe's remains in the car, we made our ways to our respective vehicles. I could see you standing near Mom and Dee, so I made my way toward you three.

"Okay, we'll see you over there, Mike," Mom said as she and Dee left for their car.

Like the others, we followed the procession of cars on the short drive around the block to the cemetery. Once there, we met up with Dee and Mom again and walked toward the gravesite. I squeezed your hand, and we looked at each other as I broke off to head to the hearse to complete my task.

After we carried the casket to the gravesite, there was a short ceremony. At the end of it all, Father Paschal announced that the family would be meeting at Aunt Ruth's house for lunch. As we all broke away to walk back to our cars, I stopped you and asked if you minded if we didn't go to Aunt Ruth's.

"We can do whatever you want sweetie," you replied.

I was happy that you didn't ask me why I didn't want to go. I didn't actually know myself. It could have been me not wanting to be social, or not wanting to eat. All I knew was that I was tired and ready to leave.

Along the way, I stopped to say goodbye to Aunt Ruth.

"You're not coming to my house, Michael?"

"No, I didn't sleep well last night. We're just going to head home, if that's okay," I said, and then hugged her goodbye.

"Sure honey. You take care," Aunt Ruth said as she gave me a kiss on the cheek, and then she looked at you.

"It was very nice meeting you Amy," Aunt Ruth said, and then gave you a hug.

"It was nice meeting you too!" you replied, and we turned to leave.

We were quiet on the way home, you giving me my space and time to deal with the events of the weekend.

"You don't mind me dropping you off, do you?" I probed.

"No, I don't mind. I know you need time," you said as you took my hand and kissed it. "Just know that I'm here if you need to talk."

"Thank you Amy," I said as I returned the kiss, then continued the drive home.

An hour later, we made it back to your house. Even though you said there was no need, I helped you carry your bag into your house. As I prepared to leave, I again told you I appreciated your understanding. You said it was no problem, kissed and hugged me, and told me you'd talk to me that evening.

While unpacking at home, I found the box from Aunt Ruth and opened it. Inside was a note, and Uncle Joe's Rolex. I, of course, was floored. I had figured that whatever was in the package was something Uncle Joe wanted me to have, but the Rolex was one of his most personal and prized — and expensive — possessions.

I remember, years ago, Uncle Joe telling me the story on how he came to own the watch. I think I was ten or eleven when he first showed it to me. Uncle Joe was very proud of it, and he told me it was a lifelong dream of his to own a Rolex one day.

"I've always loved watches," Uncle Joe said as he showed me the newly purchased timepiece. "And I always told myself that, once I had enough money, I would buy one. To me, it was a goal. A material sign that I felt I'd made it. That I'd had a good life."

At that he handed it to me, letting me hold the watch for a bit, so I could admire the craftsmanship. And I did, even at my young age. The detailing and manufacturing time put into it, the idea that someone had created something so special, something that could be considered a piece of art.

"It is really beautiful," I remarked as I handed it back.

My eyes teared as I looked over the watch and recalled our conversation from all those years ago. I eventually set down the Rolex and picked up the note to read. It was from Uncle Joe, I could tell. There was no mistaking his perfect handwriting, something I had never mastered.

"Mike, I hope this note finds you well.
If you're reading this, then the watch made its way to you.
I know how much you admired this watch when I showed it to you years ago, and know you truly knew why I bought it.
That's why I want you to have it. I think you'll appreciate it more, and care for it more than Joey will.
I know he'll be upset that I gave this to you, but these days anything I do seems to upset him. I do feel bad about that, but I'm sure I'm not the only dad that has problems relating to their son. I know I wasn't always on the best of terms with my dad.
Also, it's not like I'm not leaving things for Joey, so don't worry about this one, he'll be fine.
Mike, I also wanted you to know how much I love you and am very proud of the man you've become. I've always thought of you as a son and wish you all the best in life.
Love, Uncle Joe."

I will always cherish that watch, and who and what it symbolizes. To me it symbolizes family, and the bond between them. It also symbolizes passing along of history from generation to generation. But, most of all, it symbolizes to me the love and respect of a man that I will always be thankful that I had in my life, someone that showed me what it truly means to be a dad.

Diary: January 19

Four months, come and gone. It's hard to believe. It seems like a lot longer.

I had my first actual date yesterday. Her name is Samantha, Sam for short. We met online a couple weeks ago and met in person last night at a local restaurant. We had a couple drinks and split appetizers. She is funny and smart. She works for a firm running their IT department. She has two boys, both in their late teens and also has two cats and a dog.

Sam is quite lovely. She has long, light brown hair. Not sure if it's her natural color or not. Her eyes are brown.

Does any of this really matter? She's no you. No one will ever be you!

I do look forward to other dates with her, because she is funny and kind. I think there is potential there. But is there really? All I think about when the conversation breaks is you and life without you. And I hate that my mind keeps going back there.

The date lasted about three hours, at least an hour longer than I thought it would. I'd like to say there might be a spark there. It's really too soon to tell, way too soon. But I will continue to try.

I keep telling myself to move along even though I'm damaged. It's what we ex-military men do, right? Be strong. Be a warrior. Keep up the fight until we can fight no more.

The only thing I can do is try . . .

CHAPTER

4

"Move it! Move it! Move it you dirtbags!" the drill sergeant barked. *"Get off this motherfucking bus!"*

"You better move like you've got a purpose!" the second drill sergeant demanded.

Yes, that was the start of my first day of Basic Training. Being yelled at, I believe, is a rite of passage for all new enlistees, or a strange sort of waterboarding technique.

I should back up, though.

After I graduated from high school, I had no real direction in life. My initial thoughts were that I'd become an architect, or maybe a teacher. I knew I was decent at drawing and really enjoyed history and English, but I didn't have any drive or money. So I wasn't really sure what I was going to do with my life. I knew that being a busboy paid the bills — ok, the bills my mom gave me to pay — but I wanted more out of life.

Being from a relatively poor family, we didn't have a lot of money, and no money for me to go to college. So it was up to me if I wanted to continue my education. I tried the usual routes, at first. I looked at grants and loans, but being a mediocre student at best didn't get me far.

After about a year being out of school and working, I knew I had to do something. If not, I would probably work as a busboy my entire life. It was about this time that one of my friends from high school, Bob, arrived home on leave. Bob had joined the military right out of high school and went into the Airborne infantry.

"Dude, you should join the army," Bob suggested, knowing my predicament. "They're giving me $20,000 for school. And I hear if you join the National Guard after your initial enlistment is up, the State will pay for your tuition! That leaves the other money for books and beer!"

I normally didn't take advice from Bob, just because he was always gung-ho about ideas *he* thought were better than sliced bread, but this one actually seemed like a good one. I mean, this was almost too good to be true, the idea that someone that will pay *me* to go to school. So it took me all of, like, two seconds to be swayed.

"Okay, what do I have to do?" I asked, knowing I might regret the answer.

"It's easy. I'll go with you to the army recruiter tomorrow!"

Bob was way too enthusiastic about this, but I told myself, *Hey, what is there to lose?*

Then, again, weren't those Marie Antoinette's famous last words?

The next day, which happened to be my day off, Bob and I went to the recruiting office. We were greeted — and by greeted I mean, door-opened, escorted-to-a-seat-in-his-office, coffee-offered greeted — by a staff sergeant Billings. Not being a coffee drinker at the time, I respectfully declined the beverage and proceeded to the topic at hand.

"What brings you gentlemen here today?" Sergeant Billings asked as he sat down at his desk.

"I'm thinking about joining the army," I stated.

"Did you have a certain career in mind?" the sergeant asked as he placed a sheet in front of me containing my options for career specialties.

I didn't really need to look these over, already having picked the Airborne infantry. Bob, having up-talked his choice, seemed to have chosen well, so who was I to question. After all, I knew I still wanted to be an architect or a teacher someday, so why would I need to learn a trade while serving?

After telling Sergeant Billings my choice, I was escorted to a computer to take a pre-test to make sure I had the smarts to jump out of a perfectly good airplane. The test wasn't that hard, in my estimation, so I scored well. I found out later that my score was high enough to choose any career I wanted.

"Sure I can't talk you into a career in computers or engineering?" the sergeant asked.

"No, my main reason for joining is the money for college. Airborne infantry seems like something I'd like."

Sergeant Billings nodded at that and proceeded to pull forms out of his desk for me to fill out and sign. Less than an hour later, I was officially bound to the army.

I was all smiles when I left the recruiting office, knowing I'd made a good life choice. I couldn't wait to tell Mom and Dee what I had done, knowing they'd be proud that I was doing something with my life.

One of the things I didn't think about while signing my life away, however, was how this would affect my girlfriend Barb.

Barb and I had been dating on and off for about six months, and this happened to be one of the times we were on. Barb was a junior in high school and worked at the same restaurant I worked at as a dishwasher. Because of our conflicting schedules, our dating was limited to an occasional Friday or Saturday night, if neither one of us was working.

Knowing I'd see Barb at work the next day, I waited to tell her. Luckily, we had the same shift that day, and both got to work fifteen minutes or so early.

"You did what?" Barb asked. I could tell she was a little miffed.

"I joined the army."

"Why the hell would you do that?" she asked, a little stronger this time.

"So I could earn money for college."

"And you didn't think I'd like to have discussed this with you before you joined?"

"Well, my friend Bob was in town—"

"And you couldn't *call me*?" she exclaimed.

"I did know I'd see you today."

"You couldn't call me *before* you did it? *Uuuuhhhh!*" she screamed. I didn't think she'd be this upset, knowing how often we saw each other.

Barb stood there in front of me for a minute, arms crossed, toe tapping, fuming. All I could think to do was stand there and wait for her to calm down. Eventually she asked, "So, when do you leave?"

"In two weeks. And I'm sorry. I really didn't think you'd be upset! I'll be home on leave in four months."

"*Four months*! Four months?"

"Yeah, four months. It's not like its forever."

"I *know* it's not *forever*! It's still four *months*!" Barb exclaimed, and then, after a pause, she said the words I knew deep down were coming. "Well, if you think I'm going to sit around waiting for you, *you are wrong*!"

At that, she turned and bolted into no-man's land, aka the women's restroom. After a minute or so, seeing that she wasn't coming out, I clocked in and went to work.

That shift was the last time I saw Barb. Her mom picked her up after work, refusing the ride home I offered her. And although I tried to call her the next day, and a few other days before I left, she refused to take any of calls.

All in all, my final two weeks before leaving were pretty uneventful. I quit my job on a week's notice, which totally pissed off my supervisor and guaranteed I'd never have a job there again. I said goodbye to all my friends that weren't away at college. And I drank beer.

Mom and Dee were *happy if I was happy*, of course. I could always count on them backing me in my good and bad decisions. We had a pleasant farewell dinner at a nice restaurant the night before I left, where they told me they'd miss me, and I returned the sentiment. And the next day I was off. A hop, skip, and jump later, I was at . . .

"Move it maggots!"

In what seemed like forever, but was probably only twenty seconds, the busload of us recruits were standing in lines in front of what would be our new home for the next four months. The drill sergeants walked up and down the aisles yelling at, berating, and generally harassing us. Sergeants would occasionally stop to pick on one individual that kept *eyeballing* an instructor, or one that just couldn't seem to stand up straight.

"You maggots are going to be split into platoons. Once you hear your name called, you will form in front of the instructor responsible for that platoon! Is that understood?"

"Yes sergeant!" we all shouted.

"*What was that pathetic squeak I just heard? I said, 'Is that understood?*'" the instructor screamed.

"*Yes sergeant!*" we screamed back.

"*I can't hear you!*"

"*Yes sergeant!*" we screamed again.

"*God dammit! Drop and give me twenty! All of you!*" he barked, the veins on his forehead looking like they were going to burst.

At that we stopped and got into what I would eventually learn was the *leaning rest* and proceeded to do the lame versions of what we thought were pushups. After about five minutes, the drill sergeant got tired of this and finished assigning us to our platoons.

I was assigned to the second platoon along with about thirty others. On the plus side, they had me bunk above the guy that would eventually be the platoon leader, Jake Sampers. He and I became friends quickly. The advantage to this, of course, was that he made sure I wasn't assigned to any shit details, when he could help it.

Sampers, the use of the last name being more the norm in Basic, and life, actually, was from Detroit. Sampers was probably three or four years older than me and looked a few years older than that. He had graduated and gone onto college, getting his associates degree in business, but felt he was suited for the military. I came to find out that he also had a wife and child in Detroit.

After a few weeks, life became routine. Wake at 0500 hours. Go for PT, physical training, for about an hour. Clean up and eat breakfast. Train. Eat lunch. Train. Get picked on and do chores. Clean up and go to bed.

The busyness helped take my mind off the fact that I was one thousand miles away from home.

Besides traveling with Mom and Dee, I had never been away from home and family before. So this was a new, and somewhat scary, experience for me. Not that the drill sergeants yelling at me wasn't scary; it was, scary as fuck, actually. It was a different type of scary. A lonely, empty feeling that I'd never experienced before, except maybe with the loss of my dad. My mom and sister had always been there for me before. They had always been there when I needed help with my homework or a shoulder to cry on.

This was definitely a new experience.

Sundays were good days in boot camp. Very little PT, very little cleaning, and, as long as we didn't fuck up the barracks during the week, I got to call home. If I remember correctly, we only got fifteen minutes to call, so you had to keep it short and sweet.

Of course, I called my mom and occasionally talked to my sister. My side of the conversations pretty much went like this:

"Hi Mom! How are you?"

"Good. What's new?"

"Nothing, okay. How's work?"

"Same old, same old. Any new *men* I should know about?"

"That's good, at least. So, are you still going to come down for graduation?"

"Great to hear! I miss you guys! Give Dee a hug for me! I love you!"

Click.

Occasionally, when the line wasn't too long, I'd go back to the end of the line for another turn so I could call Barb. She was, at least in my mind, still my girlfriend. These calls usually consisted of me getting attitude from Barb for not being around. So, toward the end of training, I called her less and less.

Although I was learning a lot of new things, my mind was always on home and how I may have fucked up my life by joining the army. I tried to keep my mind focused on knowing that it was only three years, which, of course, was a big chunk of my life considering I was only nineteen. But I pressed on. And it wasn't so bad. It definitely did wonders for my cleaning skills and sleep deprivation. Plus, Georgia in March, April, and May isn't that bad. Not too hot and not too cold for the twelve-mile hikes.

Eight weeks in, I switched from Basic Training to Advanced Individual Training, AIT. It had been determined several weeks beforehand that my dexterity and knowledge were above average, so they assigned me to Mortar School. This is where I spent my next four weeks. It was cool because Sampers was in the Mortars, as well. It made the time go quickly, and we had a shit ton of fun!

It was kind of weird being assigned to the Mortars. Only about 10 percent of my Company was assigned to them, so it made us feel special. It also isolated us to some extent from the rest of our Company. A few bits of training, like hand-to-hand combat, we as Mortars didn't need to do since it was more important we learn how to fire the cannon.

Before we knew it, infantry school graduation finally arrived. And, as promised, Mom and Dee came down for my graduation ceremony. I was so happy to see them after three months. It wasn't a lot of time, but I'd get to spend the weekend with them.

We had a great time. Well, mostly great. There was the moment my drill instructor hit on my mom; yeah, I know, weird. But I digress. The hotel they stayed in had a pool, so we spent a lot of time relaxing and hanging out together.

The weekend was over too quickly, and it was on to Airborne School. It was tough saying goodbye to Mom and Dee, but telling them I'd see them in a month made it just a little easier.

Airborne School was split into four one-week sessions. Okay, it was really split into three sessions, but when most trainees arrived they didn't have a team *spot* yet, so they sat around for a week before being assigned to a team. I called this the *Buffer* week. The second week was called Ground Week. Every morning they'd run the hell out of us and then teach us how to not break a leg, or anything else, when landing. The third week was called Tower Week. Every morning they'd run the hell out of us and then teach us to make sure our chutes were attached to our bodies properly and what to do in case of an emergency, like a tangled chute or one that didn't open. The third week was known as Jump Week. No PT but a lot of sitting, waiting for good weather so we could make our five jumps.

To me, the Buffer week was the most challenging. Daily we would get assigned to go to places around Fort Benning to *clean this* or *polish that*. And, of course, I still hated cleaning. No amount of Basic Training was going to break me of that. The other weeks were just training and following orders, and not breaking a leg.

I think the best part was my second jump. The Airborne instructor separated the line right in front of me, which put me in line to be the first one out the door. It was incredible standing there while the plane was traveling at two-hundred miles per hour, just watching the scenery go by. After I jumped, I got twisted around slightly and was able to see the plane as I hurdled away from it. One of the most spectacular sights I've ever seen in my life.

At the end, I successfully performed my five jumps and received my Airborne Wings.

Like most of the guys I was with, I requested a ten day leave at the end of Airborne School before I had to travel to my first duty station. It was granted, and shortly after I received my wings, I packed my gear and headed to the airport.

Even though I was still a little exhausted from the nonstop training and stresses on my body, I still wanted to hit the ground running when I got home. And the first thing on my agenda, besides saying hi to Mom and Dee, was to stop and visit my old job, and Barb.

When I got to the restaurant, my old manager, Bobby, was working. After a hearty handshake, and a few minutes of talking about my experiences, I asked if Barb was working.

"Nah man, Barb quit about a month ago. Guess she figured she'd move to Florida with her dad."

I was kind of stunned by this. We had talked just over a month ago, and she hadn't mentioned anything about leaving. Even though Barb often talked about missing her dad and hoped to see him in the near future, I was floored. I tried not to let it show, but I'm sure I failed miserably.

And it's true when they say *you don't know what you've lost until it's gone.* I had missed Barb a lot while I was in Basic and Airborne and, in the back of my head, I never thought she'd leave me for someone else, let alone leave the state.

There would be no "An Officer and a Gentleman" ending for me here. And I was sad about that, sad about not seeing Barb again. Sad about love lost.

But, even though I was bummed a bit, I don't think I slept more than four hours a night while on leave. I wanted to do *everything* I had missed while away. I ate a *lot* of fast food, I drank a *lot* of beer, and I saw as many friends as I could. Over the next nine days I had a blast, but was over before I knew it.

My first — and what would turn out to be my only — duty assignment was at Fort Hood in Texas. I arrived at the beginning of summer, and it was already exceedingly hot. My first stop was at the post assignment office, where they would assign me to whichever battalion needed an Airborne infantryman.

To my surprise, shock really, I was assigned to the Mortar Section of a Tank Battalion. It seems there was no call for an Airborne person anywhere on Fort Hood. I was depressed by this. I was really hoping to follow in my friend Bob's footsteps and get to jump out of perfectly good airplanes.

I left the assignment office in kind of a haze and made my way to the office of my new battalion. I won't go into which one I was assigned to or any of the details about my time there, except to say it was where I spent the next two-and-half years.

After about four months there, I took leave and went home. As you may, or may not, know, we were getting thirty days of leave a year, so I tried to take ten days every four months to *even out* my time and keep me sane. At the end of four months, I was really homesick and, pretty much, fed up with the "drive here" and "drive there" I was getting on base. Also, I really didn't like Texas. As a friend's dad once told me, it's the "only place I know where you can be up to your ass in mud and have sand hit you in the face."

Along with feeling homesick, I was missing having a girlfriend. Being in a tank battalion meant I was with all guys, 24/7, and the visits I did take to town, or to Dallas, made me miss it even more. There were a couple girls I had met, through friends, but they just never my type. And there was the fact that I would be going home for good someday and that might cause problems.

I got in around 4:00 p.m., and my sister Dee picked me up from the airport. At first, she seemed really weird, like she had something to tell me but she wouldn't spit it out. I wondered if she had a new boyfriend or a new job, but she wouldn't say.

When we got home, my mom was waiting and we went right back out again for dinner; eating out was kind of our thing with a working mom. During dinner, Dee told me that she was going out that night and wanted me to come along. She was planning on meeting some friends and had told them all about her *army brother* and wanted to introduce me. She also told me that we were going to a dance club and I should probably spruce myself up a little *just in case*. Who am I to argue with my older sister?

"Haven't I met all your friends?"

"No, there's a few that you haven't. You've been gone four months you know!"

Around 9:00 p.m., we left for the dance club with my sister smiling the whole time. I knew she was up to something. When we got to the club, I immediately saw the table she was headed for. Dee's best friend Rachel was sitting with a girl I had never met before.

"Hey Rachel!" I yelled, having to scream over the music.

"Damn Mike, you look good! The military must be agreeing with you!"

It wasn't, but I smiled and hugged her anyway.

"Mike," Dee started. "This is my friend Jennifer."

"Hi Jennifer!" I exclaimed, my voice breaking slightly.

Jennifer was about five foot four, had brown eyes and brown hair, and was a tad overweight. She had on jeans and a white blouse that fit just right, if you know what I mean.

"Hi Mike! It's nice to meet you finally! Dee's told me a lot about you."

"Oh yeah? Well, none of it's true," I joked, making her laugh. A laugh I was thankful for, considering what a horrible opening line it was.

Although Jennifer wasn't super-hot, she did have a certain air about her – a vibe surrounding her that emoted sexuality. I was instantly smitten.

"How do you know Dee? And, more importantly, what has she told you about me?"

"Oh, not much . . . just that you're in the army and you're stationed in Texas. She showed me your picture from training. You looked very angry," she said smiling.

"Yeah, they don't like soldiers that smile," I jested.

This banter lasted for about twenty minutes, and the whole time it did, I could see Dee out of the corner of my eye just smiling away. Then it hit me. The reason Dee had been so aloof earlier. This was all a set-up. Dee could be sneaky when she wanted to be. I guessed I'd just run with it.

Seems Dee and Jennifer had met at Dee's work, a local restaurant, where Dee did some bookkeeping. Jennifer had been hired a month or so previously to work as a receptionist on the night shift. She told me she liked the job, and it was convenient because it wasn't too far away from home. She also liked it because it allowed her to go to college during the day.

Eventually I got up enough nerve to ask, "Would you like to dance?"

"Sure!" Jennifer said enthusiastically.

"Dee, we're going to dance," I announced, nudging my sister.

"Okay, we'll join you!"

This was not the response I wanted but should have figured.

We proceeded to the dance floor that only had a few other people on it; it was early. The floor probably wouldn't get busy until after 11:00 p.m., which was fine with me. I wanted a little bit of space and privacy

— as much privacy as you can have on a dance floor — so I could talk to Jennifer more.

I found that it was comfortable talking to her. Not forced in the least. She had a certain wit about her, and a pleasant smile. We continued to talk and dance for three or four songs, until a song came on that neither one of us liked much. Also, we were both thirsty, so we made our way to the bar for drinks and then walked back to the table where we continued to talk.

Before I knew it, the evening was over, and we said our goodbyes. Now it became awkward, because I really didn't want the evening to end. Jennifer was wonderful. I asked her for her number, which was dumb since I knew Dee had it, but hey, I can be dumb when it comes to the opposite sex.

After Jennifer said goodbye to Dee, I walk her to her car. When we got there, she unlocked the door and I proceeded to open it for her. As I reached for it, she moved in between me and the car and, before I knew it, we locked in an embraced.

Her lips tasted like cherry lip balm, sweet and savory. And I held onto that kiss for as long as I felt I should dare before moving back to open her car door.

After she was inside, I closed the door and backed away so she could leave.

I think I stood there for a minute or so after she pulled away, still reeling from the events of the evening. I know at some point I made my way back to Dee and Rachel, walked Rachel to her car, and headed to Dee's car. It was all kind of a blur.

Most of that leave I spent with Jennifer.

I wanted to spend every second I could with her before I had to go away for another four months. We went to dinner a couple times, visited my friends a few times, and made out a lot. Many of the nights we just cuddled up on my mom's couch and watched TV, enjoying a closeness I had sorely missed.

Before I knew it, my leave was up, and I was headed to the airport bound for Texas. Jennifer drove over to my house in the morning so she could drive with Dee and me to the airport. As I exited the car, Jennifer kissed me long and hard, leaving me with the taste of cherries the entire flight back to base.

The months I waited for my next leave rolled by quicker than I expected. Being able to talk with Jennifer, Mom, and Dee whenever I wanted helped the time pass. Before I knew it I was again requesting leave and booking flights.

This time when I landed, I was met at the airport by Jennifer. Meeting me right outside of security, we were in each other's arms as soon as we saw each other. Feeling her familiar warmth next to me brought back the comfort I was longing for. After we separated — quite a while later — we strolled, hand in hand, to her car.

Leaving the airport, I noticed that we weren't going toward my mom's house.

"Um, can I ask where we're headed?"

"You'll see," she replied, in a playful voice. Twenty minutes later, we were pulling into a hotel parking.

"What's this all about?"

"Well, I figured we could use some quality time together. Haven't you missed me?"

With that, I grabbed her and kissed her hard. "Does that answer your question?"

Smiling blissfully, we picked up our bags and checked in. We barely made it in the room before she was on me, attacking me, and pulling at my clothes. Within a minute, we were in the bed writhing on each other, showing each other how much we missed one another.

An hour later, we ordered room service, and spent the rest of the night in each other's embrace. Eating, catching up, making love, and just holding each other. And we slept a very restful sleep, the type of sleep I couldn't get when away from the ones I loved.

In the morning, we checked out of the hotel and drove to my mom's, where we spent the day lounging and talking with my family until Jennifer had to leave for work. As soon as she left, I borrowed Mom's car and visited a few friends, but made sure I was available the moment Jennifer was out of work.

Over the next nine days, Jennifer and I spent almost every waking moment - and a couple sleeping ones – together. As before, leave came and went in a flash. Although quicker than I wanted, I was left with plenty of great memories to take back with me to Fort Hood.

Over the four months, we seemed to talk less and less each week. I could tell that the distance was having an effect, but what could I do? I was in Texas and she was in Ohio, and I had two years to go on my contract before I could be discharged.

When the four month mark hit, I put in for another ten-day leave. As soon as it was approved, I called Jennifer to tell her the good news.

"Oh. That's nice" was all she said.

"I thought you'd be happy about seeing me!"

"Well, my mom and dad booked a vacation for us and I'll be gone."

"The whole ten days?"

"No, I'll be home the next Friday night. I might be able to see you then."

Might be able to see me then? This seemed to be a weird response, considering how much we had talked about missing each other. I guess I could understand a planned vacation with her parents taking priority over my trip, but the indifference in her voice threw me off.

Not wanting to give up on seeing her so easily, I quickly worked out another plan.

"Hey, let me check to see if I can push my leave back a week! That way it won't interfere with the vacation."

"Oh, don't do that for me. I know your family misses you! And you can still visit your friends!"

Unsure on how to respond to her cold retort, I simply said, "I suppose."

An awkward silence descended on the line as I tried to think of some way I could get to see her. I finally broke the quiet by asking, "Where are you guys going on vacation?"

"Um . . . to my aunt's house, in Michigan."

"And you're sure you can't get out of it?"

"No, it's been a couple years since we've seen her, and my parents want me to go. They're really looking forward to it, actually."

After another minute of small talk, and getting nowhere with my quest to see her, I said the only things left I could think of. "Okay. Well, I'll let you go then. I miss you!"

"Yeah, I miss you too," she replied, and I heard the familiar click as the line disconnected.

After I hung up the phone, I stared at it for a moment, bewildered. Considering she knew I was planning a trip around this time, the sudden news of a family vacation seemed very odd.

Feeling like I wasn't getting the whole story, I decided to call Dee to see if she knew about any of this. Unfortunately, she didn't.

"Actually, Jennifer and I really haven't hung out that much in the last few weeks. I've only seen her at work a few times in the last month."

After I hung up with Dee, I thought about my options. After hemming and hawing about it for a couple minutes, I stuck to my original plan. Calling the airline, I made my flight arrangements, and hoped I'd get a chance to see Jennifer while on leave.

When I exited the airport my sister Dee was there waiting for me. I was happy to see her, even though I was wishing it was Jennifer meeting me instead

As we were driving home, I asked Dee if she had heard anything else out of Jennifer.

"Actually, I talked to her the other day."

"And?"

"And she seemed really weird."

"How so?"

"I don't know. She was very evasive when I asked about her vacation."

The rest of the ride home was somber. I contemplated this new information and what I should do, and decided that - after dinner with my family - I would drive over Jennifer's house to see if she had left yet for her aunt's.

About two hours later, I borrowed Dee's car and drove to Jennifer's. As I drove by her house, it looked like they were still home. All the lights were on, and their three cars were in the driveway. In order to not seem creepy — stalking *was* kind of creepy — I drove home and called Jennifer's house. Mrs. Lindale, Jennifer's mom, answered.

"Hello Mrs. Lindale. Is Jennifer home?"

"Oh. Hi Mike! Yes she is. Let me get her."

A minute later Jennifer picked up the phone. "Hi Mike! You're here! I didn't think you were coming in until tomorrow."

"No. Pretty sure I told you I was coming in today."

"Well, I must have mixed up the days."

"What are you doing? Can I come over?"

There was a slight pause, and it sounded like she muffled the phone. After about a minute, she returned, "Um . . . we're getting ready to leave in the morning, so I don't think it's a good idea."

"Oh . . ." was all I could say. I was taken aback by her response. I just traveled twelve hundred miles to be with her, and she was blowing me off.

"Can I ask? Is there a reason you've been distant the last few weeks?"

With this there was another pause. I finally got the response I was dreading. "Mike, I'm not quite sure how to tell you this . . . but . . . I started seeing someone else."

My chin, and heart, dropped to the floor.

"I was going to tell you sooner . . ." she continued, "but we just started seeing each other, and I'm not sure where it's headed." There was another slight pause, and I could hear her clearing her throat. "I'm telling you this because I really do like you and care about you. This is just something that happened."

It was obvious to me at that point she was trying to have her cake and eat it too, like she wanted to keep me around in case things didn't work out with the new guy. And part of me, specifically the part that didn't like to lose, thought that I could make this work. I could hang on and wait for this guy to fuck up.

But most of me had too much respect for myself to do this and knew I had to move on.

"Well, I'm sorry to hear that Jennifer," I said, holding back the tears, and the rage. "I really did think there was something between us."

And, of course, for pride and sanity, I had to say it. "I guess this is goodbye."

At that I hung up the phone, ending my last call with Jennifer.

I heard a few years later, through Dee, that it didn't work out with the new guy, but she did meet someone and settle down. In my heart, I wish her the best in life, and love.

Diary: February 19

I had a good friend pass away the other day. She was a mutual friend. She was someone that we would both see when we were out and about. The wake is tomorrow. And all I can think is how we aren't attending together.

We used to do everything together.

The good. The bad. The questionable. The fun. The boring.

Everything.

And now I have to be there for emotional support for our friends and her husband.

How do I do that when my heart is just as broken as theirs? How do I tell her husband that I can't be one to lean on?

Some mornings I wake hating you for leaving. This eventually fades, and I hate myself for hating you. I hate myself for loving you. I hate myself because I can't move on.

How do I move on? Please God, tell me . . .

CHAPTER

5

I remember the first time I lost you.

Things had been going well with us the first two years we were together, or so I thought. I think every couple has issues from time to time. Ours were usually around me having ex-wives and kids. Not to say there weren't other issues. But being part of another family at one time bothered you.

"Hey Amy! My daughter's sixteenth birthday party is on Saturday. I need to go. Do you want to go with me?" This was the message I left on your voicemail.

Being a typical weekday, you usually kept your cellphone on silent and didn't respond to texts or calls until lunchtime or after work. I understood this, in most cases, so if it was really urgent I called your office to get hold of you. Sure enough, around lunchtime, I got the returned call.

"Hi Mike! You mean this coming Saturday? Why are you just telling me now?"

"Sorry sweetie. Michelle just sent me a text letting me know."

Michelle was my second ex-wife and my daughter Heather's mom. The party, which was originally slated for the following weekend, had to be moved up because of a last minute scheduling change at her work. The following weekend was chosen because it was the only available one in the foreseeable future. So, as soon as she knew, she texted me to let me know.

"Well it's kind of last minute. I was hoping we could go to the art gallery," you replied.

I knew this, of course. We had planned on going that weekend, and I knew you were really looking forward to it. And you weren't the only one. I wanted to go just as much as you, but suddenly I was put between a rock and a hard place. The only thing I could do was punt.

"Well, the party is at 1:00 p.m. at the park. We *could* go to the art gallery after. We would easily be out of there by 3:00," I said, hoping this would appease you.

"That won't give us much time at the gallery."

"Again, I'm sorry sweetie! How about we try to be out of there by 2:00 p.m.?"

"I suppose. But, do I have to go?"

"Not if you don't want to. We could make it to the art gallery earlier though, if we could leave right from the party."

"Can we talk about it later? I need to get back to work."

"No problem, my love. I love you!"

"I love you too," I heard right before the phone disconnected.

From the sound of your voice, I knew you were pissed, but I was trying.

It was like I was always trying to balance spending time with my kids and you. But I did make you the priority in most cases. This was different though. This was Heather's sixteenth birthday party.

We saw each other later that evening, and after discussing the different options, which included me picking you up from home after the party or me dropping you off at a local store before the party and picking you up after, we agreed that you going to the party made more sense. As discussed, I picked you up on Saturday at 12:30 p.m. so we could be at the party right at 1:00 p.m.

When we got there, the party was already in full swing. It was mostly Heather's friends, my son Brian, my ex-wife and her boyfriend, and assorted others from Michelle's side of the family. I had asked my mom and Dee if they would be there, but neither one could change their schedules to accommodate the last minute date change.

Heather was, as always, very beautiful. She was dressed in a spring dress and combat boots, which was the normal attire at the time for her high school peers. You were very cordial to her and her friends, even though I knew you didn't want to be there. And, actually, I really didn't want to be there either. I love my daughter, but it was really my ex-wife's family's party, and I felt like I was intruding.

Also, I really wanted this to be *our* weekend. I wanted every weekend to be *our* weekend.

On the plus side, Brian was there, and he sat with us as we ate. We talked about what Brian had been up to with work and any girlfriend update we hadn't talked about. It was good to see him; I really didn't see him enough.

About an hour into the party, Heather, and her friends, opened up her presents, which included the one I bought her. I had gotten her a new *fashionable* jacket to match what her friends were wearing so she could be *in style.* I also gave her a gift card to Applebee's because the girl does love her some Applebee's.

When all the gifts were opened and the cake was cut and eaten, we said our goodbyes to the crowd and left for the art gallery. I believe we only missed the 2:00 p.m. cut-off time by a half an hour, and I was grateful you didn't berate me for it.

After the gallery, we went to dinner at an Italian place and headed back toward my apartment.

At that point in our relationship, you were spending weekends at my apartment. Even though you only lived ten minutes away from me, you had started spending weekends so we could spend more time together. And it was way more comfortable to make out on a couch or bed than it was in the backseat of my car.

"So, anything in particular you want to watch when we get to the apartment?"

"No," you said. "Actually, could you do me a favor and drop me off at my house?"

"Oh? You brought your stuff . . . I thought you were spending the night at the apartment."

"Yeah. Sorry. I forgot that my mom wanted me to go to church with her in the morning. I hope you don't mind."

"Not at all, my love," I said, even though I did mind. "I'm sorry we didn't get to spend more time together."

At this, you were silent and I could tell that something was up, but I resolved not to question it. I loved you and had to trust that you were telling me the truth.

As I dropped you off, you were very brief with me. In the past, before you started spending weekends with me, we would park and make out in your mom's driveway for hours, sometimes until the sun came up.

"Good night. I'll talk to you tomorrow at some point," you said as you kissed me, exited the car, and walked toward the house.

"Good night!" I returned, and added, "I love you!"

But there was no reply.

After you were safely inside, I sat there for a minute pondering what had just transpired. Was I imagining things, or were you upset? Did you hear me say I love you and chose not to respond, or did you just miss it? I couldn't tell. And sometimes you held your feelings so close to the chest that I couldn't read you. I figured I was just overthinking things, so I waited until the next day to ask you.

That next day, I didn't hear from you much, which was different from our normal weekends. No matter what our plans were, we usually kept in touch and texted each other several times a day, sometimes several times an hour. But, for some reason, this felt different. I remember you texting me "Good night" in lieu of a phone call, which really bothered me, but I thought you might just be busy or sleepy, so I texted back "Good Night, my love! Always!!"

Monday, during the day, I didn't hear from you at all until just after 5:00 p.m. I waited at work until then so I could talk to you, and possibly see you. Like clockwork, just after 5:00 p.m., you called.

"Hi Mike. Do you have time to talk?" you asked.

"I always have time for you, sweetie,"

"I've been thinking it over . . ." you began. "And I'm not comfortable on where our relationship is going."

I was stunned, but I knew something was amiss.

"I'm not sure what you're saying."

"I feel that you need more time with your family."

"I'm not sure where this is coming from. I thought you were okay with my kids."

"I like Brian and Heather. I just feel you need more time with them. I didn't like going to the party on Saturday," you said, and then paused.

A thick, almost tangible weight hung in the air as I waited for your next words, words that made my breathing stop. "So, I think we need to break up."

My heart sunk on your statement. It was hard to fathom that, after being together for two years, you were getting cold feet.

"I'm sorry I asked you to go to the party, Amy. You don't need to go to any more birthday parties if you don't want to!"

"It's more than that, Mike. I think I need some time to myself. I've been ignoring work and my future."

"Amy, please don't do this," I begged. "I love you. I know we can make it work out."

"I'm just not comfortable with that. I hope you can understand."

"Amy, please!" I pleaded.

"Mike, I'm sorry. I need to let you go now. Goodbye Mike."

I heard the phone disconnect, and I felt my world stop.

I sat at work for a few minutes, not knowing what to do. I had spent the last two years getting to know and love someone, spending most of my free time with that someone, and now it was all gone.

"Where do I go from here?" I asked myself aloud. As expected, there was no reply.

When I made it home, I sat for a few minutes before the tears started to fall. They didn't last long, because, how could they? I could not fully take in what had happened or truly understand why you left. All I could do was turn on the TV and take my mind off what just happened. Like that was possible.

That night I hardly slept. I left the TV on for background noise just so I didn't feel as alone as my soul felt.

In the morning, I started my normal routine. I exercised for twenty minutes, followed by filling my coffee thermos, shaving, brushing my teeth, and showering. Total prep time: around an hour. I left the apartment and drove to work in an emotional fog.

As I drove past your street, I hoped I would see you, prayed I would see you, prayed none of this was real. I wasn't sure if it was a good thing or bad that I didn't. I wasn't sure how I would react if I did.

I worked my normal day, not taking lunch. The more I worked, the less I thought of you. At the end of the day, I drove home, changed, and drove to the gym. After working out, I drove home, showered, cooked dinner, ate, and watched TV until bed time.

This became the routine, *the new routine*, and, as you know, I was good at routine. The next day I did the same thing, and the next: one foot in front of the other, step by step trying to get through the day. And each day trying not to think of you, but failing.

Thursday, I received a text from you asking "Are we still friends?"

"Of course! I can't imagine my life without you"

Even though it hurt my head to say it, I somehow knew it was the right thing to say. I had always maintained my friendships with my exes for as far back as I can remember, all the way back to high school.

After a few silent minutes, I put down the phone and returned to my routine.

Before I knew it, it was Friday. What would I do on the weekend? How would I keep my mind off you? There was work, of course. I had a laptop and could work from home, but how would that keep me sane?

I decided to drive to see Heather. Maybe seeing her, going to a movie with her, would keep my mind off the pain. I picked Heather up mid-afternoon and headed to the theater. I don't even remember what we watched. My mind was in limbo.

After the movie, I dropped Heather off and drove home, the whole time thinking of what I would do Sunday. Maybe I could visit my mom, or Dee, or one of my friends, anything to keep me active.

When I got home, I received another text from you. "Hi Mike! How are you doing?" it read.

"I miss you and love you. I hope you are doing well," I returned.

There was no response right away, but finally it read "I'm doing well. Thank you for asking!"

Then, a few seconds later I received, "Hope you have a good weekend!"

I'm not sure what this told me, except that I was on your mind. For that, at least, I was grateful.

Sunday, I woke, hit the gym, and called my mom. I drove over to see her and spent time watching TV. After maybe an hour or so, we went to dinner at a seafood place. Afterward, I dropped her off and drove home.

And the routine started over.

Tuesday, around lunchtime, I receive another text from you asking "Did you have a good weekend?"

"Yes I did. I went to a movie with Heather on Saturday and had dinner with Mom on Sunday," I returned, and then asked, "How was yours?"

"It was good. I mostly stayed home except for a trip to the store on Sunday. I picked up a new piece of furniture for my bedroom," you replied.

"Sounds good," I sent back.

"OK. I have to get back to work," you sent, and I returned, "I Love You!" But there was no reply.

Then it was back to the routine.

As Friday rolled in, I again tried to make plans for weekend. I asked myself who I could hang with this weekend to keep my sanity. Not having a good answer, I chose to see the new superhero movie on Saturday. No sooner had I put my phone down when I received the latest text from you.

"How are you?"

"Good. You?" I replied.

"OK. Big plans for the weekend?"

"No. You?" I sent back.

I waited for a bit, staring at my phone awaiting a reply, but none came. I finally texted back "I miss you and love you!" and again waited for a response.

After a few minutes, I received "Hope you have a good weekend!"

I made up my mind not to respond, knowing deep down it was better that way. After all, you knew I was here waiting. I wasn't sure what, though. Was I waiting for you to tell me you love me back? Was I waiting for you to tell me what a great weekend you had? Was I waiting for possibly no response at all? Any of the above? None of the above? It had only been two weeks, but it felt like a decade.

Friday night I stayed home, figuring there was enough on TV to keep me interested, to keep my mind off you. On the way home, I picked up some NyQuil, hoping that a dose might help me sleep. I knew it was a crappy way to solve my insomnia, but I was starting to become desperate. The long, restless nights were taking a toll on me.

When I woke on Saturday, I did the usual, getting home around noon. After showering, I sat down and looked up the *Movie Times* for the superhero movie, selected the 7:00 p.m. showing, and watched TV until it was time to leave.

As I pulled into the theater parking lot, a text came through from you. "Are you having a good day?" it read. And, like every other time, it knocked the wind out of me.

I looked at the screen for a few moments wondering what I should reply. Knowing it would do no good to reply the truth or a lie, I shut off my phone, walked into the theater, bought a ticket, and headed into the show.

The movie was decent, entertaining, and more importantly it kept my mind off you for three hours. When it ended, I left the theater and returned to my car, not realizing until I got there that I hadn't turned my phone back on. I hit the power button and, after a minute of booting, the main screen popped up. A few seconds later, two more texts from you came through. It was after 10:00 p.m., so - knowing you normally went to bed early - I didn't text you back.

When I got home I watched some TV, took some NyQuil, and fell asleep in my lounge chair.

Sunday was more of the same. This time, I picked up Brian and went to a sports bar. We ate dinner — if you can call chicken wings dinner — and watched some sports. After, I dropped Brian off and drove back to the apartment. I thought that you might text again, but there was nothing. I also thought that maybe I was better off, maybe it was time to really move on.

But then the same questions that had been bouncing around my head came to the surface: how do you move on when you know you can't? When you love her and only her? I had no answer, not even a clue.

Sunday night, as I prepared the coffee pot and my clothes for the next day, I realized that, since I hadn't heard from you, the pain of missing you was a little less than the day before. It dawned on me that each text from you felt like a hand that pushed a knife deep into my chest. And without them, I felt that I could loosen the knife and heal. It didn't mean I would heal anytime in the near future, but given time, I actually might.

In the morning, I left the apartment about three minutes later than I usually did. Not quite sure why, but it was as if something was telling me to wait.

As I was driving past one of the side streets that I knew you normally took, I saw your car rounding the corner and pulling up to the stop sign. Sitting there, we briefly made eye contact before I waved for you to go first. For the rest of the mile long drive, I followed behind you, hoping to pull up beside you just to have one glimpse of your face. Unfortunately, because of traffic, it didn't happen.

That day, I worked through lunch. Something I had been doing to keep my mind off you. It was right before the end of lunch that I received a text from you.

"Hi. Can I see you after work?"

My heart dropped again. I wasn't sure what was going on or why you wanted to see me. Had I done something wrong? Was there something I left in your car? Regardless of the reason though, I wanted to see you.

"Sure," I replied, and then added, "What time?"

"Can you come over to my office around 5:30?"

"No problem," I answered.

My whole afternoon was spent half on work, half on me thinking about seeing you. Questions like how I would react or what we would talk about kept jumping into my head. Was there anything I should or could say to change your mind and take me back?

I was so nervous. The minutes seemed like hours.

As 5:00 p.m. approached, people slowly started to leave work, eventually leaving me alone in the office. At 5:20 p.m., I couldn't wait any longer, so I sent you a text asking if it was okay to come over.

"Yes" was all I received.

"Be there in 5," I replied, and shut down my computer.

I'm sure I was pale. I felt all the blood draining from my extremities, and I hoped the walk to my car would help. My legs felt like butter as I got in my car, started it, and left the parking lot.

As I approached your work, I could see you standing outside pacing back and forth. I pulled my car into my *usual* spot, right beside the door near where you were standing. I noticed right away that you had tissues in your hand and you had been crying. Turning off my car, I got out and walked toward you. As I got closer, I noticed that you were starting to cry even more. I hoped that nothing bad had happened like your mom passing away or you getting fired.

I stopped in front of you with my arms by my side, and asked, "What's wrong Amy?"

"I'm sorry . . . I fucked up," you sobbed, dabbing at your eyes with a tissue.

"Why? What do you mean?" I asked as the multitude of possibilities ran through my head.

"Us. I fucked it up."

I'm sure I looked at you with my head slightly cocked as I thought, *Could this be real?*

"I should never have broken up with you," you continued.

Without a word, I approached you and put my arms around you, hugging you, and holding you. You returned the hug hesitantly as you broke into heavy weeping, slowly increasing your hold on me when you realized I wouldn't back away.

"It's okay. It's not unrepairable. I'm here now."

After a minute or so, when your crying slowed, we separated slightly so you could blow your nose and wipe your tears, my arms still around you, never wanting to let you go. We looked into each other's eyes. How I had missed those eyes.

"I didn't know what I was thinking . . ." you started. "I was just scared that we were getting too close . . . maybe. I don't even know," you said, starting to cry a little more. "All I know is, when you didn't text back Saturday night, it scared me that I might never talk to you again."

"I'm sorry. I was in a movie when you sent the text, and by the time I got out, it was late and didn't want to disturb you."

"I'm sorry. Can you forgive me?" you asked, dabbing at your eyes again.

I pulled you in close to hug you, my head resting on your shoulder. "Amy, I love you. There's nothing to forgive. I want you in my life, always."

With that, you hugged back hard and wept. When your crying slowed, I turned my head slightly so I could kiss your cheek. I tasted the warm salty tears that had made their way down your face. I then moved to your other cheek and kissed it, wanting to kiss all the tears away.

As your crying stopped, we loosened our embrace and faced each other and met each other's lips. As soon as we did, I felt complete again.

We moved to my car so we could sit. After we were both in, I started the car so we could have some cool air and then turned down the radio so we could talk.

"Do you have any more tissues?"

I opened my glove compartment and handed you the box. After you wiped your eyes, you asked, "Can you forgive me?"

"Asked and answered. We're fine," I replied. You just looked at me, wordlessly.

"I never want to lose you again," I continued. "I love you Amy. I've loved you before I knew you. I want you in my life forever."

"Can we go somewhere . . . for dinner maybe?" you asked as you dabbed at your eyes once again.

"Of course. Are you all locked up?" I asked, nodding toward your work.

"Uh huh," you said, and inquired, "Would you like to go to Charley's?"

"Sounds perfect," I said and put the car in reverse to start our adventure.

As we drove to the restaurant, I contemplated the last two weeks and all that had transpired. I thought about all the hurt and pain that was slowly fading away — not all healed, but fading — and I hoped they'd never come back again.

That's when I looked at you and said, "Promise me you'll never do this to me again. I don't know if I could take it."

You squeezed my hand as an acknowledgment as we turned into Charley's parking lot.

Less than a month later you moved in with me, and I felt like my life was complete.

Diary: March 19

I went to the art museum yesterday . . . the first time I've been there since I lost you.

It was difficult walking the halls and seeing the art that we both loved.

The whole time it felt like there was an empty space next to me, a void that needed to be filled. I kept looking over to see what I was missing. I eventually realized it wasn't what I was missing, it was who I was missing.

If only there were some way to get you back. If only there were some way to go back in time and change life.

I would do anything to have you back.

I literally feel like I'm in hell, every moment of every day, and I wonder why the universe is punishing me. Was it something I did? Something I didn't do? Something I did to one of my previous relationships that caused this?

I would do anything, anything, to have you back.

CHAPTER

6

When I started ninth grade, I didn't know too many people and was kind of a loner. My family had just moved to town, and I was starting in a whole new school system. I guessed this was fine because it was high school, and there were a lot of new kids that didn't have any friends there either, let alone where the hell their first class was.

Dee had it a little rougher than I did since she was in tenth grade when we relocated. She had already been through the trials of freshman year, so, for her, this was like freshman year all over again. But having her back in the same school gave me a little bit of comfort.

For me, high school was just another drain on my outside activities. I wasn't much of a school person, you could say. There were only two subjects I liked and considered myself good at: English and drawing.

Knowing this, my Uncle Joe had given me a drafting table and drafting tools the previous Christmas, and it gave me the perfect outlet for taking my mind elsewhere.

And, as it so happens, having this hobby led me to the group of friends I've had my entire life.

As one of my electives, I chose Beginning Drafting, which gave me a place to vent during the school day. On my first day, I entered the class-room and looked for a seat as far away from the front of the classroom as possible. I always did; I hated being the center of attention.

Upon choosing a seat, I noticed that all the others around me were vacant, the way I preferred it, except for the one directly to my left. There sat a kid about my same height and age, with reddish brown hair and what looked like an attitude waiting to happen.

I didn't know it then, but this kid would turn out to be the guy that would become my best friend for life.

I was never shy, except when it came to girls, so I introduced myself. "Hi. I'm Mike."

"Jim Larkman," he said as he stuck out his hand. "It's nice to meet you."

We shook, and instantly hit it off.

Jim and I both had the same sick sense of humor and didn't fall into the usual cliques you normally see in high school. We weren't jocks, but we weren't geeks. And we weren't in band or choir. I guess you could say we were part of that in-between group, but I'm not sure we were that either. The only extra-curricular activities we wanted to do were watch science fiction, draw, build models, and blow stuff up.

For the next two years of high school, Jim and I were inseparable. In school, we had a few classes together and sat together at lunch. After school, we'd walk to his house and hang out in his room or basement until dinnertime, unless I was invited to stay. On weekends, I'd help him with his paper route in the morning and we'd hang out at his house or mine all day.

In the summers, we'd sleep over at each other's houses, unless family time interceded — family vacation time and such.

During this time, Jim's family became like a second family to me. I called his mom *Mom*, and his younger sister Sarah, who was two years younger than us, was like a baby sister to me. And, just like me and Dee, Jim and Sarah fought a lot, although I could tell they actually liked each other.

We were about halfway through our junior year when we finally hit a crossroads where Jim and I started growing apart, that crossroads being girls.

It was in April that year — spring time, of course — when I met my first girlfriend. It was a normal school day, mid-week I believe, and Jim and I were walking to his house. When we got close to the house, we could see Sarah and another girl sitting on the steps of his front porch. As we approached, the girl kept staring at me with a puzzled look.

When we were within speaking distance, she said, "Hi Mike. This is my friend June."

June had brownish blond hair, blue eyes, and a devilish smile, the kind of smile that looked like she had more on her mind than freshman homework and band practice.

I was instantly smitten. I mean, at the time I was captivated by pretty much every girl I saw, especially if they smiled at me, but this was different.

I looked at her and said, "Hi June!"

"Hi Mike," she said, and then her eyes narrowed. "Are you related to Scott Sloan?"

"No. Who's that?"

"He was someone I knew in middle school. You look just like him!" she said, and then asked, "You sure you're not related?"

"Nope."

Sarah whispered something in June's ear, and before I knew it June said, "Okay, it was nice meeting you, Mike!"

At that, Sarah and June turned and walked away. As soon as they left, Jim and I continued our trek into the house and up to his room to hang out.

The next day, when Jim and I were walking to his house, we ran into Sarah and June about halfway there. As we approached the pair, I noticed that they kept looking back over their shoulders, and I suspected that *maybe* they'd been waiting for us to catch up.

"Ladies," I said, giving them a slight bow. Yeah, maybe I watched too many knight movies in high school, but it made them both giggle and smile.

"Sarah. Don't you have someplace to be? Like, not near my face?" he asked as the older brother. At this, I quickly turned and bumped his arm. I was perfectly fine being around June, and if that included his baby sister, so be it. He gave me a but-it's-my-little-sister look, but I just smiled.

"What are you two up to?" I asked, turning my attentions back toward the girls.

"Not much," June said in a perfect *high school apathetic* tone.

"Same here," I said, returning the tone as Jim and I continued our walk.

June and Sarah joined us, much to the chagrin of Jim. A junior walking with a freshman was bad enough, but an older brother walking with a younger sister was scandalous, and may be cause for immediate dismissal from the Cool Kids Club. He wasn't having it and started walking at a faster pace. I quickened my pace to catch up.

June, who had been walking behind us with Sarah, also quickened her pace so she could get close to me. I felt sorry for her, but she eventually sped up to join us.

"So . . ." June said so close to my ear it startled me. "Any big plans for the weekend, Mike?"

"No. Not really. Just planning to hang out with Jim. And you?"

"Marching band practice tomorrow morning, then nothing the rest of the weekend. My mom talked about us going to the mall, but I'm not sure I want to go."

"Wait, a girl not wanting to go to the mall? What kind of alternate reality world is this?" I exclaimed.

June laughed at this. She was really cute when she laughed.

"No, it's not that I don't want to go to the mall! I just don't want to go with my mom! That's lame."

To that I could relate. My mom often wanted me to go to the mall with her, and I almost always turned her down. If she forced the issue, I often bartered with her, asking her if Jim could also go, so it didn't feel like the proverbial *having your face washed in public by your mom.*

"Gotcha," I said as we continued our walk.

As soon as we rounded and were within sight of his house, the girls split off so they could go up to Sarah's room. Jim and I, in turn, headed to the basement to melt plastic soldiers in mock battles.

Yeah. Don't ask.

When dinner time came around, June and I were given the nod that we should leave, so she and I walked out the door at the same time. I was pretty sure she liked me, though I could never really tell. So I made the decision to be bold.

"Would you like me to walk you home?"

"Sure! I live on Richland. It's near the middle school," June said. After a minute or so, she asked where I lived.

"I live on River Street," I answered, hoping this wouldn't scare her off.

River Street wasn't in the best of neighborhoods. Meaning that for the hoity toity city we now lived in, it was considered the *bad side of the tracks*, if you know what I mean. It was near the mall and there was hardly ever any crime, but the apartment complex we lived in was only one of a few within the city limits.

"My friend Katie lives near there. We go to the mall all the time," she stated.

We continued our conversation as we walked, talking about life, her telling me about her family and her four brothers, me telling her about my small family. I made sure not to bring up anything about my dad. I didn't want her feeling sorry for me like so many people did when the subject was breached.

When we reached the middle school, June turned and started walking behind the building. Although I didn't know what she was doing, I followed her. It was getting late - close to 6:00 p.m. - and the sun was just starting to set. The school was vacant of students and staff, and it even looked as if the cleaning crew had left because the parking lot was empty.

As we rounded the back of the school, June walked toward a slight gap between the old building and the new addition added a few years before. The gap itself wasn't big, but it faced away from the street and was pretty well masked from the parking lot. Following her, June stopped us just inside the gap and then turned to face me. With a huge smile, she looked at me and asked, "Do you want to kiss me?"

"Well . . . um . . . yes. But I'm not really good at it. I haven't kissed a lot."

I know it was lame to say, but it was the truth. The last girl I kissed was probably Heather, and you know how that turned out. I really did want to kiss her, but after watching probably too many *coming of age* movies, I didn't want it to be bad. It could, after all, be the death blow that would kill the relationship before it even started.

"It'll be okay," she said as she leaned in, and her lips found mine.

I'd like to say I kissed her back, but I was kind of in shock. I was pretty sure this was the first non-relative girl to have ever kissed me on the mouth. My lips pressed hers for about thirty seconds, and it was done. I looked at her, slightly embarrassed, and I felt like I had just screwed up our first kiss. Seeing me like that, June looked into my eyes and smiled.

"Don't worry," she said as she leaned in for another. "It'll get better."

And it did. I loosened up a bit on the second, and even more on the third. After a few minutes that went by way too fast, we separated. Satisfied with our first encounter, June reached down, took my hand, and started walking us toward her house. When we got there, we said our goodnights and exchanged phone numbers before she walked through her doorway.

I'm not sure how I got home that night. I might have floated. I was definitely on a cloud.

The next morning, I didn't show up to help Jim on his paper route. I hoped he wouldn't be mad, but my bigger hope was I would get to talk to June. When I was a no-show, he knew something was up and called around 10:00 a.m.

"Dude, what's up? Where were you this morning?"

"Sorry man. I woke up late and am a little under the weather," I blatantly lied.

"Okay. Sorry to hear man. Hope you feel better soon!"

We talked for another couple minutes and then hung up, and I was pretty sure we were okay. Sometimes it was hard to tell with Jim. He could be an emotional weather vane at times.

After I ate breakfast and watched some TV, I tried to call June. Lucky for me, she was the one that answered. I guessed she had made her case on how uncool it was to go to the mall with your mom, because she was home alone, and we made full use of this time.

We talked about school. We talked about Jim and Sarah. We talked more about our families and where we grew up.

All in all, I think we talked on and off for six hours, only breaking for dinner, bathroom, and family needs such as letting someone else use the phone. When it hit 9:00 p.m., she said that her mom wanted her off the phone, so we started to say our goodnights to each other.

"By the way, do you want to hang out tomorrow?"

"That'd be cool," I said, trying to act nonchalant.

"Okay! Want to come over?"

"I guess . . ." I said tentatively. "Who will be home?"

"I think just my mom. The boys are all going to some sort of truck thing. We don't have to stay here long."

I wasn't sure if this was a good or bad thing, meeting her mom. But if she wanted me to and it would put me in her good graces, how could I say no?

"Okay. That sounds good. What time?"

"How does just after lunch sound?"

"Works for me. See you then!" I said and hung up the phone.

The next day, as promised, I was at June's house right after lunch. I rang the doorbell and was hoping that June would answer.

Unfortunately, I didn't get my wish.

When the door opened, there was a gentleman standing in front of me who was about six foot five inches tall.

"Can I help you?" the giant looming in front of me asked.

"Hi. I'm Mike. I'm here to see June," I said, my voice noticeably cracking from fear.

"Mike, huh? Here to see June? Can I ask what this pertains to?" the skyscraper asked.

Next thing I knew June was at the door pushing the hulk away. "Bob! Stop! You knew who he was!"

"Hi June!" I said, relief washing over me.

"Sorry," she said apologetically. "The boys haven't left yet for the truck thingy. Come on in."

June opened the door for me and proceeded to introduce me to her brothers and dad. Fortunately for me, after some quick hellos, her brothers and dad left, leaving me alone with June and her mom.

Mrs. Peterson was a nice, somewhat chubby lady who, after offering me food and drink which I politely declined, strolled back to the kitchen to continue cooking what I guessed would be dinner.

"Mom. We're going to my room," June said as she grabbed my hand and guided me toward a bedroom.

As soon as we entered her room and the door was shut, June pushed me onto her bed. Within seconds, she was pressing me down against her mattress and kissing me.

Not knowing how to react to this, I kissed back. Every now and then I opened my eyes to look around to see if anyone was watching. I was frightened that any minute June's mom would pop through the door and yell at us for making out on her daughter's bed.

Luckily though, it never happened.

After maybe ten minutes of this, June stopped and showed me her room. And it was like any other teenage girl's room. The walls were painted white with pink accents, music and *hot guys* posters decorated the walls, and clothing decorated the floor. It was obvious June had attempted to clean a little but gave up after realizing the extent of work it would take to organize the multitude of pants and shirts that were strewn across the room.

Sitting on her bed, we talked a bit, then made out for a bit, and then talked a little more. And after maybe forty-five minutes, June got up, opened the door, and announced to her mom that we were leaving for a walk.

"Okay honey. Be back for dinner" was the only reply, and we were out the door.

As we walked, June held my hand, aggressively. It wasn't quite a death grip, but I could tell she wanted to be the one in charge.

Our first stop was the middle school, where we made out for a bit until we heard some kids. So we left. The next stop was some bushes behind the shopping center, where we made out some more. After about twenty or thirty minutes, we left the bushes and walked around for a bit. It was a beautiful day, after all, and we couldn't spend it all day in the brush. I mean, we could, but my lips were starting to get sore and needed a short break. After all, they had not been this active, in, well, never.

As we walked, June and I continued our discussion about our lives. And I was surprised at how pleasant and knowledgeable she was for her age. Maybe too knowledgeable, based on the amount of making out that had been occurring.

Although she was aggressive, I could feel that there was a bond growing between us. And I enjoyed listening to her go on about her take on life, family, and, well, just about everything.

Somewhere around dinnertime, I walked her home, making one more stop at the middle school. When we got to her front door, we said goodbye and agreed to talk before bed.

The next day, Monday, I knew would be a d see Jim in first period, and I was *sure* I'd have to tell h I'm not a very good liar, and I was sure it would show

Especially with the ear-to-ear grin I had been carry

"Hey man! Feeling better?" Jim inquired when we sa the hall between classes.

"Yeah. I was feeling better by lunch Saturday," I said — a other blatant lie.

"Oh, dude! You should have called!"

"Well, I actually got a call from June. I ended up hanging out with her yesterday afternoon," I stated.

Jim's face went blank. "June. As in, Sarah's friend June?"

"Yeah," I replied, not knowing how else to respond.

Jim just looked at me, stunned. And I wasn't sure what was going on in his mind, but it didn't look good. Was he looking at me that way because he felt betrayed? Or maybe it was because he couldn't fathom me, or anyone our age, being attracted to someone Sarah's age?

"Dude, is that okay? June is cool."

"Yeah. I'm just a little shocked. I always took June to be a cold fish, if you know what I mean."

"Dude. She's anything but that . . ." I said and proceeded to tell him about my afternoon with her. Not *all* the details, obviously. But enough to let him know that she was *not* cold by any stretch of the imagination.

After school, Jim and I hung out for a bit, but I could tell there was something bothering him. I eventually broke the ice.

"Dude, what's up with you? You've been in a mood since school."

"It's nothing," he said as he painted the wing of the model jet.

"I'm crying bullshit here. I *know* something's up with you. Now spill."

y. I've hit on June before, and she didn't seem interested in guys."

"Oh," I replied, giving it a minute to sink in. "Dude, I had no idea. You never told me you liked her before."

"I was afraid you'd make fun of me for liking one of my sister's friends. She is a freshman."

"You've known me for two years. You should know me better than that Jim." At that I bumped him with my shoulder, making sure I didn't mess up his paint job.

Jim stopped painting for a minute, waited a few seconds, and said, "Yeah. I know. Sorry."

"No biggie. How much longer are you going to work on that? This M80 is burning a hole in my pocket!"

After that, the mood lightened, and a few minutes later, we went to the woods and blew up a perfectly good model airplane.

As we were watching the plane and some leaves and twigs burn, he asked, "So, does June have another friend I can date . . . *besides* my sister?"

Good thing he added *besides my sister* part; I'm sure he knew I would have jumped all over that one.

That night, June called me after dinner, and we talked for an hour or so. Then we called it quits for the evening so we could go to bed. Before hanging up, we made plans to meet after school the next day, near the middle school, so we could spend more time together.

I think it was about a week later, when June and I were in the bushes again, that I popped the question.

"June, do you want to *go* with me?"

"Well, yeah! I thought we were already *going steady*!" she stated and looked at me confused.

"Well, I *thought* so too . . ." I lied. "But I wanted to make it official."

She laughed at this for a moment and then proceeded to make out with me some more.

It was about a week later that June started getting spooky.

We started meeting more at her house or Jim's house, but the making out trickled off and stopped. We'd still hold hands and sit together, but whenever I'd make a move, she would cut it off right away. And we were seeing each other less frequently, only a couple times a week.

This really confused me. Had she stopped liking me? Did she not like our kissing, or anything else, anymore? Was I moving too fast for her? Was I moving too slowly? Did she have too much schoolwork? Marching band practice? I really had no clue.

It was about this time that Jim and I started hanging out with Glenn Fields. Glenn was a guy we met in our Advanced Algebra class. One day during class, Glenn overheard Jim and I talking about blowing stuff up and wanted in.

Since Glenn only lived two or three streets over from Jim, it was easy to call him up last minute and say, "Hey, we're blowing up a model M-60 tank; wanna watch?" No sooner would you make the call than he'd be on his doorstep, lighter in hand. He also started hanging out with us when we weren't blowing stuff to bits.

When both Jim and June were busy the following Saturday, it didn't take a second's thought for me to make the call.

"Hey, I'm bored. I was thinking about hitting the little league game at the ballpark. Do you want to hang out?"

"Sure!" Glenn replied eagerly.

"Cool. Meet me there in a half hour?"

"Cool!" Glenn replied. After a slight pause, he asked, "Do you care if my friend Mary hangs too?"

"Who?"

"You know, Mary Masters," Glenn said as if I should know her.

"Sorry, I don't know her. But, more importantly, does she like to blow stuff up?" I jested.

"I don't know."

"Yeah, she can come along," I replied since he didn't get my joke. "See you in a few."

"Cool. See you then!" Glenn said and then hung up. True to his word, about thirty minutes later, Glenn and Mary met me at the local base-ball field.

Being that it was baseball season, the ballparks around the city were always busy with games and spectators. Hanging at the ballpark wasn't what I considered a great time, compared to blowing stuff up that is, but it was a decent enough place to waste time. Each ball field usually had a stand selling hotdogs and sodas, and there was a lot of eye candy to be had, so it didn't suck too much. And the one where we were going was no different.

As I pulled my ten-speed up to the bike rack and locked it, I spotted Glenn on one of the stands watching a game. As I approached, I had to do a double take when my eyes fell upon the girl sitting with Glenn. Whoever she was, she was hot! She had dirty blond hair and a killer body. And, as she turned toward me, I saw that her eyes were a shade of light blue that could melt your soul. They certainly melted mine.

"Hey Glenn!" I said as I walked up.

"Hey Mike! What's up?" Glenn said as he stuck out his hand for a fist bump.

"Oh, and this is my friend Mary Masters," Glenn said as he gestured toward the afore mentioned *hot girl*.

"Hi Mary!" I said, trying to keep my composure.

"Hi Mike!" she said as she looked at me quizzically.

After a few seconds, I said "Should I ask?"

She snapped out of it at that point and said, "Sorry. It's just you remind me of a guy I knew in middle school . . . Scott Sloan. Any relation?"

"No, no relation," I stated, and thought it was weird I was being asked for a second time if I was related to Scott Sloan. I also noted that I really needed to meet that guy someday.

For the next two hours, we watched the baseball game, drank soda, and talked about our lives and school. Eventually the game ended, and we got ready to leave the park. I ran off to use the restroom, and by the time I got back, Glenn was gone.

"He left," Mary said, noticing my questioning look at the bleachers. "He said he had to get home . . . something about a chore."

"The jerk! At least he could have said goodbye!" I said jokingly.

"Yes he is!" she laughed. After she dismounted the bleachers, she looked at me and asked, "So what are you doing now?"

"Nothing much. I can be home for dinner whenever. What are your plans?"

"I was just going to walk home. Do you want to walk me home?" Mary inquired, practically batting her eyelashes.

"Sure," I replied, and we were off.

Having walked from Glenn's house, Mary didn't have a bike, so, being a gentleman, I walked my bike alongside her as we made the trek to her house. It was probably two or three miles, so we had plenty of time to get to know each other.

It turned out Mary lived in a gated community near the lake. The first thing I noticed as we approached her house was the guard shack, complete with a guard, and barricade blocking the driveway. When we got there, I was ready to leave, but she asked, "Would you like to come up and watch some TV?"

"Sure!" I said as the guard let us through the gate.

As we walked toward her house, I was dumbfounded by the prodigious houses in the community. Each house was three or four level high, and most extended out over the lake to accommodate boat docks under the houses. She told me that her stepfather was a doctor, and I guessed a pretty damn good one based on the cost of living in this neck of the woods.

When we got there, I left my bike by the side of her house, walked through the door, and followed her up to her game room.

She had a *game room!*

The game room had a pool table off to one side and a dartboard on one wall, along with a large leather couch that sat against a huge window overlooking the lake. Mary turned on the massive TV mounted on the wall across the room from the dartboard, and seconds later MTV popped onto the widescreen. We sat on opposite ends of the big leather couch for a while watching TV and chatting about our summer plans and their other house in Florida.

When the conversation lulled, Mary asked, "Would you like something to drink?"

"Sure. Please!" I answered.

"We have Pepsi . . . is that cool?"

I nodded, and Mary got up and left the room. She came back a minute later with two cans of Pepsi that she set down on the table in front of me. This time, instead of sitting on the opposite end of the couch, Mary sat down inches from me. I was perfectly fine with this, even though I was really nervous. She was, after all, very beautiful. And I was pretty sure she was coming onto me.

As we watched TV, I could feel her moving closer to me. I wasn't totally sure what to do at first. I eventually went for broke and put my arm around her. With that, she nuzzled into my arm, and before I knew it, we were kissing. She tasted sweet, as if she had been just eating my favorite candy. We kissed hard for several minutes. Mary was almost as aggressive as June had been that time in her room.

June . . . *Fuck!* What was I thinking? I *had* a girlfriend! Why was I here making out with Mary when I had a girlfriend I *should* be making out with?

Then again, June didn't want to make out like this anymore, even though I had tried. I *had* made multiple efforts to kindle the spark we had when we first started dating, but she didn't seem interested anymore.

That's when it hit me; I needed to break up with June before I saw Mary again.

I know it's weird, but these are all the things I was thinking about when I was making out with Mary. Those things and the fact that I loved the video they were playing on MTV.

About an hour later, I left Mary's house and biked home lost in thought. My mind raced between thoughts of Mary and the wonderful time we had on her couch, combined with the guilt and dread that arose when I thought about June and what I would say. The trip, which was only thirty minutes, flew by in a heartbeat, and I was thankful that I made it home without getting my head hit so far into the clouds.

As for the problem with June, I was befuddled.

How would I approach her with the news that I'd found someone else? This dating thing was all new to me, and I had no frame of reference to go by. I had seen plenty of breakups on TV of course, but they were all staged. So I couldn't rely on them for any guidance. And the only other experience I had was from my mom's breakups with guys. And, thinking about them, those were of no help either.

After thinking about my possible choices, I finally opted to call her and tell her the bad news in lieu of confronting her in person. I know it sounds like a shitty thing to do — and it was — but having no experience in breaking up with someone, my mind told me that would be the least harmful for all the parties involved.

And before I made that call, I went to Jim's so I could talk to Sarah first. I was kind of hoping she'd have some words of wisdom or advice for me when it came to her friend. When it came down to it, I liked June a lot. I just liked Mary more.

That night, I called June and told her about my day, leaving out any hint of Mary, of course. She, in turn, told me about her day: about marching band and how much she missed me. At the end of the conversation, I wished her goodnight and hung up, guilt weighing heavy on my shoulders.

Luckily for me, Sarah was home the next day. I called her ahead of time and asked if she had any plans with June. When she told me she didn't, I asked her if I could come over and talk to her. She was curious as to why, but I told her I would explain everything when I got to her house.

With that out of the way, I hopped on my bike and rode over.

"I met someone else yesterday. Someone I really like. How do I go about breaking up with June?" I asked the minute I walked in the door.

Stunned by my announcement, Sarah stood there for a moment before she answered, "Oh man. That's not an easy one, Mike."

After showing me to their living room couch, she continued, "June is gonna be pissed. She really likes you. I mean, she really, really, likes you. We were just on the phone last night talking about you."

Okay, that sucked to hear, but I was resolute. I needed to break up with her, and I needed to do it in the kindest way I could. I've always hated to burn bridges, but there was no getting around this.

"Can I use your phone?" I inquired.

"You're gonna break up with her by phone?" she asked, a quizzical look appearing on her face. After I nodded, she smirked and said, "Alright . . . your funeral."

We stood and made our way to the kitchen, and a minute later, I was on the phone with June.

"Hi June. It's Mike."

"Hi Mike! Whatcha up to?" June asked cheerily.

Hearing her tone, I fumbled slightly over my words as I continued. "I'm over Sarah's house. I-I wanted to call and talk to you about . . . about something."

"Sure. What's up?" June inquired, happiness still in her voice.

"I'm . . . I'm not sure how to say this, b-but . . . um . . . we need to break up," I announced.

There was a bit of a silence before she asked, "Why?"

"Because . . . I . . . I met someone else," I said, trying to steady myself.

"Can I ask who it is?" she queried in a quieted tone.

"Her name is Mary. Mary Masters."

There was another pause on the phone, and then the line went dead. After saying hello into the phone a few times, I hung up and turned toward Sarah and saw that she was standing in the doorway, her eyes wide and jaw agape.

"Why didn't you say it was Mary Masters? Oh man . . . oh crap," she said as she lowered and shook her head.

"Why? Do you know Mary?"

"You bet I do. We went to middle school together before she transferred to the all-girls' school. There's quite a bit of history there between Mary and June," she expounded.

"Back in middle school, June was dating Scott Sloan. She dated Scott for a few weeks or so, and then Scott met Mary. Like, a day later, he broke up with June.

"About two or three days go by, and then June attacks Mary at her school. Well, tried to attack her, I should say. It wasn't much of a fight. It probably lasted thirty seconds before a nun stepped in and stopped the fight," she said as her expression turned from dread to humor.

"Oh man, I'm sure June is way pissed! I better call her," she said, trying not to laugh.

Now, with my jaw agape, I just stood there as my brain went into overdrive.

If I didn't know better, I'd swear this was a set up. But knowing Mary had never seen me before, I think, and Glenn not having a clue, because he was normally clueless, I'd have to leave this up to chance.

Oh universe! Why do you vex me so?

A minute later, Sarah came out of the kitchen. "I called June. Her mom said she wasn't home. She said she stormed out of the house a few minutes ago."

No sooner did she say that than the doorbell rang. She went to the door to answer it, and then returned a minute later with a worried look on her face.

"Mike, June is at the front door," she said, and my heart stopped. She then added tentatively, "She wants to see you outside."

My eyes shifted from her to the front door, and all I could do was stare as my mind ran through the options. I knew I was in over my head, and something told me to bolt. I had no clue how I could face June. I had no idea what I could say to her that I hadn't already said.

I finally snapped out of it, decided to man up, and headed to the front door. I opened the door to June pacing back and forth near the front steps, and she certainly did not look happy. Her face was red and full of anger, and I could tell that she had been crying. As soon as she saw me peak through the front door, she walked up the front steps and I could see every muscle tensed in her arms and torso.

"How the hell can you do this to me?" she roared through gritted teeth.

"It just . . . happened," I replied; my head hung a little low.

As I looked down, I noticed her clenched hands and, more importantly, her right hand, which had something pointy in it. Could it be?

Yes it was. It was a butter knife.

I barely had a chance to look up before she raised the blade and bolted at me. I'm not quite sure how I managed it, but I grabbed her right wrist — you know, the one with the butter knife — and held it in place about six inches from my chest. As she raised the other fist to hit me, I grabbed that one as well. June moved her wrists and body back and forth trying to escape from me, or to stab me, either case not good for me.

"June, drop the knife," I said sternly as she thrashed back and forth, trying to free herself. After ten seconds or so, she finally relented and dropped the knife on the porch. I continued to hold her arms as her rage turned into sobbing.

"Why her? Why *Mary*?" she pleaded.

"Again, I don't know. It just happened," I said, not knowing how else to answer.

After a minute, her sobs dissipated, and I released my grip on her arms. Wordlessly, June lowered her head, turned, and walked back down the steps. Then she mounted her bike and rode away. I stood there and watched her go, the only thing I *could* do. As soon as she was out of sight, I bent down, picked up the butter knife, and went back into the house.

Even though I'm pretty sure Sarah witnessed the whole thing, I handed her the butter knife and told her what had happened. After saying my goodbyes, I exited the house, depressed and a little shaken, and headed for home.

When I got home, I plopped down on my couch, still in shock, and thought about what had just transpired. I didn't go out the rest of the night or talk to anyone. I needed some time to myself.

The next day, I woke in a relatively good mood. The mood that darkened my spirits the previous evening had left, replaced by thoughts of spending time with Mary. And, even though it was a school day, I had a smile on my face and a song in my heart.

As soon as I got home, I called Mary and made plans to meet at Glenn's after dinner. Glenn was okay with this, since his social calendar was rather sparse from not having a lot of friends.

We spent the early evening with Glenn, just hanging out and watching TV, as Mary and I held hands. When it started getting late, I walked Mary home, stopping in secluded spots along the way so we could make out. She still tasted like candy, every time.

As instructed, I called her when I got home. After relaying what a fun evening we had with each other, we discussed her plans for later in the week and weekend. Mary told me that her parents had planned a family get-away that weekend to Catawba Island. She told me the plan was to boat up to the island late Friday night, spend the weekend, and then boat home late Sunday night. And although it was a school week, and she would be gone all weekend, she said we could get together Thursday night.

While we waited for Thursday to arrive, she and I talked every night after dinner. We talked about all the things she was taking at school, the differences between the all-girls' high school and public high school, and our families — the usual banter teenage couples have.

Although I felt like she was out of my league, I knew we liked each other and that's all that mattered.

Right?

Thursday arrived and, as arranged, we met at the ballpark right after school. There we ate pizza and watched baseball a little, but eventually made our way back to my house, and my room, for some kissing and cuddling. When it got late, I walked Mary home and kissed her goodnight.

"Hey . . . hope you have a great time this weekend!"

"I'm sure I will," she said as we uncoupled. After giving me one last peck on the cheek, she added, "I'll try to call if I can."

"Okay," I said as Mary turned and walked through the gate.

As soon as she was safely in her house, I started my walk home, smiling the entire way.

I tried to keep myself as busy as I could that weekend, in order to keep my mind off missing Mary; it was rough. I hung around with Jim and Glenn making and destroying stuff and even got in a little drawing time. I also hung out with my mom and Dee, going to dinner and a movie Saturday night.

It felt like the weekend dragged on forever.

The worst part was not hearing from Mary the entire weekend. Although she said she *might* call, part of me understood why she didn't. She was boating with her family, after all, and probably not near a phone. But I was a little surprised I didn't get a call Sunday night, assuming she made it home alright.

I was antsy all day Monday, wanting the school day to be over so I could see Mary. Although it had only been a week since we started dating, I missed her a ton. She was so pretty and fun, and mine.

As soon as I got home from school, I called Mary's house, and she answered, "Hey Mike! How was your weekend?"

"Good! I hung out with Glenn and my friend Jim mostly. How was yours?"

There was a delay in response, and she finally said, "Good. I had a lot of fun, and got some sun."

"Well that's good. Hey, do you want me to come over?" I posed.

There was another delay before she answered, "I'm not sure that's a good idea."

"Why's that?" I asked, confused.

After a pause, she said the words that were furthest from my thoughts, "Well . . . I met someone when I was on the island."

This time it was my time to give a delayed response.

"Oh" was all I could muster.

"I'm sorry Mike. I think you're a really great guy. I'm sure you'll find someone soon."

"Are you sure about this?" I asked, hoping she'd take a minute and change her mind.

"Yeah," she said immediately, which led to an awkward silence. It was ended a minute later when Mary said, "Hey, I gotta go. You take care now."

"You too," I replied and hung up the phone.

I sat alone there by our kitchen phone for a bit, as depression set in, thinking about how much life can change with a short phone call or only a few words. I'm pretty sure I didn't cry, even though I had felt like it. In my mind, it just didn't make sense to. In my mind, she was always out of my league, and I had already unknowingly convinced myself that something like this might happen. So, after a short break from life, I moved on.

Being friends with Glenn, I did see Mary a few more times over the next few years. I heard that she moved to Florida with her family right after high school, and I've never heard from her, or about her, again.

June, on the other hand, I did hear about. We wound up back together a month or so later, and we dated on and off throughout high school. Eventually, the relationship petered out, like most things from high school do, and we haven't seen each other since.

You never do forget your first loves, though.

Diary: April 19

I tell people I'm fine. I'm not.

There are so many things I miss about you since you left.

I miss falling asleep next to you. I miss having my hand barely touch you and feel your warmth. I miss waking next to you and seeing your beautiful face. I miss having coffee with you in the morning.

I miss the fantastic coffees we shared in Cape Cod. How I'd wake every morning and run down to the coffee shop and pick us up coffee and I'd get those cookies with the big chunks.

I miss seeing your face light up when you'd see me return with the coffee and cookies.

Why can't we have that again? Why can't you be here with me? Why can't the universe bring you back?

I would do anything to have you back. I would sell my soul to have you back.

CHAPTER

7

I remember when we first started talking about spending the rest of our lives together.

It was the year that my best friend got married.

As you know, my friend Jim never found direction in life. He dropped out of college after a year or two, deciding it wasn't his thing, much to the chagrin of his parents. After moving back in with them and leaching off them for a few months, they knew he was old enough to make his own mistakes and kicked him out, giving him about five thousand dollars to get him on his feet.

Living on his own, he bounced from job to job for many years.

He worked for a library as a maintenance man for a few years, and then moved on to retail sales, selling men's suits. He also spent a few years in restaurant management.

It was somewhere around the time I met you that Jim finally went back to college and got his business degree. This, of course, made his parents ecstatic, and they ended up paying for his college so he could better himself.

After earning his master's in business, Jim went into sales with his dad. His dad owned an import company that distributed textiles and such around the United States. It wasn't too long before he was promoted to regional sales manager of the north-eastern United States.

I was very happy for him, happier than he was for himself, I think. He never liked talking about his job. Or at least he didn't like talking about his as much as I liked talking about mine.

When Jim got his promotion, he moved to Boston, since Boston was pretty much in the center of his territory and there wasn't a lot to hold him here beside his few friends and immediate family. It sucked not having him live local any more, but he traveled back to Cleveland about once a month for sales meetings, which gave us the opportunity to catch up, aka, drink.

A few months after Jim moved to Boston, he met a woman there named Brittney. Seems he was alone at a bar one night and met her after he overheard her talking about Cleveland. As it happened, Brittney was originally from Cleveland and, like Jim, had also relocated for her job.

I met Brittney for the first time a few months after they started getting serious. He had scheduled a sales meeting back in Cleveland, with some vacation tacked on, and Brittney came with him to meet his parents.

That's when I got *the call.*

"Dude! Whatcha doing tonight?" Jim asked as soon as I answered the phone.

"Why, are you in town?" I inquired excitedly.

"Yes sir!" he replied enthusiastically. "And I brought Brittney with me. We were hoping you and Amy weren't busy tonight."

"Dude, you're priority one. Did you want to do dinner?"

"That'd be great! Are you in the mood for Mexican?"

"Only always!"

"Cool! Cancun at 7:00 p.m.?"

"Just need to check with the chick, sir. I'll call you back if there's an issue."

"See ya then!" Jim replied and then ended the call.

I called you at work and you said it was all good, so we met the two at Cancun, our favorite Mexican restaurant, as promised.

When I first saw Jim, he looked . . . joyful. He emanated a type of joy that came from the inside, and not just the exuberance that he wore as a mask most days. Maybe it's just something a best friend can sense.

As we approached the table and I saw Brittney for the first time, I knew right away that she was truly his dream girl. She was everything he had said he wanted in a woman when we were young. She was about six inches shorter than him, had strawberry-blonde hair, green eyes, and was built on the petite side.

After we got our bro hug out of the way, he introduced me to Brittney.

"Hi Brittney! It's nice to meet you," I said, giving her a hug, and then turning toward you. "This is Amy."

You two hugged briefly, and we sat down for a night of burritos and booze.

Watching Jim and Brittney was a delight. Together they made such a cute couple and looked like they were made for each other. They finished each other's sentences, they held hands all night, except for when they were eating, and laughed at jokes only the two of them knew. And they kissed a lot. I was very ecstatic for Jim, for both of them, really.

When we finished our meals and a second round of beers, he stood and broke the news to the table. "So, Brittney and I are getting married."

"Dude! Congratulations!" I said as I got up to give him a hug. "I am so happy for you two."

"There's more," he said as he hugged me back.

"Oh yeah?"

"Yeah. Since both of our families mostly live here in Cleveland, we're getting married here!" he replied in delight.

"Cool! I can't wait! When is the big day?"

"We talked to our families, and if it all comes together, we're looking at three months from now."

"Three months?" I queried as the smile left my face a little. "I mean, that's fantastic, but, isn't that a little . . . fast?"

"No. Not really. We just figured . . . why wait?" Jim said as he looked over at Brittney.

I watched him for a few seconds, looking for any change of expression. After knowing him for so many years, I could usually tell if he was holding back the truth. I could see something in his expression as he looked back at me, but nothing that would tell me he was holding back anything critical, you know, like a surprise pregnancy.

"Gotcha," I said as I sat down to finish my beer.

"So, are you in?" he asked as his face became serious.

"What do you mean?" I inquired, looking up from my drink.

"Are you in . . . as best man?"

It took me a minute for the lump in my throat to subside before I said, "Well, hell yes! I would be honored!"

"Great! My work here is done!" he said as he sat back down, pretty satisfied with himself.

"Oh? How's that?"

"Well, since we don't live here, my parents said they'd make all the arrangements," he replied as he took another drink. "You know how anal my parents are about stuff."

It was true. Jim's parents, mostly his dad, were very controlling when it came to their family and family functions. When he said they were making all the arrangements, I could only imagine the wedding that they would unleash. And I was also sure that he would not have to do anything but show up.

"So," Jim said. "Are you ready for another round?"

Around 11:00 p.m., the restaurant started to wind down, and so did we. We finished our drinks, paid the check, and had another brief hugging session in the parking lot before we drove home.

I didn't see Jim again during his vacation, or for the three months before the wedding, but it wasn't unusual for me to go months without seeing him. He always seemed to be busy when he had a significant other in his life, and this was no exception.

And I can't say I was any different. I always had problems keeping in touch with friends when I had a girlfriend or wife. There were always demands in a relationship that took precedence over seeing a friend here or there.

About a month before the wedding, Jim called me to see what my thoughts were on tuxedos. Having been to, and through, a few weddings myself in the past, I guess he thought I'd have some valuable input. I didn't, really, but reviewed a few options he sent me that were listed on a website.

"Oh, your family is letting you pick them out?" I joked as we perused the site.

"Ha. Ha. That's really funny . . . dick."

"Hey, I had to," I said, laughing. "But I am glad you get to pick out your own clothes. How old are you now?"

Jim laughed at that, and I was glad I could make him laugh. After talking to him several times since the wedding announcement, I knew he was on edge over the upcoming nuptials. As his best friend, it was the least I could do.

"By the way, does it bother you having, like, no control over your wedding?" I probed.

"Why would it bother me? There's like a million and one things to do for a wedding, and Mom and Dad want to handle them all. I just need to show up sober. Oh, and get tuxes."

"Cool," I replied, figuring if he was happy, I was too. "So, when are you coming into town?"

"Brittney and I are taking two weeks of vacation for the wedding. One week to spend with friends and family, and one week for a honeymoon."

"Nice! I can't wait, man!" I said, then noticing one tux that I thought he would like. It was kind of traditional but had a steampunk flare to it. "Hey, what about model 237?"

"Dude! That is perfect!" he said, elated. "Thanks!"

"Least I could do man!"

"It is? You're not forgetting my bachelor party, are you?" He asked. I wasn't, of course. Being the best man, and more importantly the best friend, it was my duty to plan and execute a fantastic party for him.

Unbeknownst to Jim, I had made arrangements with his family - aka got approval - for Jim, me, and two of our high school buddies to go out to Cancun for food and then hit a strip club. After discussing it with all the parties involved, sans the groom, I determined the best day for the party would be Wednesday. This left two days of recovery time for us *just in case* things got out of hand.

"No sir. Everything's covered. Wednesday night."

"Well, until then," Jim said as we ended our conversation.

And, pretty much that was it.

Even though Jim and Brittney flew in Sunday night, they were busy with wedding plans, so we didn't see them. I texted him on Monday to confirm they had made it, to which he replied they had, indeed, made it to town and he would call me as soon as he could. On Tuesday, he texted me that the tux fitting was Thursday, and we could talk about it Wednesday night. Besides that, there was no word from him.

I guess I was a little pissed that I felt like I was being put on the back burner and not being given more information, but I resigned myself to the fact that Jim had a shit ton of items he needed to accomplish before the wedding. Also, I'm sure there were a bunch of people he had to pacify besides me, others that weren't as understanding as I was. But it doesn't mean I wasn't a little put out. So I did what had to be done. I made sure that the bachelor party, or at least the start of it, happened as it was supposed to.

The four of us — Jim, me, Bob, and John — met at Jim's parents' house at 6:00 p.m. to start our festivities. I had arranged for a limo for our evening transportation, and I made sure it was stocked with enough crappy Mexican beer and whiskey to satiate four men for one evening. At about 6:20 p.m., we loaded into the limo and set our course for adventures, well at least for tacos.

I do love when my plans work out. Sometimes I really think I should have been a professional party planner instead of being an engineer. Pretty sure my college debt would have been way less. But I digress.

I will try to recap the evening for you as quickly as possible, mostly because I'm not sure if everything I say here is correct. So, please bear with me; I'll get us through this.

On the way to Cancun, we all cracked a beer and toasted the groom-to-be with a shot of whiskey, thus officially kicking off the bachelor party. While at Cancun, we each consumed two additional beers — not bad for only being there about an hour or so.

This is where things start to get a little fuzzy.

We left Cancun around 8:00 p.m. and went to The Lucky Horse, a strip club I had selected down in the Flats, an area near downtown Cleveland. Not having been to many strip clubs, I thought this one was as good as any other, and, in fact, I was pleasantly surprised. The club had two levels, with the second level open in the middle so it looked down onto the main stage. This allowed for viewing of the stage from almost everywhere. That was the most interesting thing I found at the strip club, except for one of the bartenders I just happened to run into.

Being the most sober of us, I staggered up to the bar to get another round of drinks. That's when I saw her.

At first, I wasn't sure it was her, having not seeing her since high school, but there was no mistaking her voice. And, after all, do you ever really forget your first love?

"Yes, sir, can I help you?" Heather asked in a sultry voice.

I paused, taken aback for a minute as my brain matched voice to memories. As soon as it hit me, I responded, "Excuse me, but is your name Heather?"

She looked at me for a few seconds, also trying to match face and voice, and when it dawned on her, she said, "Mike?"

We both smiled at the recognition, and then bellowed out in unison, "Yeah! How *are* you?"

She smiled at this and was the first to answer. "Good! How are you? How is Dee?"

"I'm good, so is Dee!" I said, my smile equaling hers. "It's so great seeing you!"

After a few more seconds of staring and reliving our childhoods in our minds, we both got back to the business at hand.

"Great to see you! What can I get you?" Heather asked as she wiped the surface in front of me with a towel.

"Yeah . . . sorry. Can I get four Dos Equis?"

"Sure!" Heather replied as she grabbed four bottles from the fridge. Setting them down in front of me, she asked, "You here with anyone I'd know?"

"I don't know . . . just a few of my friends from high school. It's my friend Jim's bachelor party," I said as I gave her my credit card.

"Yeah, not sure I remember Jim. It has been a few years," she joked as she ran the card.

"Yeah, a few." I laughed, and then asked, "How's your family? I thought you guys moved out of state?"

"We did, but moved back a few years later after my mom and stepdad split," Heather said, handing me back my credit card. "Do you want me to leave this open?"

"Yes please. And I'm sorry to hear about the divorce," I said, but then realized there were other people wanting beverages and I had a bachelor party waiting for beers. "Hey, I better let you get back to it."

As I started to leave the bar, Heather stopped me, "Mike, how long are you guys going to be around tonight?"

"Not sure. Why?"

"Stop back up, and see me before you leave," she said, smiling, and then shifted her attention to another patron.

"Will do!" I replied as I moved back to the table of thirsty groomsmen.

Two hours later, when I saw that Jim was sufficiently inebriated and smiling from having had a couple lap dances, I patted myself on the back for having performed my job adequately. After talking it over with the party, we called it an evening - mostly so we could get his home before he would vomit on us. I told the gang I would be right back and walked back to the bar to close out our tab.

"Hey Heather, can I close my tab?" I asked as I wrote on invisible paper.

She rang up the bill and handed it to me. After I briefly reviewed it, I added a fifty percent tip — she was practically family, after all. As I handed it back to her, she grabbed my hand and pressed a note into it.

"What's this?" I asked as I opened up the paper. Inside I saw a phone number next to her name.

"It's my cell number. Figured you, me, and Dee could get together some time. I'd like to see you guys again, if you're available."

"Dee actually lives out of state right now with her husband. But *I* could call you sometime, if you don't mind just hanging out with me, that is."

"That would be great, actually!"

"Okay! Take care," I said as I nodded to her and turned to leave.

"Wait!" she said as she ran down to the end of the bar. She made her way out and around the bar, approached me, and hugged me.

As soon as I got back to the table, I contacted the limo driver and told him we were on our way out. And with the help of John and Bob, we were able to get him out of the bar and into the limo. Somewhere along the drive back to his parents' house, Jim had fallen asleep, so when we got back to the house, the three of us carried him in and placed him on his parents' couch. Mrs. Larkman wasn't too happy about his condition but let us drop him off anyway.

When I got home that night, I woke you up briefly to let you know I was home. I kissed you goodnight and climbed into bed. It had been a great night, and it was fantastic seeing Heather. I couldn't wait to tell you how awesome the night was and looked forward to telling Dee who I ran into.

The next morning you woke me up before you left for work, and I briefly told you about the festivities. I mean, you knew we were going to a strip club and I knew you weren't too happy about it, but you smiled as I told you about the night.

"And the best part, besides getting Jim hammered, was seeing Heather," I said joyfully.

"Who's Heather?" you asked.

"She's a childhood friend. She gave me her number so we could hang out sometime. I can't wait for you to meet her."

"So, you meet a woman in a strip club and you want me to meet her?" you asked indignantly.

"No! I've known Heather for close to forty years! She's a friend of the family," I said to try and appease you.

"Well, I suppose. Just seems weird to me," you responded a little upset and not knowing how to take this news.

"She's cool. You'll like her," I said hoping to calm you down.

"Okay," you said, looking at the time. "I need to leave for work. Can we talk about this when I get home?"

"Sure thing, my love!" I said kissing you goodbye. "Hope you have a great day today! I love you!"

"I love you too. Hope *you* have a good day, Mr. Best Man," you quipped as you turned to leave.

It wasn't a lie though. *I truly am the* best *best man ever*, I thought to myself before I fell back asleep.

I woke to the alarm about two hours later with our conversation about Heather on my mind. Before I did anything else, I sent a text to Dee telling her about the previous evening's events and about seeing her. After sending Dee her number, I realized I was running late, grabbed coffee, threw on some clothes, and left for the tux shop to meet Jim.

The rest of the day was pretty uneventful. We were fitted, went out for a quick beer, and then headed our respective ways until the rehearsal dinner. When I got home, I sent Heather a text to let her know that it was great seeing her the previous night and that I had relayed her number to Dee.

Heather responded almost immediately saying that it was great seeing me as well and thanked me for Dee's cell. She also asked if I'd like to get together in the near future. I told her I'd have to bounce it off my girlfriend, letting her know that I had a girlfriend so there was no miscommunication. She responded that she would have to do the same with her boyfriend, but it shouldn't be a problem. When you got home after work, I let you know what had transpired that day, including my text to Heather.

"So, she has a boyfriend?" you asked as you walked toward the bedroom to change out of your work clothes.

"That's what she said. What are your thoughts? Maybe we can double date with them?"

"That'd be okay, I guess."

"Cool. I'll see if they want to do something next week, after all these wedding shenanigans are complete," I said as I approached you and gave you a hug. "So, are you ready for dinner?"

It felt like the weekend came and went by in a flash. Friday night, of course, was the rehearsal and rehearsal dinner. Everyone that was supposed to show up at the church did, which I considered a Christmas miracle. Our friends weren't always as reliable as we would have liked.

The vows and positions were rehearsed, Jim and Brittney looking cute as can be as they exchanged their vows. The whole thing probably took an hour, to everyone's delight. I could tell that Jim and the rest of the bachelor party, having recovered successfully from drinking two nights previously, were ready to drink again. I do love my friends.

Everyone left the church as quickly as they could, and we reconvened at a local gourmet burger joint for dinner. No, it wasn't the fanciest, but it's one of the only things that the bride and groom got to pick. The place had a wide selection of whiskeys and beer, which suited everyone's wants just fine.

After a few toasts and a couple rounds, we called it quits for the evening knowing we all had to *show up* the next day. This was fine with me because I knew you wanted your beauty sleep, and we had to be at the church at 11:00 a.m.

We woke early the next day so we could have our Saturday morning coffee ritual. This mainly consisted of us waking, drinking coffee, and cuddling on the couch, with a possible move back to the bedroom for more cuddling. We had to forego the latter, of course, because of time constraints.

At 11:00 a.m., we arrived at the church, me in my tuxedo and you in a black dress. As we entered the church, we were surprised with the changes from the previous night. There were red carpets up and down the entrance aisles, floral bouquets adorning each of the pews, white silk near the alter, and banners and ribbons everywhere. We could tell that Jim's parents put out enough coin to really have one of the best weddings I had ever been to.

"Wow! This is beautiful!" you said as we walked in. As we did, I felt you increase the grip on my hand, as if you were holding on for dear life. I'm not sure if it was because you were excited for them or scared.

"I know, right? I think I told you the Larkmans come from money," I said, and it was true. Jim's parents were loaded with some old school money inherited from a few generations back, and at least for this occasion, they weren't afraid to show it.

As we had been instructed the night before, we proceeded to the back rooms of the church to meet up with the rest of the wedding party. Two rooms had been set aside, one for the groomsmen and one for the bridesmaids. Since I was already dressed, I sat outside the groomsmen's room with you to keep you company.

We were seated only a minute or two before Mrs. Larkman came out of the bridesmaids' room. She was wearing a light blue dress and a small hat with lace that, along with the heels she wore, made her out to be five or six inches taller than she actually was.

"Hi Mom! You look beautiful!" I said as I rose to hug her.

"Thank you Michael!" she said as she looked the two of us up and down. "You both look lovely."

"Thank you!" we both said in unison. At that Mrs. Larkman walked over and took your hand.

"Why don't I show Amy where she can sit," she said as she started to lead you back out to the sanctuary. "Michael, can you go check on Jim?"

"Will do, Mom!" I replied as I turned and entered the grooms-men's room. As I entered, I could see that Jim was nervously pacing back and forth.

"Dude . . . chill," I said as I approached him and gave him a bro hug. "It'll all be over within an hour or so."

"I know. It's just . . . I'm getting married in an hour!"

"It'll be fine. You got this, man! I'll be by your side the entire time."

"You better be!" Jim said, trying to smile.

I convinced him to sit for a couple minutes, reminding him that he'd be on his feet a lot today and he needed to rest while he could. A few minutes later, the other groomsmen started arriving. His tension eased noticeably as each came over to hug him and wish him well.

Before we knew it, we were all assembled and were ushered out to wait at the back of the church with the rest of the wedding party for our big entrance. As promised, I stood by Jim the entire time.

When the music started, I thought Jim was going to puke, but he didn't. We each, in turn, walked down the aisle hand in hand with our bridesmaid partners to stand by the altar. I was paired up with Sarah, which made me happy. He walked down the aisle by himself to stand and wait for the bride.

When Brittney walked out from the back of the room, we were all floored. She was dazzling in her white gown and veil. Being a guy, I couldn't really tell you what made this dress elaborate or expensive.

The wedding itself went off like clockwork. Brittney's father walking her down the aisle to Jim, he and Brittney exchanging vows and rings, the kiss, and then it was done. We all exited like we had come in, and I could see Sarah trying to hold back the tears until we made it to the church doorway.

"See, you did it!" I remarked as I entered the foyer. Jim looked at me and pretended to wipe sweat from his brow.

"Congratulations you two!" I said, and then backed away making room for the others in the wedding party to offer their well wishes.

After a few minutes, everyone but the bride and groom were directed outside to wait for the married couple's big exit. I found you almost immediately, standing by yourself, anxiously waiting for me to join you. A smile lit your face as soon as you saw me.

"How'd we look?" I asked as I hugged you.

"You all looked great! Brittney's dress was beautiful!" you said as we turned and waited for Jim and Brittney. I could tell how excited you were by the tone of your voice, and the way you kept squeezing my hand like you were afraid you were going to lose me, like that could ever happen.

A minute later, the bride and groom exited and ran to the waiting limo as we pelted them with rice. Jim never looked so happy in his life, to include the times when we were blowing stuff up. As the limo started away toward the Metro Parks for pictures, I gave you a kiss goodbye and handed you my car keys.

"You're okay getting there?"

"I'll follow the crowd," you replied as I was herded to a waiting limo so we could meet the bride and groom for photos.

To explain, I was always a little afraid when you were driving somewhere on your own. I'm not sure if it is the protective side in me or the side of me that knows how bad you always were at directions. I knew in the back of my head that you were an adult and had driven for years without me being around, but it still made me nervous. Luckily, the pictures didn't take too long, and before I knew it, the limos were taking us to the reception hall.

Once we reached the hall, we each entered it in the same pairs as we did at the church, the men escorting their counterparts to their positions at the wedding table. When I got to my seat, it took me a minute to find you. As soon as I did, though, I was able to relax. I'm sure you saw me smile when I found you, glad that you had successfully made it to the reception.

One of the only things that sucked about the reception was being away from you. We were told at the rehearsal that, once we arrived at the hall, we would be sat at the dinner table and would not be allowed to join our spouses until after dinner. To me, it just didn't seem right that the wedding party should be separated from their significant others. I mean, this was a wedding, a joining of two people. Why couldn't we be joined as well? So, I bided my time as the evening progressed.

Each table was served. We ate, drank, and toasted the married couple a hundred times. And as we finished our dinners, I was called upon to give my best man speech. I won't go into the details of it, because I'm sure you remember it. I will say it appeared to be a big hit and I made Jim and Brittney laugh.

After everyone else had made their speeches and toasted them, I was able to get up and make my way to you. I was on such a high from my speech and the champagne, I couldn't wait to be with you. I was able to barely kiss you before I was called for the groomsman/bridesmaid dance, my final responsibility for the evening.

Eventually, I was announced and joined Sarah on the dance floor for our dance right before the married couple. They looked so wonderful dancing together and smiling. You could feel the love permeate the room.

Finally, it was our time. I said my goodbye to Sarah and made a beeline straight for you for another kiss. I then escorted you onto the dance floor so we could be together.

We just smiled for a bit, losing ourselves in the dance, losing ourselves in each other. I so wanted to capture that moment in time: us dancing and holding one another as we smiled and kissed. Just kissing and being one. I can still picture how perfect you were right at that moment.

"I love you," I said as we moved in time with the music.

"I love you too."

"Do you think we'll ever do this?" I asked tentatively, knowing how adverse you were to the thought of getting married.

"Maybe," you said, smiling at me. "I do know I want to spend the rest of my life with you."

At this revelation, I almost stopped dancing because it felt like the world shifted under my feet. *My* world had just shifted under my feet. I almost fell to my knees at this utterance. I was glad that you were there to help hold me up. To kiss me and hold me until my world caught back up with my surroundings.

When it did, I wanted to tell you that my thoughts were the same. That, from the day we met, I too wanted to be with you and only you for the rest of my life. But I was tongue-tied. I couldn't find the right words that would express how I was feeling in that moment, how I felt every moment we were together. No words could ever cover every thought and emotion that you meant to me.

But, somehow, you knew. We just held each other and continued our dance until the music changed.

After that, everything happened quickly, maybe because I wanted it to. All I could think of was getting you home and making love to you forever.

The bride and groom eventually left to start their honeymoon, and we left for ours in the comfort of our apartment. It had been a long, crazy week, and all I wanted to do was be home with you.

I, indeed, took you home that night and made passionate love to you, my heart keeping the exhaustion away until we had had enough, until we held each other content and satisfied.

The next day we slept in, eventually getting up and doing the coffee routine. This time, however, it included intimate time back in bed. After we awoke for the second time, we made our way out of the apartment for a walk. A walk with the only person I wanted to be hand in hand with for the rest of my life.

That night, too, ended with us making love, still on a high from the wedding, still on a high from our profession of love for each other. And, again, we fell asleep in each other's arms.

The next day I sent a text to Jim and Brittney telling them to have a great honeymoon and letting them know we would see them soon, knowing it was probably not a true statement. Life always had its way of getting in between friends, after all. His reply mirrored the sentiment. And life moved on.

Funny, but no sooner had I put down the phone than a text appeared from Heather asking how the wedding went. I told her "Fantastic," of course, and that I was the greatest best man ever. I got back some LOLs, which made me happy.

I told Heather I had checked things out with you and that you were open for a double date if she was. She said that's be perfect, and we made preliminary arrangements to meet at the mall the following Friday night for dinner.

"So, is that okay?" I asked when we both arrived home that night.

"Do we have any other plans?"

"Not that I'm aware of. So, is it cool?"

"I suppose," you said, knowing that I wanted to do it.

That Friday, we met Heather and Rick, her boyfriend, at one of the mall restaurants for dinner. As we sat through dinner, we explained how you and I had met. She did the same, telling us about her and Rick and their time together. When she finished, I explained how she and I had met, omitting the failed kiss, but letting you and Rick know we'd known each other for years.

When we finished with dinner, the four of us wandered the mall for a bit and then headed to a bar for a nightcap. All in all, it was a great time. I was pretty sure you had a good time and felt more comfortable with Heather.

It was the following Tuesday when I spoke to Heather again, her texting me to let me know that Rick and she had had a great time with you and I and would like to do it again in the near future. I told her I would run it by you but it shouldn't be a problem. We chit-chatted on and off during the next few days, asking each other's likes and dislikes, how we got into the careers we were in, and about our significant other.

Heather, it seems, was a secretary for an engineering firm but didn't make much money, so she bartended to make ends meet. Rick, on the other hand, couldn't keep a full-time job, which made it a little rough on her. But she had confidence that he would find something he could stick with in the near future.

When Friday rolled around, you called me at lunch, which was unusual for you, to let me know that your friend Susan was ill and being admitted to the hospital and you wanted to fly to Georgia to be with her.

"Oh. Sorry to hear. When were you thinking about going?"

"I was thinking about taking next week off and flying down Sunday, if that's okay?"

"That's fine with me sweetie. I hope she's okay soon."

"Me too!" you said, adding, "Well, I better get back to work. I love you!"

"I love you too!" I responded as I hung up.

When we got home that night, you made the flight arrangements for that Sunday morning, asking if I could drop you off at the airport. I told you it wasn't a problem as we went onto our weekend activities.

On Sunday, I took you to the airport as planned, and I stayed by the ticket booth having coffee at Starbucks until your flight left, just in case. When you were safely in the air, I left and drove home. I was probably home for two minutes when I received a text from Heather asking what I was up to. I told her I had just dropped you at the airport and I was a bachelor for the next week. She then asked if I'd like to get together that evening for dinner, so I didn't have to cook. I said that was fine, and then I let you know what I was doing as soon as you landed.

"Just you two?" you asked.

"I think so. I'm not sure though. Hold on, I'll text her and ask."

A minute later the reply came in that, yes, it would just be me and her. Rick was visiting his parents and couldn't join us.

"So, is that okay?" I asked, hoping it wasn't an issue. I really didn't want to cook that night.

"Yeah, that's fine," you answered. "Just text me later when you get in. I love you!"

"I love you too! Give my love to Susan!" I said as I hung up the phone.

Two hours later, around 5:00 p.m., I met Heather at Cancun. We also had a couple beers with our meals and talked about our life goals and significant others. We had a great time laughing, drinking, and enjoying each other's company. We eventually called it an evening around 7:30 p.m., knowing we both had to go to work the next day.

As I walked her out to her car, she asked, "Do you want to hang out Tuesday night? That's the night Rick works late."

"I don't see a problem with it, but just to make sure I'll bounce it off Amy."

"Okay, sounds good. Let me know tomorrow. Cool?"

"Will do," I said, closing the car door for her.

That night we talked, and I told you what a fun meal it had been with Heather. I knew you were a little jealous, but what was the harm. Both she and I were in committed relationships and had no intentions for each other.

"So, she wants to hang out again on Tuesday. Is that okay?"

"Wait a minute. I go out of town for a few days and she wants to hang out with you? I don't know if I feel comfortable with that," you said.

"She said it's the night Rick works late. I swear I won't make it a late night," I promised.

"Okay. I guess. Hey, I've got to run. Have a nice night's sleep! I love you!"

"I love you too!" I replied and ended the call.

That Tuesday was pretty much like Sunday. Heather and I met at Cancun, we ate, we talked, we drank, we laughed, and we left. No big fanfare or to-do, just two old friends meeting for dinner and drinks. This, of course, I mentioned to you when we talked that night.

"Okay. Sounds like you had fun."

"How's Susan? Is she feeling any better?"

"She is, actually. She's being discharged from the hospital on Friday."

"So, you're still on schedule for coming home Sunday? I miss you."

"I miss you too! I am so looking forward to coming home."

"Me too!" I said. And, after talking for a few more minutes, we said our goodnights and hung up for the evening.

The rest of the week was pretty uneventful. Work then home, work then home. Friday morning, I received a text from Heather asking if I wanted to meet for drinks at Cancun after work. I, again, told her I'd check with you but it shouldn't be a problem. I sent you a text but didn't hear back from you. I figured you were busy, but, based on the last couple times, I assumed it shouldn't be an issue. When 5:00 p.m. rolled around, I kept my plans and met Heather at Cancun. About twenty minutes after I got to Cancun you called.

"Hi honey! It's been a weird morning," you started. "Sorry I didn't get back to you."

"No problem sweetie. Everything okay?"

"Yeah, I guess. Susan had an issue this morning, but they still decided to release her. I've been in the hospital all day so I couldn't call."

"No problem," I said, taking a sip of my beer. "Just wanted to let you know that since I didn't hear back from you, I ended meeting Heather for a drink anyway. Cool?"

At this, Heather chimed in with a "Hi Amy!"

This, in hindsight, was probably the worst thing she could have done.

"So you didn't hear back from me and went anyway?" you asked, and I could hear the anger in your voice.

"You were okay with the other times. I didn't think it was a problem," I replied tentatively and could tell by the long pause that followed that you weren't happy with my response.

This was also the moment I knew I had fucked up.

"I'm sorry. I seriously didn't think it was a problem. If I did, I wouldn't have come."

The pause then ended with your question. "So, what time do you think you'll be home?"

"I'm going to finish up my drink and head home . . . maybe less than an hour?"

"Okay," you said with a chilled anger in your voice. "Please call me when you get home."

"Will do! I love you!"

"I love you too," you replied and hung up.

Heather looked at me and asked as soon as I put down the phone, "Is everything okay?"

"No, not really," I said as I finished up my beer. "I've got to get going. I hope you understand."

"I suppose. Does she normally keep you on that tight a leash?"

"Excuse me?" I said, being taken aback by this comment. "I don't consider it a tight leash. She just didn't know what I was up to."

"Sorry. I didn't mean to offend you," Heather said. "But it just seemed like you got in trouble over nothing."

"Not really. It's just that Amy doesn't know you well," I said as I downed my beer. "Plus, she's got a lot going on with her friend Susan. I'm sure her mind is running a thousand miles a minute."

"Gotcha," she said, but I wasn't sure if she truly believed me.

"Well, I better go," I commented as I finished the last of my beer and slapped a tip on the counter. "We'll talk later in the week . . . cool?"

"Sounds good. Take care and drive safe!" she said as she gave me a goodbye hug.

"You too!" I said as I made my way toward the door.

A few minutes later, I was on the road traveling home for the tongue lashing I knew was coming. And I guess I deserved it. Here I was, out with another woman having drinks, while you were visiting a sick friend. Even though it was innocent, I understood how upsetting it was for you.

"I am sorry," I said into the cell phone. "I didn't mean to upset you."

"Are you planning on seeing her again?"

"No. We have not made any plans besides the one today."

I paused for a minute, to let that sink in, and then said, "I miss you! I am so looking forward to you coming home."

"Me too. But I really don't want you to see her again. I don't feel comfortable with her. It just seems off."

"She's just a friend. You know that, right?"

"Yeah, I know that. But you're too caring of a person."

"What does that mean?"

"It means that you're too easily swayed. I'm just afraid she'll take advantage of you."

"Take advantage of me?" I scoffed. "I'm a grown man, you know. I make up my own mind."

You paused, and then said, "Can we just leave it at *I don't want you seeing her again?*"

I thought about this for a minute. I really wasn't doing anything wrong, but I didn't want to mess up our relationship. I loved where we were at. Talking about marriage, talking about being together for the rest of our lives. And I wanted that. I wanted all that.

"Okay. I won't see her again. I promise."

You and I talked for a few minutes more and then said goodbye until later that evening.

I sent a text to Heather a little while later to let her know about your feelings, and about mine. I felt really bad doing it, since we had just rekindled our friendship, but it was for the best. She wrote back she was upset but understood. "Not all women can handle guys and girls being friends." I wrote back that I appreciated the understanding and that maybe we would run into each other again someday. In my heart, though, I was pretty sure we wouldn't.

That night when I called you, I explained that I had dropped the friendship and that I was okay with it, even though I really wasn't. I could hear a little relief in your voice, and we moved on to other subjects.

Sunday came and I picked you up from the airport, and it was like nothing ever happened. I was glad about this. I was so afraid that you would hold a grudge. But I guess that true love forgives almost anything. And you were always more important to me.

You were always the most important thing in the world to me.

Diary: May 19

I think my biggest regret is never marrying you. Not that I didn't ask; I did, multiple times. I don't know if you just felt like you needed more time or that we had more time.

I guess neither worked out for us.

I mean, we practically were married. Being together so long, in each other's lives so long. We grew together, both as people and as adults.

I remember how many people said we were that "cute older couple". The way we held hands as we walked through the mall or through the dance club. We were perfect for each other, so I thought.

I wish we would have had more time. That's all we needed . . . more time.

CHAPTER

8

It had taken a while after being cheated on to start dating again — almost a full year, in fact. It wasn't a bad year, though. I had just been promoted to Specialist 4, which meant more money in my pocket and people below me to shuffle work to if there was something I didn't want to do. Also, there were cut backs in the military, so they were letting people go early and we weren't going into the field as much. All in all, I couldn't complain.

I was doing my usual, working for four months and then taking leave for ten days. And the time for me to take leave again was fast approaching. I decided this time around I'd take leave during Christmas. Being on base during Christmas was a little depressing, at least for me as a single guy. Don't get me wrong, there were plenty of things to do, of course. Places to eat, clubs to go to, and hobbies you could get into. But I thought, what the hell, a white Christmas was a thing of beauty; why waste it?

My plan was to not tell Dee or Mom and just surprise them by showing up. So I made flight arrangements to fly Christmas Eve. The flight was a little more expensive, but I thought it would be worth it. And the flight I chose would get me in around 4:00 p.m., just in time to join them for Christmas Eve dinner at our favorite Chinese spot. It was weird, but it was our family tradition.

That day, the plane landed about an hour late because of the snow in Cleveland but got me in just in time to meet Dee and Mom at the restaurant. As I entered the restaurant and walked over to their table, their jaws dropped. It was priceless. All except for the tears — I hate it when women cry more than I hate it when I cry.

When we finished hugging, we all sat down and stuffed ourselves with Shrimp Fried Rice, and then left for home to open presents. I had the forethought to send their presents by express post so they arrived, guaranteed, two days earlier. Dee had called me when they arrived and *begged* me to let her open her present. But knowing I'd be home, I told her and Mom that they had to wait until Christmas morning while I was on the phone. I'm such a sneaky devil.

The minute we got home, Dee made a beeline to the parcel I sent. It was huge! It had cost me a bundle to ship, but I was a single guy and seldom went out. I could afford it.

"So, is this all mine?" Dee asked as she knelt down next to the box.

"You wish!" I said as she examined the parcel. "But no, there are presents for you and Mom in there."

"Crap," Dee said jokingly.

"If you want, you can open it . . . all the presents in there are wrapped."

Dee was like a five-year-old. She opened the outer box and saw all the wrapped boxes inside. Dee reached in, grabbed them one by one, and shook each of them as she removed them from the carton and placed them under the tree.

When she was finished, we waited for Mom to finish putting our jackets away. I think she knew it was almost impossible to have us do it ourselves with all the presents looming in front of us. I opened my bag and pulled out the package my mom had sent to me that contained my presents. Thankfully, they had arrived just in time for me to throw them in my bag to bring back with me on the plane.

"Which one can I open first?" Dee asked.

"If it's okay with Mom, open the one from me," I said, turning my attention to Mom for agreement.

"Oh, sure," she replied, and Dee tore into the box. Mom and I just looked at each other and laughed.

"A new guitar!" Dee exclaimed as she opened the box, revealing its contents.

Sometime in the summer, Dee had taken up guitar at her boyfriend's behest so she could join his band. She had tried out and gotten the job as the singer for the band, but he figured it'd be "way cool if Dee could wail on the strings as she sings". To accommodate his request, Dee had gone out and bought a cheap-ass guitar to play. After seeing the guitar on my last vacation, I figured she needed a better one.

"This is perfect, Mike! Thank you!" she practically screamed as she hugged me, almost breaking a rib.

"Mom, it's your turn!"

At this I handed Mom the gift I bought. Tradition usually called for us to open in order of age, but I guess you could say I passed my opening privileges. I just traveled over a thousand miles, and I wanted to see the joy the two would have opening my gifts first. It was, after all, one of my favorite things about Christmas.

"Mike! You shouldn't have!" she said as she opened the package with the diamond earrings I purchased.

"Yes I should have! Aren't they great?"

"They are beautiful! Thank you!" she said as she came over and kissed me on my forehead.

The two of them looked at me now, and I guessed I had to bite the bullet and actually open one of my presents.

"Which one?" I asked the pair.

"That one! It's from me," my sister said as she pointed to a present wrapped in green.

"I hope it's okay!" Dee said as I un-wrapped the gift. It was a paperback of Stephen King's *Pet Cemetery*.

"Dee! This is perfect! Thank you!" I replied. Stephen King was one of my favorite authors.

The rest of the evening was spent like this: opening presents, eating snacks, and enjoying each other's company. I had really missed being home.

We eventually turned on the TV to watch *Charlie Brown* and *It's a Wonderful Life*, our traditional Christmas Eve movies. I think I was the first to start falling asleep on the couch. My mom nudged me to wake me, and without having to be told, I said my goodnights and ambled to my own bed.

As soon as I woke the next day, I called Jim to see what he and his family were up to.

"Dude! You said you weren't going to be home! You dick!" he exclaimed.

"Yeah, sorry. I wanted to surprise Dee and Mom and figured you'd blab."

"Yeah, you're probably right," he said, laughing.

"So, what's up for the day?"

"Not much. We already ate, and Sarah is going to her boyfriend's house. Wanna hang out?"

"Yes! But I need you to come pick me up!" I demanded into the phone.

"Okay, I'll be there in twenty. Be ready!" he said, knowing it always took me time to find my shoes.

"Okay. See ya then!" I said, finishing our conversation.

True to his word, exactly twenty minutes later Jim was at my door. And we spent the day visiting our friends and seeing the sights. Four months doesn't seem like a long time, but it's amazing what can change in that brief period: businesses closing, new stores opening, new restaurants. We drove around all day seeing everything I'd missed. We eventually went to his house for dinner. It was great to see Sarah, his dad, and of course my other mother.

"So, what's up with the love life?" I asked. The last he had told me he had broken up with Ann, a girl he had dated for about two months.

"Nothing, really. There's this one girl at my work. We've been talking. That's all."

After a few seconds of silence, he asked, "And you?"

I just stared at him at this point. It hadn't been that long since we talked, and I'm pretty sure he knew my stance on dating a woman not in our area.

"Well, I've only been home a day," I jested. "Guess we'll have to see!"

"Game on!"

"Game on," I replied laughing. This was our typical saying before we hit the mall, or street, or wherever to go *girlfriend hunting*. But this would have to wait for another day, maybe tomorrow.

Jim and I chatted for a little while longer before we headed for my house. It was decided we'd stop for beer to take home, and he would join me, Dee, and Mom for snacks and movies. He was part of my *family*, after all. We spent the rest of the evening drinking and talking, just the four of us, and eventually called it quits around midnight.

The next few days were spent in search for girlfriends. Yeah I know, it sounds crude, but it's what single guys in their early twenties did for fun. And we did have said *fun*. We hit the mall a few times. We hit a few bars. We also went to a couple parties friends were having. After about eight days, we were not having any luck. Jim's approach to his coworker was going nowhere as well. Just two single guys with no luck.

"Dude, I leave the day after tomorrow. It's time to stick a fork in it," I stated as we drove back to my house from the mall for dinner.

"Never say die!" he bellowed as we drove on. "I'm still going to be here when you're on your way back to Texas. Take one for the team, man!"

How could I deny this logic? "Alright, what's next then?"

"The Mining Hole," he stated. "I say we hit the club tonight and see what we can find!"

Again, logic.

"Okay," I relented. "Let's see what we can see."

At 9:00 p.m. that night, we entered the dance club, dressed to kill. Well, dressed up so we could maybe get laid was more like it. The Mining Hole had two levels, three bars, and hundreds of women, mostly college students on winter break. Jim and I grabbed a couple beers and looked for a table near the dance floor.

"Damn. Place is *packed*," I said, surveying the establishment.

"If we can't get girlfriends here—"

"Girlfriend! We're in this for you tonight, dude," I said, perfectly happy with my *wingmanship*.

"Dude, you have one more day here. *Anything* could happen tonight. You never know."

It was the 80s, so every night was 80s night. That night had a DJ from the local popular radio station, playing *all the hits, all the time.* This type of music really wasn't our thing, us leaning more toward Alternative or New Wave, but the ladies liked it, so we dealt with it.

After thirty minutes or so, Jim and I saw a table of four women — a bachelorette party — just out to have a good time. So we set our targeting sights and, as the wingman, I moved in to break the ice.

It was obvious that the ladies had come in two sets of two. One pair would get up to dance while the other two sat, and vice versa. Knowing him like I did, I knew almost right away which one he liked. And, lucky for me, the girl with her was just as attractive, giving off a *naughty librarian* vibe. She would be the one I approached first. Best part was I felt no pressure. This was something I was doing for Jim, not myself. As soon as the other two ladies left for the dance floor, I grabbed my beer and made my way to their table.

"Bachelorette party?" I inquired. At this, both ladies turned toward me.

"Yes it is! Our friend Andie is getting married next weekend," the naughty librarian said, nodding toward the dance floor.

"Cool!" I said, not really thinking it was. But hey, what do you say?

"I'm Mike," I said, sticking out my hand for a shake. She took it without hesitation.

"Amanda," the librarian said, and we shook on it.

"It's nice to meet you Amanda. The gentleman over there is Jim," I said loud enough for both ladies to hear. At this I turned my head, looked at him, and signaled for him to come over to the table. He was there in an instant.

"Hi, I'm Jim," he said as he stuck out his hand to the future Mrs. Larkman.

"Becca," she said as she hesitantly shook his hand.

"A pleasure, Becca," he said, lightening her tension.

"Would you like to dance?" I asked. And before we knew it, we were on the dance floor with the lovely ladies: me with Amanda and Jim with Becca.

As we danced we gave each other space so we could divide and conquer. Okay, it really wasn't like that, but military sayings were always running through my head. But it was nice having some semi alone time with a beautiful woman. And, that she was. She had shoulder-length light brown hair and blue eyes. Her body was on the petite side, but not waifish. And she was probably about four inches shorter than me, which was good because I'm not a tall guy. Finding a woman shorter than me can be a chore sometimes.

We danced relatively slow, considering the music being played. We were kind of ignoring the music anyway, wanting to get to know each other.

"So, what do you do for a living?" I asked as we danced.

"I'm a librarian," she answered, as I mentally said, *Nailed it.* "And you?"

"I'm in the army at the moment," I answered. "I have one more year, and then I'm moving back here to go to college."

I added this trivia so she wouldn't get scared off, in case things happened between us. I know I said I was in this for Jim, but the girl was hot. And smart. And hot. Maybe I could find someone local!

Watching her move along the dance floor, it was as if the world was slowing down so I could take in every second in a minute's time. She had on a cocktail dress that ended about two inches above her knees. As she danced, the dress would twirl slightly allowing me glimpses higher on her thigh. It was beginning to become difficult to dance.

It didn't help that she was giving me this sensual look. Smiling at me as we danced, looking deep into my eyes, dancing so close that we occasionally touched. And each time we touched, she smiled at me just a bit more.

The music changed and we backed away from each other slightly, which was good. It allowed me to look over the amazing body that she had. She was perfect, or perfect for me. Either way I liked what I saw.

And then, I noticed it. As I looked down her left arm, taking in every inch that was Amanda, I saw a glint on her left hand, on her ring finger. Yes, ladies and gentlemen, she had on a wedding ring.

I believe this is the point where time sped back up. Or my jaw was dragging on the floor making me move slower. Either way, the song ended quicker than I expected, and we walked back to the table.

"So, you're married?" I blurted out, wanting to put everything on the table.

"Yeah." she confessed.

"Okay," I said, trying to play it off like it didn't bother me as much as it did. "How long have you been married?"

"About a year."

When she said this, I was ready to call it quits and go back to our table. But out of the corner of my eye, I saw Jim and Becca walking toward the restrooms, so I made the decision to stick with Amanda until they came back. It was, after all, the gentlemanly thing to do.

I took a drink of my beer to clear the dread that was in my throat. I didn't know how to feel about this. Was I wrong in her attraction toward me? It felt real. With all the contact and smiling as we danced, I knew in my *soul* this girl was attracted to me. Knowing that, I asked the question that still haunts me to this day.

"So, are you happily married?" I joked. Or it was meant to be a joke. "No" was all she said.

I think this was the point where I gave up on the evening, gave up on making Jim happy, gave up on having a good time before I left for Texas.

To give you some back story on me — not that you haven't been reading all this anyway —I've always been pretty monogamous. Maybe it's because I'm no good at juggling. Maybe it's because my mom had affairs with married men, and I hated that she did. Maybe it was just because I never ever wanted that happening to me. I'm not sure.

But I did know this is where my evening ended.

Eventually, Jim and Becca came back to the table, stating they had used the restrooms. I'm pretty sure that also meant that he had gotten her phone number, which meant my part this evening was complete. With my job well done, it was time to call back the troops.

"Dude, time to go?" I posed. He looked at me quizzically at first, but he could see from my eyes something was up so he nodded.

"Well, it was nice meeting you ladies! But we have to go."

"Oh really?" Becca asked with a slight pout on her lips.

"Yeah. I have to work tomorrow . . . early," he said, and he wasn't lying. But I think the ladies knew something was up.

Before we started for the door, we both gave hugs to the ladies. It was, in fact, really nice meeting them. And had I met Amanda a year earlier, we'd be in business. But timing can be everything.

On our trek home, I explained to Jim what had happened. And being the friend that he was, he accepted my reasons for wanting to get the hell out of there. Those are the things best friends are made of, after all. And he did, in fact, score a number. I made his evening, performing my wingman job with distinction.

I was tired, body and soul, when he dropped me off. I don't think I said two words to Dee and Mom when I strolled in. I just headed for bed, hoping sleep would come and take away all the thoughts and events of the evening.

The next day, being my last day of leave, I spent all my time with Dee and Mom, or as much as I could with their jobs interfering with my family time. It was sometime after dinner that Jim called up and wanted to hang out. Even though I really wasn't in the mood after the previous night's events, I resolved to hear him out.

"Dude, it's your last night. Let me take you out," he pleaded.

"Man, last night took the wind out of me. I don't want to go clubbing," I said defiantly.

"No! No clubs. Just you, me, and a pocket full of quarters we can use at the arcade."

Now we were talking.

Growing up I ruled, *ruled*, at video games. Said rule was most evident in a game named Defender, which was also one of the most difficult games to play. With your left hand you have to control the joystick that moves you up and down, with a button to switch you left and right. With the right hand you have to shoot, thrust, and drop smart bombs. The object is to guard ten *humans* walking around on the surface of the planet while being chased by dozens of various flying creatures. If you lost all ten guys, the world would blow up and you had to then face *hundreds* of flying creatures that wanted to kill your ass.

Like I said, it was hard, and Jim and I were the best we knew at the game. Most people trying the game for the first time get blown up in a minute and never play again. He and I, however, could play for hours. No, I'm not joking with you, I do mean hours. The best run I ever had was eight straight hours on one quarter.

"Okay. You're on" was all I said and, twenty minutes later, we were making our way to the local arcade.

We did have a great time that night. We probably spent only five dollars apiece in three hours of play, all of which came out of Jim's pocket. When a movie costs five dollars and the soda and popcorn even more, this was a value you could not beat.

We left after those three hours knowing we had successfully defended the universe from all extraterrestrial threats. It also helped that I kicked Jim's ass in every game we played together. I always did. And he was okay with it.

"So, where are we off to now, Mike?" he asked, hoping the evening was not over.

"Not sure . . . are you hungry?"

"I could use a snack," he said and drove us to McDonald's.

It was probably around 11:00 p.m., close to closing, when we pulled into the lot. We went in even though it was late, knowing it was kind of a dick move to mess up the dining area this late at night. But, we did just save the galaxy, so what did we care?

After we ordered our food, we sat down and destroyed it in seconds. I guess killing blimps on a screen for three hours builds up an appetite. After the food was gone, we sat there and drank our *free refill* sodas, determined to stay until they kicked us out.

That's when I met Katie. I knew this because it was on her name tag.

Katie was the assistant manager at McDonald's. Her task, at that point of the evening, was to clean the dining room and force out any stragglers that might cause the store to run past closing time. And, Jim and I were those guys.

"Hey guys. Can you wrap it up so we can close?" Katie asked, in a more than nice fashion.

"Do we get free food if we do?" Jim said, intentionally giving her shit because she was in a manager uniform.

"Ha ha ha. You're funny. If you go out to your car, I can see what we can do."

"Good ploy. Don't worry, we were just leaving," I laughed.

Katie smiled at this, a very pleasant smile, at that. One I could get used to. And she actually looked kind of hot in the manager's uniform, which was really weird. Made me wonder how good she'd look in street clothes, or without clothes.

"Hi . . . Katie," I said, testing the name just in case the nametag was a fake. "I'm Mike. This is Jim. It's nice to meet you."

She didn't blink, so I assumed the nametag must have been accurate.

"Hi. What brings you into Mickey D's so late?"

"We were just at the arcade and got hungry," I said, kicking back in the booth a little.

"Cool! I'm glad someone was having fun tonight."

"And you weren't?" he chimed in, smiling at Katie. Katie giggled. Here we go again.

"Yeah, lots of fun. Can't you tell?" she asked jokingly.

As Katie talked to us, she walked around the dining room cleaning here and there. Wiping down tables, putting chairs on tables, all the while answering questions he and I posed, all the while looking at me. At least I'm pretty sure she was looking at me more. I'm not sure Jim picked up on it right away, but when Katie was finished, she came over and sat with us, next to me.

"What are you doing after this?" I asked Katie.

"Nothing. I'm just going home after this. I'm beat," Katie stated, but then looked at me and asked, "How about you?"

This is the point where Jim realized that Katie had a thing for me. Part of me felt bad because he got shut down, but most of me was happy for *me*. There was actually a not-married — pretty sure she was not married — woman interested in me. But I *was* leaving for Texas the next day. Great timing on the universe's part, I must say. But he understood he became the wingman.

"Nothing, really. I'm in the army. I head back to Fort Hood tomorrow," I replied, knowing this was the last *hurrah* for the evening.

"Oh, that's sucks."

"You're telling me . . ." I replied back because, well, it did.

"How long will you be gone?"

"I'll be back for ten days around April."

"Cool!" Katie said, as she pulled a piece of paper and pen out of her pocket. She scribbled something on it and handed it to me. "Here's my number. If you'd like to go out when you get back, call me."

At that, she rose and walked toward the door. We followed suit, knowing it was our time to leave. As we exited the restaurant, we heard the lock click behind us and we walked to Jim's car. I was on cloud nine as we drove home. And I think he was happy for me, even though he was shut down.

When we reached my house, I left the car and said goodbye to Jim as we shook hands.

"I'll see you in four months dude!" he said before I closed the door and walked into the house. This and saying goodbye to Mom and Dee, of course, were the saddest parts of my vacation. But all good things, they say . . .

The next day Dee dropped me at the airport, and I flew back to Texas, very satisfied I had had a great vacation and left with the potential of a date when I returned.

The next four months dragged, and I mean, they *dragged*. It seemed like every week was the same. Wake, PT, shower, breakfast, formation — which was the battalion standing in the cold for almost no reason — clean vehicles, lunch, clean weapons, afternoon formation, return to barracks and wait for dinner, dinner, return to barracks to watch TV, sleep. On the weekends, I'd travel to Dallas or down to Austin for fun one day, laundry and phone calls one day. Then the next week would roll through.

The phone calls home were the only respite from monotony, and the phone calls to Katie were the highlight of my week. From the first week I returned to the base, I was calling Katie regularly. It turned out that she usually had Sundays off, so every Sunday at 2:00 p.m. we talked, usually for hours. She would catch me up on all things Cleveland, her family, and the joys of working for McDonald's. She would also let me know what days she had off that week, and I made every opportunity to call her on those nights as well.

Eventually April arrived and I requested ten days of leave for mid-month. I then made my flight arrangements, as I had multiple times before, and arranged for Dee to pick me up from the airport.

"So you're coming home on Thursday?" Katie asked with excitement.

"Yep! My flight lands at 4:20 p.m."

"Awesome! Will you be busy Thursday night? I have that night off."

"I probably should stay home for dinner, but I can leave maybe around 8:00 p.m. Would you like to do something?"

"Hell yeah!" Katie yelled into the phone. "Want to come over my house?"

"I could . . . if you want me to?"

"Would love you to!" she replied. And the date was set.

Four days later, Dee picked me up and took me home, where I had a quick dinner and asked to borrow Mom's car for the evening.

"No problem. Just make sure you're home by 7:30 a.m. so I can go to work," Mom jested.

I waited until 7:00 p.m. before I called Katie to make sure she was home and, more importantly, wanting company. After a squeal of delight, she said she was there waiting and proceeded to give me her address and apartment number. Around 8:00 p.m., I left my house bound for hers.

When I arrived, I rang her apartment, and she buzzed me in. Upon reaching her door, I barely got a knock in before the door swung open and she shuffled me in. The apartment was small, containing only a single bedroom, small kitchen, bathroom, and living room. The living room was sparsely finished, holding only a couch and TV.

At first, I thought it was dreary only having the bare necessities. But, then again, how much more does one really need? Okay, maybe a bed, which I hadn't seen yet, but with any luck . . .

But I'm jumping ahead.

As soon as the door was closed behind me, I was locked into a bear hug. I had no problem with this, really, but it did seem quick.

"I'm so glad you're back. I missed you!"

"I'm glad to see you too Katie!" I replied as I wrestled my way out of the death grip. "So, this is your place, huh?"

"Yep! I don't have much, but what there is, is mine," she stated proudly.

As I assayed the rest of her apartment, I spied the dining room table near the kitchen. It was adorned with what appeared to be two lit candles and dessert, for two.

"Very nice," I said as I took off my coat and looked for a place to stash it. Katie pointed to a coat rack by the door, so I hung my coat and proceeded to get comfortable.

"As you can see, I made dessert. You like banana cream pie, right?"

"Wow! You remembered!" I answered surprised. Dessert had been the topic of one of our multiple conversations, but I didn't think she would have remembered. I mean, I know she told me what her favorite dessert was, but I'd be damned if I could remember what it was.

Katie took my hand and guided me toward a waiting chair. After we were both seated, Katie updated me on the events of the past few days as we ate our slices of pie. As she talked, ranting about this or laughing about that, I thought how nice it was to hear her voice in person.

When we were finished eating, she asked me if there was anything in particular that I wanted to watch on TV. There really wasn't, I replied, so she turned on a sitcom. We sat and watched it for about an hour, just the two of us next to each other, enjoying each other's warmth.

I eventually put my arm around her, and she put her head on my chest. It felt . . . right. Working up the nerve, I finally made the decision it was time. Turning my head toward her, I raised her head slightly with my hand, leaned in, and kissed her. We both tasted like banana, which didn't suck.

Within a minute or so, she was sitting on my lap, straddling me. Deep, wet, banana kisses that aroused me, and pleased her, from what I could tell. My hands worked their way up her shirt, and I cupped her warm breasts. I thought she might stop me, but a few seconds later, she lifted her shirt, took it off, and threw it to the floor. All the while she was grinding on me, something that made me think of something out of soft porn.

This lasted for five or ten minutes before she dismounted, grabbed my hand, and led me to the bedroom. And, yes, there was a bed. It was kind of small, but we made use of it for the next few hours.

Around midnight or 1:00 a.m., I figured it was time to go home. I used the excuse that I had to return the car, but that wasn't totally it. I felt weird that we had practically just met, talked, albeit a lot, and now we were sleeping together. It just felt too . . . fast? I've never considered myself old fashioned, but I was definitely feeling that way at this point.

"I should go," I said as I found and put on my clothing. "My mom wanted me home about now, since I just got into town."

"Alright. Is everything okay? I didn't upset you, did I?" She must have known something was off.

"No, not at all! I'll see you tomorrow . . . err . . . later today. Cool?" I asked as we walked to her door.

"That'd be great! I work 4:00 p.m. to 10:00 p.m. tomorrow. After that . . . or before? It's your call," she said as she handed me my coat.

"How about after? It'll give me some time to hang with Jim," I said, laughing. "He doesn't even know I'm home yet."

We kissed one more time, and I walked out the door.

The next day, as promised, I called Jim and let him know I was in town. He wasn't too surprised because he knew of my timetable but reprimanded me on not calling him as soon as I got in. He picked me up after dinner, and we visited his family for a bit and then proceeded to the arcade for a rematch.

He also informed me that he did, in fact, ask the girl from his work out on a date. He and Abby had been on a few dates since then and were getting serious. I really did need to talk to him more often when I was away. We also discussed my seeing Katie, and I briefly went over the events of the previous evening. When we left the arcade, after me crushing him, I mentioned I was headed over to her house at 10:00 p.m.

"Dude, do me a favor and drop me at Katie's house . . . cool?"

"No problem. Are you spending the night?"

"Maybe. It seemed like she wanted me to stay last night, but I figured it was rude to my mom and Dee."

"Dude, do what feels right" were his words of wisdom. If only life were that simple.

Twenty minutes later, right around 11:00 p.m., Jim dropped me off at Katie's. He waited until I was inside the apartment and waving from the window before he left — a true gentleman and best friend.

After kissing for about five minutes, Katie and I said hi to each other and moved to the couch to watch TV. Things progressed from there to be a replay of the previous night. And, again, I had no problem with this.

"You know," Katie started. "I don't have to work until 11:00 a.m. tomorrow. You can spend the night if you want."

"Only if you're sure it's okay. I don't want to impose."

"It's no problem. And I want you to," Katie said giving me the full puppy dog eyes. I told her I would, and I wanted to as well.

I figured I'd better call home and let Mom know so she wouldn't be worried. Dee answered the phone — thank God I didn't wake Mom — and I told her. For some reason, she wasn't surprised. Maybe I'm too predictable.

It was nice sleeping next to her, spooning, enjoying each other's contours. The little noises she made while sleeping. All the while trying not to choke in the middle of the night on hair, and yet loving every minute.

We spent the rest of my leave like this: me spending every day hanging with Jim, Dee, Mom, and my other friends and then spending almost every night with Katie. I was very morose when it came time to leave. I had gotten used to sharing my time, and a bed, with Katie. It was going to be tough to leave her for four months.

The last night I spent at my mom's house but was able to talk my mom into letting Katie spend the night. In the morning when it was time to take me to the airport, Dee drove me and let Katie come along for the ride. Dee even played chauffeur letting Katie and I sit in back so we could cuddle and kiss.

"I'll miss you!" Katie said through tear-filled eyes. I can't say I was much better.

"I'll miss you too!" I replied, kissing her one last time. I gave Dee a hug and strode in to catch my flight.

Four hours later, I was back at Fort Hood, and the four-month clock was reset.

These months, of course, were worse than the previous. Having a relationship with Katie made it tough being away, though tougher than the other times. Even the times leaving Jennifer didn't seem as bad as this. I think this was because Katie and I had a closer bond than Jennifer and I had. Not really sure. I did know these months were dragging, and I missed Katie immensely. I couldn't wait to get back home.

Katie and I did talk every couple days, which kept me from losing my mind, but I wanted her with me, wanted to be *with* her. And it wasn't so much I loved her — too soon to tell — as I was lonely without her. I was tired of being alone day in and day out. I had roommates, sure, but it wasn't the same. When August hit, my unit had nothing planned so I scheduled my next leave.

Dee picked me up from the airport and drove me home like before. When I got there, I immediately dropped my bags, borrowed Dee's car, and drove to Katie's. From our conversations, I knew Katie would be home and I practically attacked the minute I got there. From our previous encounters, I knew she would have no problem with this, and she didn't. Katie was supposed to work that night, but she resolved to call in sick and we spent the night, and almost my entire leave, together.

Sometime, maybe mid-leave, I asked her, "Have you ever thought about living in Texas?"

"Actually, I have. I miss you when you're gone. You know that, right?"

"I know. I've just been thinking lately that maybe we should move in together."

At this, Katie's eyes grew wide, as did her smile. "Really? Because I thought the same thing!"

And that was it.

When my leave ended and I got back to base, I put in for off-post housing. It wasn't always granted, but because I was friends with a few of the people in battalion admin, mine was approved. A week later, I found an apartment and contacted Katie.

"I found a place!" I said, very proud of myself. "It's not too far from post, so I can walk to work most days, and it's right down the street from a Mickey D's."

"That is awesome! I'll see if I can request a transfer."

And, less than a month later, Katie was all moved in.

Times were tough, financially, during this time. Katie wasn't able to get a job as an assistant manager like she had when she was at home, so she had to settle for part time crew. The pay increase for living off post wasn't a lot either. The increase was only the difference in food pay. Guys living off post didn't get meal cards like the guys that lived in the billets, so making ends meet was tougher than I thought it would be. After being together two months, we weren't sure how much longer we could afford rent, or food.

"Well, we have an option," I said one day.

"Oh?" Katie said, wanting me to go on.

"We could get married," I said flat out.

Katie's eyes went wide. "But I thought you didn't want to get married?"

It was true. I hadn't. My plan was to go to college as soon as I got out of the military, and I figured getting married would put a damper on my educational plans. But the military would increase my pay by 50 percent if I had a spouse. That would allow us to make rent, and with the little bit Katie was making at McDonald's, we'd have comfort money.

"Well, I mean, we are already living together. It wouldn't be that big of a leap if we got married," I said, liking the thought more and more as I ran it through my head.

"Will your family be okay with it?" Katie inquired.

"They won't be pleased, but once I explain it to them, they should be alright," I said, knowing this was a blatant lie. They would be pissed.

When I posed my thought about having Katie move in with me to my mom, her first words were "Is that all you have planned? You're not planning on getting married to her, are you?"

"Well, I wasn't planning on it, but at this point, it is the best plan," I explained to Mom, and Dee.

"Have you really thought this through?" Mom asked.

Katie and I had discussed it. I knew Katie wanted to get married from the minute we moved in together, but I didn't mainly because I wanted to go to college and thought that it would be difficult to have a family while going to school. Katie insisted that we could make it work. And being an optimist, I figured we could, as well. One of the things we agreed to was Katie being the bread winner while I went to school. If she could support me through school, I would support her after I graduated to support any college or career she wanted to pursue.

"Yeah. We discussed marriage, and college, Mom. We can make it work."

Katie and I had also discussed divorce if the plan didn't work out. I did want to make sure I had all my bases covered. Oops, sports analogy again.

"Well, okay," Mom said hesitantly. I knew she just wanted the best for me. "When is the big day?"

"We're planning on going to the Justice of the peace at the county courthouse . . . probably next Monday, if I can get an okay from my platoon sergeant. Ian is going to take us and be my best man."

Ian was one of my roommates, and kind of a dick, but I understood him and considered him my best friend in the army. He always had my back, and always good for a joke. What caused him to be *dickish* was him being a bit of a womanizer. This pissed me off to no end and was the main cause for many of our arguments.

"Okay . . ." Mom said hesitantly again. "It sounds like you know what you're doing. Call me to let me know how it went! I love you!"

I gave her my love and hung up, feeling that I had her approval, or as much as she was willing to approve. And, as planned, we were able to get married that following Monday. Ian was on his best behavior, performing his duty with merit. As we left the courthouse, however, he couldn't help but revert to his normal self.

"So, am I just dropping you off so you two can fuck tonight?"

"Ian . . . really?" I asked harshly.

"What? I just thought you two would want to make some babies tonight," Ian said as he snickered.

"Fuck off Ian!" I retorted.

"That was my plan," he stated, in his true dickish form.

Our honeymoon was spent in the apartment, not being able to afford anything else. I was able to pinch pennies well enough to buy us two lobsters and a six pack of beer, albeit cheap beer. It would still be at least a month before the military paperwork would catch up and increase my pay. Katie's pay from McDonald's helped, but things were really tight before the pay increase hit. And it took two months, but it finally happened. I was so relieved when I saw the additional funds hit my direct deposit.

This relief was short lived, however. About a month later, Katie lost her job at McDonald's.

"What happened?" I asked, concerned.

"They said they didn't need me anymore. I wasn't working many hours, so they cut me. And I was the last one hired."

"Well that sucks" was all I could think to say. So much for making ends meet. I guess it was time to tighten the belts, again.

And that's what we did. We cut out fast food, for the most part. We cut out beer runs, which wasn't really an issue. Ian was kind enough to pick up the slack by bringing beer with him when he visited. Mostly because he hated cheap beer and he figured it was his way of *paying us back* for putting up with his misogynist ass.

I guess you could say I was okay with Katie not working. Most of the other soldiers' wives I knew didn't work, mainly because they had kids. So I didn't press her to find another job. It did start to bother me when money started to go missing. When I questioned Katie, she always had a good excuse for where the money went, though.

When other monies, like those left around the apartment, disappeared, I asked her, "Honey, did you see the twenty I had lying on my dresser?"

"Didn't you take that with you yesterday?"

"No. I know I left it on the dresser," I replied.

After maybe the fourth or fifth time that happened, I started questioning myself if I was crazy or whether Katie was using it. I finally made the decision to leave a twenty on the dresser and see if it went missing. The first day I left it there, it was there when I came home. The second day I took it with me so it didn't look like I was just leaving it there. The third day, however, when I left it, it was missing.

"Katie, did you see the twenty I left on the dresser?"

"No honey, I haven't" was the reply.

"Are you sure? I know I left it there this morning," I stated emphatically.

Katie just looked at me like a deer in the headlights, and then said, "No Sweetie, didn't you pick it up this morning? I'm almost sure I saw you take it."

This pissed me off since I *knew* what I did, but I didn't want to cause more of an argument. I resolved, from that point forward, I wouldn't leave money lying around. I felt shitty for being like this too. I never had this issue with my family. One of the things that sucked the most about this was, if Katie asked or said she needed the money for something, I would have given it to her. I would give her the world if I could. But the fact that she felt like she needed to lie about it hurt. And I didn't want to start calling Katie a liar. I didn't want to lose her.

Besides this little problem, life with Katie was fantastic. I loved being able to come home to her at night, to sleep next to her at night. It was perfect. Life was perfect.

The last year I was in the army, I made the decision not to take leave to go home. It did depress me that I didn't get to see Mom and Dee, but it saved a lot of money. And there was always the telephone, for a while at least. About two months after I solved the missing cash issue, I got a phone call from my mom.

"Mike, I just got a huge phone bill in the mail. Have you been using the calling card for anything?"

During my first visit home from Fort Hood, my mom had given me a calling card that billed her home phone so I could call whenever I wanted. It came in handy during the time before Katie and I moved in together. I used it sparingly, of course. Only calling home on weekends and limiting friend phone calls. After Katie and I moved in together, we had a home phone, and Katie and I limited our phone calls home the same way.

"No Mom. You know when I call. Why?"

"Because we just got the bill, and it's about one-hundred dollars more than it's been in months. The calls are all to local numbers here."

"I have no idea . . ." I said, thinking about it for a minute. "But I can ask Katie when she's finished with dinner, if that's okay?"

"That's fine. It's probably just a mistake. Thanks sweetie!" she said as she ended the call.

When Katie was finished cooking dinner, I asked her about it.

"No, not sure what you're talking about."

"You know . . . the calling card that charges to my mom's home phone."

"No! Why would I use that?"

"I didn't think so . . . just wondered sweetie," I replied and dropped the subject. I probably shouldn't have.

The next month rolled around and, about the same day of the month, I got another phone call from my mom asking the same question. This time the bill was closer to two-hundred dollars. She, being generous and not wanting to cause waves, didn't question the previous month's bill figuring it would get sorted out by the phone company. She just paid the bill and moved on. This time, however, she had no choice but to cancel the card.

"So I canceled the card," Mom said. "Sorry sweetie. I can't afford to keep losing money."

"Oh, I understand Mom. Like I said, it wasn't me or Katie using it."

When I hung up the phone, I mentioned the call to Katie, and she again looked at me with a blank stare. Again, I dropped the subject and moved on. I obviously couldn't blame her for something that wasn't her fault. But it nagged at me. Something about the way she looked at me or something in her response just felt wrong. And looking back on it, I probably should have questioned it. But I'm trusting, maybe too trusting. After all, you're supposed to trust your spouse, your soulmate, the person riding with you on the train they call life.

Like I said, life with Katie was mostly fantastic. But there were always little things like these that popped up from time to time. Like a little too much being spent on groceries or things that went missing around the apartment. The most notable being my wedding ring.

My habit, like some of the other married guys, was to leave my wedding ring at home when I went on maneuvers. One reason was so I didn't accidentally lose it in the woods someplace. Another being if the ring was too shiny it would reflect light, which could make you visible when you were trying to be stealthy. Some guys put them on a chain around their neck. I wish I had done this. But I didn't want to take the chance that the chain would break.

I took all this in stride. I was a trooper, after all. And before I knew it, the year was up. It helped that I didn't use any leave the last year, too. Because I had thirty days saved, I was able to get out of the army a month earlier. It was like a paid severance where I could look for a part time job, look for an apartment, and apply to college.

The first step was to send Katie home. I booked a flight for Katie so she would arrive about two weeks before I left Texas. I also made arrangements with my mom and Dee so Katie and I would stay with them while we looked for a place of our own. She could also be at home to start looking for a job and be there when our furniture arrived from Fort Hood. I would stay a day or so after I got out in order to ship the furniture and clean the apartment, for maximum deposit reimbursement.

All went according to plan, and at the allotted time, I flew home for good. I was so over Texas, and so happy my service was over. Unfortunately, I flew right into a shit storm.

"Mike, she's a fucking liar!" Dee said, almost the first sentence she uttered when Dee picked me up at the airport. There was, of course, a good amount of hugging and tears from both of us before my sister went off.

"She admitted that the phone card was used by her sister," Dee fumed. "Mom and I called a few of the numbers, and we eventually put two and two together!"

I was floored. I knew Katie talked to her sister, almost weekly, but I had no idea that she would share the calling card number with her!

"And that's not the only thing she's lied about," Dee continued. "She hasn't even been looking for a job since she's been back. She spends most of the time at her parents' house. I know because I drop her off and pick her up from there almost daily! She said you knew about it and it was okay."

As soon as I got home, I said hi to Mom and hugged and kissed Katie. I was very happy I was home with my family, my whole family. After about thirty minutes of greetings and sobs, I took Katie aside to talk to her. When we were alone, I confronted her on the items Dee had brought up.

"I gave my sister the card number so she could call me. I didn't know she was going to use it for calling friends in other states!" was Katie's reply.

"Why would you do that without asking anyone?"

"I don't know. I just thought it'd be easier for her to have the number. I didn't think it would matter if I was calling her, or she was calling me."

I guess I couldn't argue with this logic, really, but it was questionable judgement. It's not something I would have ever done, *especially* without asking the person the card belonged to. But there was more to discuss. I then asked Katie why she hadn't been looking for a job.

"I thought you wanted me to wait until you got home," she said. At this point I was livid.

"*That was the whole reason you came home two weeks early!*" I shouted. "We *talked* about this!"

"I thought I was coming home to receive the furniture," she rebutted.

"You were, *and* to look for a job!"

"Oh. I'm sorry. I didn't know."

I was extremely frustrated at this point, but I was willing to accept that she didn't truly understand what I thought we had discussed. Call me a sucker, but aren't we all suckers when it comes to love? Sometimes it's better to give up a losing battle and move forward. We discussed her getting a job. She agreed, and we hugged and kissed. I was home, and that made up for a lot.

The next month was busy for me. I applied and was accepted to college. Katie found a job at a McDonald's full time. It wasn't the same McDonald's, and it wasn't a manager position, but it was full time work.

Things were settled between my mom, Dee, and Katie. And my mom for-gave the three-hundred-dollar debt. All seemed better, for a while at least.

Over the next two months, I noticed the same things going on that had happened while in Texas. Items started to go missing, which included a small diamond ring that my mom really loved. And cash that was laid around the house went missing without explanation.

We — Mom, Dee, and I — knew Katie was the cause for these dis-appearances, but we never really had proof. Every time we tried to discuss it with Katie, she emphatically denied she had anything to do with it, even when she was the only one that could be blamed. Dee and my mom were at their wits' end, and I had no choice but to agree with them.

I wasn't much different. All the lying and stealing had caused a huge rift between us. I was pissed at her every day. And every time things appeared to get better, something else would get stolen or another lie was created.

One day Katie came home early from work, stating she had been *let go*. When I asked her why, she said she wasn't really sure. She thought it was because they had a full staff, but she was full time, which made me question if this was true.

The next day I called her manager, Dave. He and I had met a couple times when I had gone in to visit Katie at work. He always seemed like a decent guy, so I called him to see what was going on. That's when he gave me the bad news.

"Katie's drawer has been short several times over the last few weeks. We finally decided she had to be let go," he said, confiding in me.

When I confronted Katie about this, she said, "Dave's lying. I think he let me go because he likes me and I wouldn't sleep with him."

I was obviously upset and confused by this, because I knew Dave had a wife and two kids, and I sincerely doubted that he'd risk losing his job by hitting on an employee and firing her when she wouldn't respond to his desires.

Even this wasn't enough for me to end things with her, to end our marriage. For better, or for worse, is the way the vows go, and I was intent on keeping them. But it just kept getting worse and worse, without any real effort on Katie's part to rectify the situation.

The straw that broke the camel's back came a couple weeks later when Katie caused a misunderstanding between Jim and me.

It happened about a week or so before spring break. One day I received a phone call from my friend Ed letting me know he was in town. Ed was another one of my close friends from high school. He had been accepted by, and went away to, Ohio State for college.

"Mike, hey! I just got home on spring break and will be in town tonight before I leave for Florida to party. Want to go out tonight?"

"Dude! That would be fantastic. I'm supposed to have class tonight, but I can blow off one night. When are you available?"

"How about 4:00 p.m.? We'll get an early start!" Ed said. I was in.

I proceeded to tell Katie what my plan was and asked if she minded.

"No, I don't mind at all. But don't you have class tonight?"

"I do, but I'm far enough ahead in my class, and I've done the extra work. I'll be okay."

"Okay, if you're going out, I think I'll spend the night at my parents' house, okay?"

"That's fine with me, sweetie!"

Katie thought for a moment and asked, "Mike, does Jim know Ed is in town? Won't he be jealous?"

"Nah, he should be okay. Jim told me he had plans tonight so sure he'll understand," I said as I proceeded to get ready.

Ed and I had a great time that night. We caught up on each other's lives, reminisced high school, and talked about our mutual friends. We ate and drank and eventually got tired around 10:00 p.m. Ed and I said our goodbyes, and he dropped me off at home. When I walked in the door, I noticed there was a note from Katie that Jim had called, so I called him up.

"Dude, how was school?"

"I didn't go to school tonight. Ed was in town so I went out with him. Didn't Katie tell you?"

"No. She told me that you were at school."

"Not sure why she told you that," I said as I leaned into the fridge to grab some water.

"You sure you didn't tell her you were going to school?"

"No. We specifically talked about me going out with Ed and her going to her parents' house."

"Well, why would she tell me that then?"

"I don't know. That's exactly what I told her."

"Are you sure?"

"Yes! I'm sure! Why, don't you believe me?"

"Isn't it weird she would say that?"

"I don't know. Maybe she just liked to cause problems," I said, and the thought occurred to me: she *did* like to cause problems. A minute later, I ended my phone call with Jim and headed to bed.

The next morning, when I woke, I was still pissed that Katie had lied about me going out, so I had a talk with my mom about the conversation. It seemed like such a stupid thing to lie about, but she did little things like that all the time. She lied about the job. She lied about the missing items and cash. And now she was lying about this. She had also stolen from us for months. It finally came to me, and I knew what I had to do.

I discussed it with her briefly, but it was pretty obvious to both of us. And it couldn't be put off any longer. So that morning, I went over to Katie's parents' house and had *the talk* with her.

"Katie, I'm tired of all the lying and stealing you've been doing. You need to move out," I said, resolute in my decision. She was noticeably upset and tried to talk her way out of it, but enough was enough. She had made her bed, and she needed to lay in it.

So that's where an eighteen-month marriage ended. Born out of need, and then destroyed by distrust.

Later that day, Katie and I picked up her things from my mom's house and we moved her into her parents' house. It was difficult, more difficult than I can relay in this brief story. It's tough when you give someone so much love and attention, someone that was there for you when you needed them, and they return that love by lying and stealing.

Part of me will always love her no matter what she did. For the hole she filled in my life when I was at my loneliest. And I believe she still loves me and regrets the way things turned out. But she's never really admitted it.

It was just another lie, though — this time, to herself.

Diary: June 19

I wish there was some way to tell you how I feel.

Each night when I climb into bed to a sleepless night, I look back on all the things I did that day without you, and wish you were here doing them with me.

Most times I find it hard to breathe. The longing to have you here is like a weight on my chest, slowly crushing my soul, slowly draining my life.

I wish I would have told you I loved you more often. I know I told you daily, morning and night. In every text message I sent, in every kiss goodnight, in each and every smile . . . and yet it still wasn't enough. Nothing was enough to keep you here.

Many nights I sit in the dark and remember all the fun we had no matter where we went. The times we went to the park to swing on the swings, or to the lake to watch the sun set, or to the valley to walk the trails, or even to the dance club to dance.

How you loved to dance.

But then the memories fade, and I'm left alone again. Alone with my thoughts. Alone with my shattered dreams. Alone in the dark.

Alone . . . without you.

CHAPTER

I remember our best year together. It was also one of the worst years of my life.

I had so much that was good and pure in my life, it was hard to not smile all the time. Every day with you was fantastic, filled with fun and dancing, drinking and love making, great restaurants and great vacation spots. You and me — how could it have been anything else but *wonderful*?

It was our ninth year together, and we had just moved from our old one-bedroom apartment into the two-bedroom luxury apartment south of Cleveland. It had its own workout facility and great restaurants all around it. The building we lived in even accommodated dogs. Not that we had one, but if we wanted one, we were set. Someday, when we retired, it would be just you, me, and a little dog. That day, we hoped, wouldn't be too far off.

"So, what do you think?" I asked as we looked over the vacation information.

"I'm not sure . . ." you said, continuing, "I still want to go to Cape Cod later this year. I'm just not sure if I want to use all my extra vacation time on this trip."

"I understand, but I really would like to get some beach time in," I said as I continued to review the brochure on the Bahamas. "I mean, doesn't it look fantastic?"

"It does," you said as you perused the documents.

"And it's not a far flight. Only one hop from Cleveland to Nassau," I said, trying to sell my point.

I could see your mind in overdrive, trying to reconcile the cost versus the fun, also weighing in a trip to Cape Cod in September. How you loved the Cape in the fall. But I knew you wanted me to be happy as well.

"Well, let me go online and look at flight costs before we make a decision," you said, trying to lessen the load. "I also need to check it out with work."

"Okay. We can discuss it later, or maybe tomorrow. Nassau isn't going anywhere," I said trying to ease your mind.

"And your work is okay with you taking the vacation?"

"Yeah, we're slow right now. It's a perfect time for me to go. And I've got plenty of vacation saved up, so we can do both," I replied and started to walk toward the living room. Just then my cell phone started to ring.

"This is Mike," I said answering the phone with my standard greeting, not bothering to look to see who was calling.

"Hey dude!" Jim's voice came booming from the phone.

"Dude! Good to hear your voice! What's up man?"

It had been a few weeks since I had talked to Jim. With our busy work and home schedules, it was difficult to keep in touch sometimes. But we did try.

"Not much. Just figured it'd been a while since we talked. Trying to keep the communication lines open, you know?" he joked.

"I hear ya. Glad you rang! Amy and I were just planning a Bahamas vacation. You in?"

"Yeeeaaaah. No can do sir. I'm swamped at work. I can barely take the time to call you!"

"Well, glad you did! How are Brittney and Jim junior?"

As it turned out, the wedding that was rushed for *no particular reason* was for a definite reason. Brittney had been pregnant. Although the two only knew each other for a short while, they knew they wanted to keep the baby and get married. Jim's parents, knowing these bits of information, thought it would be prudent if the two got hitched before Brittney started to show. When he and Brittney got back from their honeymoon, he gave me the lowdown on the whole series of events. I mean, whether I knew before or after didn't matter to me; the only thing that mattered was Jim's happiness.

"They're good. Little Jim is still in the terrible twos. Brittney is enjoying being a stay home mom. Life is good!"

"Glad to hear sir! Glad to hear," I replied.

He and I continued our banter for about a half hour before Little Jim started screaming. "Well, guess that's my cue sir! Sounds like I have to run."

"Alright man. It was good hearing from you!"

"Good talking to you too dude! Don't be a stranger . . . and let me know how your vacation was!" he said just before we hung up.

It really was good talking to him. Jim had been ultra-stressed since Little Jim was born. Also, the year previously he had been thrust into the role of acting CEO for his dad's company, his dad having mostly retired. I could only imagine what he was going through. But from the sound of his voice, he appeared to be doing okay. This made me smile. This, and the fact that, after so many years being friends, we still called each other dude.

"Was that Jim?" you asked as you entered the living room.

"It was. He said hi," I said, even though he didn't. I knew Jim liked you — liked us — and the thought was there.

"Okay, so back onto the Bahamas . . ." you started. You could be very persistent.

Three weeks later, we were in the Bahamas. You were able to get the vacation time, as was I, and picked dates so we could avoid spring break but also be back for yours and my mom's birthdays. Although it had cost a little more for the late flight booking, it was worth it. Plus, I paid. You always liked when I saved you money.

We were able to book an all-inclusive hotel on Paradise Island right next to the Atlantis Resort. It was about half the cost of Atlantis, but it shared a beach with the expensive resort so that was good enough for us. The inside of the resort was great. It had four bars and seven restaurants, all free, to include tips. Our room came with a Jacuzzi, liquor dispensers, and a balcony overlooking the resort pool. I'm sure this wasn't as plush as Atlantis, but it was still fantastic.

"So, what do you want to do first?" you asked as we dropped our bags and shut the door.

"You have to ask?" I replied, like there was any other thought on my mind besides making love to you.

"Nope!" you said, grabbing my hand and leading me to the bed.

When we were finished, we quickly showered, put on our bathing suits, and headed to the pool for some much needed sun. As we arrived at the pool, we could hear a mixture of steel drum music and hip hop. Something for everyone, I guessed. The pool area had a grill for burgers and nachos and various other snacks one would want whilst basking in the sun. There were two sets of stairs leading down to the beach so you could swim in the surf for a bit and then go back to the pool to relax.

The pool itself was round and had a swim-up bar in the middle. We picked a couple lounge chairs close to the bar, dropped our things, and jumped in the pool. About an hour or so later, we had had our fill of sun and liquor and made the decision to clean up for exploring. It didn't take us long before we were on the street and making our way to Atlantis.

Atlantis was over-the-top immaculate. Glass sculptures adorned the ceiling, and expensive stores and restaurants filled the halls. We decided to hit the indoor aquarium first because we had heard how amazing it was, and it did not disappoint. We spent an hour or two walking around the aquarium and resort, the parts we could access not being guests there, just enjoying the hoity toity atmosphere.

Around dinner time, we left Atlantis and went back to our resort for dinner and more drinks. After some discussion, we chose the sushi bar restaurant, knowing we still had six more nights to try all the other restaurants the resort had.

After dinner, we went out to the beach to take in the Bahamas' night air. A cool breeze was blowing across the water, and the moon was creating sparkles in the surf. To say it was beautiful was an understatement. It was perfect. You and I just held each other for a while, absorbing the scenery, savoring each other's company. Lightly kissing and nuzzling occasionally to share the warmth between us.

We eventually left the beach and journeyed back up the stairs to the resort to watch the entertainment provided. We watched jugglers twirl flaming batons and swords while dancers showed off their acrobatic movements. Eventually we got tired from all the excitement and fun and strolled to our room. We poured ourselves a nightcap, undressed, and climbed into the Jacuzzi to rest our sore muscles and sun-kissed skin. This lasted only a short while, both of us finding it nearly impossible to keep our eyes open. We dried off and climbed into bed, too tired to even make love again; that would have to wait until morning.

The rest of the vacation was spent much like that day. We traveled the island enjoying the beaches and sights, hitting the occasional bar or restaurant, or just choosing to eat at our resort. For seven days it felt like time had stopped for us. Work and home were both miles and days away. We could just be ourselves and enjoy what our hard work had purchased.

But, like everything else, vacation was over before we knew it, and it was time to fly back to Cleveland and our responsibilities.

The next couple months were pretty normal. Nothing out of the ordinary happened. Careers taking hold of us during the week, time with each other on the weekends, both of us just biding our time until our next vacation.

Not to say we didn't have fun. There were art shows and concerts, along with friends to hang out with and family to spend time with. We filled our time and lives with things that we both cared about and loved.

During these two months I didn't talk to Jim much, which was not an unusual thing. There were several times throughout our many years of friendship where we went for a month or so without talking to each other. Not sure if it was an *out of sight, out of mind* thing or if both he and I were too preoccupied with family and/or work to pick up the phone. But when we did reconnect, it was like no time at all had passed.

And I know it sounds weird, but if it did go too long without talking to him, I'd get an itch in the back of my mind that I should call him. Like there was some reason I should call. I liked to joke that it was a cosmic link we shared. And maybe it was, because almost every time I got that itch something had happened in his life. I'd get on the phone with him, and he'd tell me he was "just about to call me" because he got a promotion or someone in the family died. It was weird, for sure; of that I had no doubt. One Sunday afternoon in August was one of these times.

"This is Jim."

"Hey dude! What's up?" I said jovially into the phone.

"Hey man . . . not much . . . just the usual," he returned plainly. I could hear clicking on the other end of the phone as if he was typing as we talked, so I asked.

"Are you at work?"

"Yeah, unfortunately," Jim responded, sounding preoccupied.

"Man! What are you doing working on a Sunday?"

"There's a lot going on here Mike" came the reply.

"But, aren't you like CEO or something? Can't you have a peon do whatever you're doing so you can enjoy life?" I jested.

"I wish. Us CEOs have to work too, ya know," he retorted. At least he hadn't lost his sense of humor while at work.

"Well that sucks. What's new?"

"I . . . I really can't talk right now Mike. Wish I could."

"Oh, okay man. Give me a call when you have a chance!" I said, knowing that tone in his voice meant he was fixated on something.

"Will do! Bye" was all he said, and he hung up.

I didn't think too much about it, knowing Jim could get stuck on something easily. And he was running a company with a couple hundred employees. That's enough to stress anyone out. So I gave him some space and wait for him to call me, feeling that he would realize how short he was with me and want to fix it.

In the meantime, it was time for you and me to book our September trip to Cape Cod. You were so excited that we were going, and frankly, so was I. It had been a stressful few months at work, with it being rush time for companies to get their budgets in for the new fiscal year. I looked forward to sand and surf time with you again in the Cape.

It was about three weeks after my brief phone call with Jim, the night before our trip to the Cape, that the itch started. Since it had only been three weeks, though, I just sent him a text to see how he was doing. Kind of as a friendly reminder that he owed me a phone call.

"I'm okay. I'll text back soon." was all I got back. I then texted to tell him we were traveling to the Cape the next day but to call whenever he wanted. To this there was no reply. I thought it was funny but figured he would text back when he was ready.

The next morning, we flew into Providence, picked up a rental car, and drove the two to three hours to Provincetown, our favorite city. For those who haven't been there, Provincetown has a huge gay community. And I always found it funny how we, a straight couple, were the minority. I remember getting leered at a few times while walking hand in hand with you.

As we entered Provincetown, our first stop was the grocery store so we could pick up provisions for the week. Even though we usually ate out most nights, you liked to make sure we were stocked with breakfast foods and some lunch supplies.

When we completed our shopping, we headed to the place we were staying this time around, and I was stunned by your selection. This time, you had rented us an elaborate condo with two bedrooms and two baths — much more than we had had in the past. It came with an amazing view of Cape Cod Bay. I was literally in awe. But I promised that next time we could stay in a little cabin like you liked.

After dropping our bags, putting the groceries away, and getting a lay of the land, we walked along Commercial Street to see what we could see. First stop — coffee!

Of course, not a whole lot had changed from the last time we were here. A few stores had closed with new ones opening in their places. There was a new coffee place that used to be a bar, if memory serves. But mostly it was just as we had left it two years previously.

On our way back to the condo, you suggested we stop at the dune tours place to see if we could book something for the next day. There were two spots open for the next morning at 10:00 a.m., which was perfect. We never really slept in there. There was always so much to do and see in seven days!

Having been successful, we walked toward the multitude of art galleries and shops. Eventually, we got tired and hungry, and we trekked back to the condo for a drink and to change for dinner.

One of the new places we saw along our afternoon journey was a sushi place. Luckily, when we got there, they had a table for two available. And it was a good choice, because the food and wine were fantastic.

Considering it was our first day in the Cape and we got up really early for our flight, we strolled back to the condo to drink and enjoy the night air. As we sat out on the deck overlooking the bay at night, I couldn't help but just look at you. I was awestruck by how lovely you were, just sitting there in the moonlight, enjoying your wine and our conversation.

As the evening grew cold, we adjourned to the inside of the condo to finish our drinks and get ready for bed. That night we made love, as we did most nights in the Cape, relishing in the smell of the sea air and our bodies. Every moment enveloped by our passion for the Cape and each other. We ended our evening of love falling asleep in each other's arms.

The next morning, I woke, threw on clothes, and walked to the nearest coffee shop to buy us both our required caffeine boost for the day. I loved waking that early and walking Commercial Street. Watching the shop owners and employees clean, joggers and other early risers appreciating the quiet and solitude before the shops opened and the tourists filled the street.

I purchased two hazelnut coffees and, as always, also bought you a chocolate chip cookie, the one with the most chips, to have with your coffee. The delight I got to see in your eyes every time you saw what I brought was like heaven to me.

When we finished consuming our breakfast treats, we changed and headed out for our dune tour. When we arrived there, I checked us in at the front desk and joined you outside on the benches to wait to be called. The morning was a little chilly — it always was on the Cape — so we hugged each other to share our body heat.

Eventually our names were called, and we walked down to meet our driver, Rob, who would show us the sights for the next two hours. Rob loaded us and the other three passengers into one of the waiting Suburbans, and off we went. We traveled along the main roads for a bit before we reached the entrance to the Cape Cod National Seashores.

As we traveled up and down the paths, seeing old dune shacks, building ruminants, and ancient landmarks, Rob pointed out all the different plants, trees, grasses, and animals living within the historic sands. Every inch of it gorgeous, every dune an amazing work of art made by wind and time.

I couldn't help but watch your eyes as you surveyed the landscape and how you were enjoying every new sight. You were like a kid in a candy store viewing all the flowers and foliage growing in the rough terrain. Seeing you that happy and content always brought love and joy into my life.

About halfway through our tour, we stopped at the top of a crest that overlooked a beach stretching out toward the Atlantic. Here we were able to exit the trucks and roam for a few minutes, being able to touch dune grass and run our toes in the sand.

As we held hands and walked the dunes together, you asked, "Isn't this the most amazing place on Earth?"

I could only nod in agreement. I did love the Cape, maybe not as much as you, but certainly a lot. It just has a special feel to it, one of history and memories, of pirates and pilgrims. Everyone who has come here over hundreds of years for pleasure and discovery lives in the dunes and lighthouses.

"Someday, I'd like to move here. Like, when we retire," you said to me as we stood there overlooking the ocean.

"Really? You wouldn't be too cold here?"

"Maybe," you said, thinking about it. "But with this view . . . this feel, it would be worth it."

We took another minute to breathe in the atmosphere and surroundings and then walked back to the waiting vehicles.

"Do me a favor?" you asked as we made our way through the sand.

"Sure . . . anything," I said, and meant it.

"When I die someday, can you bring my ashes here?" you asked with a serious look on your face.

To this I smiled and jested, "I'm going to go way before you do."

You stopped us then, turning me so we could see eye to eye. "Please? Just promise me?"

I dropped my smile and said, "Of course I will. I would do anything for you."

"This spot . . . right here," you continued. "This view . . . this is my most favorite spot on Earth. I want to live here forever."

"I promise my love" was all I could say. You seemed so adamant about your choice, how could I deny it?

You smiled at this, and we turned to continue our trek back to the Suburban.

We finished the tour, having driven along a beach to see seals frolicking and hunting in the surf, eventually traveling back along the trails and out onto the main road. As we arrived back at the dune tour office, I could see both happiness and sadness in your face, knowing the visions you saw but realizing it would be another year before we were back on the protected sands.

"Well, what do you want to do now?" I asked as we exited the vehicle.

"I'm not sure. Maybe everything?" you jested, but it pretty much was true.

The rest of the trip was spent doing, well, everything. We hit every restaurant we could. We drove to Truro, Wellfleet, Eastham, and Orleans. We saw the fishing boats come back in in the evening. We toured three lighthouses. We even saw a couple shows at different bars and nightclubs. We walked different beaches and collected seashells at every one.

For our last night on the Cape, we went to a beach and watch the sunset. Making sure we dressed warmly and had dirty clothing on, we picked a spot and sat on the sand as the sun went down. As the sun set into the waves, we held onto each other like the world was ending, knowing that tomorrow we'd have to travel back home to our jobs and lives.

"I really do wish I lived here year-round," you said as tears started to stream down your cheeks. All I could do was lend you my sleeve and caress your back in hopes that you'd know that I was there for you, and that I would always be there for you.

We left the beach and headed back to the condo to make love one last time. And I held you all that night like it truly *was* our last night on Earth.

The next morning, we woke and had our last coffee as we finished packing the car. We then straightened up the condo so the cleaners could prepare for the next visitors. And I hoped, whomever it was, that they loved the Cape at least half as much as we did.

It wasn't long before we were on the road driving to the airport. I could see you taking in all the sights along the way. Every now and then, I reminded you not to be sad that we were leaving, because we knew we would both be back.

The flight home was uneventful, thank goodness, and we landed safely in Cleveland in what felt like no time at all. After picking up our car, we drove home, you calling your mom along the way to let her know we were safe and sound. From there on, it truly was business as usual. We unpacked our bags and washed our clothes as we prepared for going to work the next day.

The next few weeks were a blur to me as I became immersed in work and the daily routine. I wish I could say that there was something, anything, that made this time stand out, but I'd be lying. Or at least I don't remember anything until that Saturday in October when my life changed.

I remember we had finished our coffee and I was watching something I had recorded on the DVR the previous night. I was engrossed in the show when my cell phone started ringing, making me jump a little in my seat.

"Wow, scared the hell out of me!" I remarked as I answered the phone. "This is Mike."

"Hey Mike" came the reply from the phone. "It's Sarah."

This surprised me. I couldn't remember the last time Sarah had called me, if ever. Then it hit me.

Jim.

"Hi Sarah . . . what's up?" I asked hesitantly, thinking I heard a waver in her voice.

"It's Jim . . ." she said, pausing for a moment. "He . . . he killed himself."

"What . . . when?" I asked, as if it truly mattered but not knowing what else to say.

"Earlier today. I got the call from Brittney a little while ago." With every word my heart continued to sink. "He parked his car in the garage and left it running with the doors closed. He suffocated."

I couldn't believe — didn't want to believe — what I was hearing. It had only been a month since I heard from him. Why wouldn't he call me? I was his friend! His best goddamned friend! How could he do this? How could he do it to his family? How could he do this to *me*?

"I'm going to let you go," Sarah said, starting to break down. "I'll let you know when we hear more. I just . . . I just thought you should know."

"Thank you Sarah. Please send my love to your parents," I said, the only thing I could think to say. "I love you!"

"You too," I heard her say before the line disconnected.

I sat down, in shock, wanting to cry but still not truly processing the news. You must have seen me turn white, so you came over to me to ask.

"Honey, what's wrong?"

"It's Jim. He killed himself," I said, the tears starting to well as I said this out loud.

You lowered to your knees in front of me, taking my hands in yours as you said, "Oh, my God . . . when?"

"Earlier today," I replied through tears. "He left the car running in the garage and asphyxiated."

"Oh my God Mike. I'm so sorry!" you said, pulling me close and hugging me.

That's when I truly lost it. I started crying uncontrollably, tears streaming down your back as I held you tightly, not wanting to lose my grip on the world. My world felt so fragile right now. I had just lost someone that had been my anchor in tough times, someone that always had my back, someone that I loved as a brother.

And yet, it couldn't be real. How could it be real? It must be some sort of prank. The best prank Jim had ever thought of. I looked through tear filled eyes at the phone on the table. Jim would call any second now to reveal his jest. To let me know it was some elaborate plan to scare me so close to Halloween. I just talked to him a month ago. He was still there for me, just on the other side of the wires. This can't be real. This *can't be real.*

A while later, when I was able to calm myself, I called all the friends I could think of to tell them the horrible news. I started with my mom and Dee, of course, knowing he had been part of our family for thirty plus years. My mom was very supportive, as she always was, telling me if I needed anything she was there, which I knew. Dee was noticeably shaken when I told her. Jim was like another younger brother, so she felt the loss almost as much as I did.

Next, I contacted the guys. Bob and John had both moved to Tampa years back, and I was in contact with both of them a few times a year. I even got to visit them about once a year. They, too, were shocked when I told them the news. Although they didn't see Jim as much as I did, they still kept in touch with him as much as they could. I also tried contacting Rob, knowing he talked to him almost as much as I did, but the number I had for him had been disconnected. I just hoped that Sarah knew his new number or knew how to get hold of him.

"Honey!" I called to you. "I think I'm going to go for a walk . . . to clear my head."

"Okay sweetie," you replied as you peeked your head around the corner. "Do you want some company?"

"No . . . I just need some time alone, if that's okay."

"Of course," you said, walking over to hug me. I was so glad you understood.

A few minutes later, I left the apartment for a walk around the apartments and local development. I seriously needed to clear my head, because it felt like it . . . I . . . was going to explode. I had so much pent-up energy from the sadness and anger at the moment I needed to just blow off steam. Part of me was saying I should go for a run to release the energy, but part of me just wanted to walk. Maybe if I walked long enough or far enough I could leave all the hurt and frustration behind.

My mind was racing with thoughts of Jim, thoughts of our lives together, and of his family and mine. Everything we had done and said and felt. All the future conversations we'd never have. All gone now, all wasted.

You hear about teenagers taking their lives from time to time, but hardly ever anyone our age. Jim appeared to have so much to live for. What reason or reasons could he possibly have had to do this selfish act? Why would he leave his wife of three years, not to mention his son?

His *son* — oh my God, his son.

What about Little Jim growing up without a dad? I couldn't even imagine how Brittney and he would cope.

The walk lasted about an hour-and-half. At the end I was no closer to an answer or internal peace than I had been, but at least my anxiousness had diminished. As I entered the apartment, you were there, and I felt happy about my life. There would be no way I could understand suicide.

You approached me cautiously and asked, "How are you?"

"As good as I can be, I guess," I answered. "Thank you . . . thank you for always being here for me."

You came over and hugged me for a while, even though I'm sure I smelled of sweat and road. We both knew I was done for now, until more information came our way. So we agreed on a restaurant to eat at, showered, dressed, and we were out the door to help take my mind off the tragic event.

The next day, I called Sarah to see if there was any update. She informed me that Brittney was getting help from her parents on the funeral arrangements. Since both families mostly lived in Cleveland, it made sense to fly him here. There was already a plot of land set aside for Jim, and Sarah, here, and a local funeral home was selected. The plan was to fly him in on Monday, Brittney and Little Jim on Tuesday, have the wake on Wednesday and the funeral on Thursday. To me, this all felt too fast. But I guess that's the way these things go.

"So, should I call your mom?"

"I'm sure she'd like that. She and Dad are at home, if you want to call now," I agreed that I would, and hung up with Sarah.

"Hello?" Mrs. Larkman answered after a couple rings.

"Hi Mrs. Larkman," I said, forgoing calling her Mom like I normally did. "It's Mike."

"Hello Michael," she said, always preferring to call me by my formal name. "How are you?"

"I'm..." I said, pausing. "I'm okay. How are you? How's Mr. Larkman?"

"We're as good as can be expected. I take it you've talked to Sarah?"

"Yes ma'am. She said it would be okay to call. I . . . I just wanted to tell you how sorry I am for . . . well . . . you know."

"I'm glad you called Michael," she said, her voice turning more professional. "We've been sitting here making arrangements. Did Sarah share them with you?"

"Yes ma'am, she did."

"Well, if you're available, we'd like you to be a pallbearer. And, if possible, can you check with some of your friends to see if there are available to help?"

"I'd . . . I'd like that," I said, feeling stupid the minute the words came out of my mouth. "And I'll check with Bob and John. Not positive if they're coming up or not, but I'm sure they'd help out."

"If they can't, the funeral home said they'd be able to provide people."

"Okay. I'll check with them as soon as I get off the phone."

"Well, I better go," Mrs. Larkman said, preparing to hang up. "Please let Sarah know if they can help out."

"Will do, ma'am," I said "It was good to hear your voice."

"It is good to hear yours as well," she said, continuing. "And Michael . . . it's okay for you to call me Mom. I've always thought of you as, well . . . a son."

"Thank you . . . Mom," I said, starting to cry. "I've always . . . always . . ."

"We'll see you soon Michael," she said, saving me from bursting into tears on the phone.

"See you soon Mom," I said as I hung up, barely keeping it together.

When I composed myself, I called John and Bob to let them know about the arrangements. And without being asked, both said they would make arrangements to fly up. Also, they both said they'd be honored to be pallbearers with me, which I was glad for. I would need their strength over the next few days.

I called Sarah when I had finished making both calls, telling her about my conversation with her mom and told her the three of us would be honored to be pallbearers. I also mentioned to her if there was anything else I could help with I would.

"Thank you Mike. I know the family appreciates it."

Just then something came to mind. "Sarah? I hope this doesn't upset you, but . . . do you know why?"

There was a long pause, and I was about to say her name thinking the connection might be faulty when she answered, "I'm not positive, but I think it had to do with the business.

"I talked to my dad earlier today, and it seems like the company had lost a lot of money in the past few months. It was nothing specifically that Jim was doing. Business was down and he was under a lot of pressure to get more business, or he would have had to lay people off."

I could hear her take a drink, and then she continued, "I guess he was at his wits' end, between the pressures at work and the pressures at home."

"Pressures at home?"

"Yeah. Between my dad pushing him to right the business, bills, and Brittney and Little Jim he felt torn . . . like he had nowhere to go."

"That doesn't make sense," I said, slightly aggravated. "I've always been here for him. Why didn't he say anything?"

"I'm not sure Mike. Is there ever a reason for people thinking differently than we think they should? Maybe he felt he didn't want to lay the pressure on you? Who knows . . . I wish I knew," Sarah said as we both pondered.

"I wish . . . I wish he had let me be there for him. I would have, you know that, right?"

"I know Mike, as I would have been. And I think, deep down, he knew it too. But sometimes the things right in front of your face aren't as obvious."

"Yeah . . . I guess," I said, feeling we had reached the end of this topic. "Well, I'm gonna go. If anything changes, or you have anything you need help with, please let me know, okay?"

"Will do Mike," Sarah said, adding something I've never heard her say before to me. "And, I love you!"

"I love you too!" I said as I disconnected the call.

"You okay sweetie?" came your voice from the other room.

"Yeah," I said, excluding the words *as much as I can be.*

I guess the thing that bothered me most was I always thought I was there for him. I always called to let him know I was around. I always took his calls when he called me. I made time for him when he visited. And I even traveled to Boston every year or so to spend time with him. Didn't he remember this? Didn't he see that I was here, just a phone call or flight away? I guess Sarah was right. We'd never know for sure. The only thing I could do is be there for him now.

I made the decision that Monday I'd go into work, to help take my mind off things, but I'd take Tuesday through Friday off for everything that had to be done. I knew Bob and John were flying in Tuesday, and I'd want to meet up with them Tuesday night someplace for dinner if they were available. Considering how close we all were, I was sure they'd want to get together before the wake, and they did.

"Damn Mike! That's fucked up!" John said as he took a drink of his Angry Orchard.

"Tell me about it. I mean, man . . . I can't imagine my life *ever* being that bad. You?"

"It's sad," Bob responded as he took as drink. "Dude had it all, and he just wasted it."

"That's harsh," I said, starting to get pissed at Bob, which was nothing new. "Dude had problems. Don't judge him. We don't know what he was going through mentally."

"I understand that. But you have to admit that he had so much going for him."

"He did. But he also had a lot going against him. His dad has never been the easiest to get along with, and inheriting the business in a bad economy didn't help. I'd like to see how you'd handle the pressure . . . imagine having two hundred employees you were responsible for. I don't know how I'd handle it."

"But you wouldn't kill yourself," Bob retorted.

"No," I admitted. "I wouldn't kill myself. But that's me."

"That's most people."

"Walk a mile in a man's shoes . . ." I countered.

"Can we stop arguing and just do shots?" John chimed in. And we did just that.

The next day, you and I slept in, me because it helped me not think about Jim, you because you liked to sleep in. When I woke, I called Bob and John to make sure they weren't as hung over as they looked like they were going to be the night before; both were fine. We talked about meeting up before the wake and heading up together, which I was more than happy with. This was definitely something I didn't want to do, and I'm glad they, and you, were there for moral support.

I've got to admit, I believe I kept my cool during most of the wake. Even seeing Jim's body only fazed me a little. When I felt it appropriate, I went over and kneeled, saying a small prayer. You came with me and knelt with me, which helped greatly.

Near the end of the wake, the pastor of Jim's family's church spoke for a bit, followed by his dad. And they did say some nice things about him. But their speeches just didn't sound or feel like they knew him. Like they really knew him, like his friends did. They didn't mention his love of science fiction or comic books. They didn't talk about how he loved motorcycles or firearms. In fact, the movies or adventures they did mention were really based on their experiences of him, the pigeon hole that was their view of his world. And I knew these experiences that they spoke of. The persona that was Jim at work, or Jim at home, or Jim at church. But they weren't the real Jim.

Toward the end of the wake was really when I came close to losing it. It was when I finally had a chance to talk to Brittney and Little Jim. And it all came flooding back how he wouldn't be there for them anymore. He wouldn't be there to see Little Jim grow up, or play baseball, or have a crush, or fall in love. How he wouldn't be there for me.

"Amy, can we get going?" I said as soon as Brittney walked away.

"Sure honey," you said, knowing I was upset. "Do you want me to get John and Bob?"

"Yeah," I said as you took my hand and led me toward my friends.

We left together, forgoing the after-wake drinking we had planned, so we could go home, so *I* could go home to decompress. I just hoped I could handle the funeral. I was so glad you were going with me. I don't know how I would handle this kind of weight by myself. I'm so glad I didn't have to.

The next day, the funeral started at 10:00 a.m., starting with a service at the church. Bob, John, and I got there early, as requested by Jim's family, so we could go over our tasks as pallbearers. When the service was over, the family, which included me, were allowed to say our final goodbyes to him. This was one of the toughest things I've ever had to do in my life. For me, that was when everything hit home, when his death became real to me. That this would be the last time I ever saw his face. And although he was already gone, that was the moment I truly felt like I lost him.

I only hovered for a moment, looking at his face, before my world started to spin and I needed to walk away. I knew I still had obligations, so

I only moved twenty or thirty feet away, just far enough so I didn't have to look at them closing the casket.

Knowing what I was going through, you followed me over to where I was standing and hugged me from behind. Even though I felt cold, colder than I had ever been, I felt the warmth of your touch, your body pressing against mine, and my world slowed and became our world. I took your hands in mine, pulling them across my chest so I could pull you in tighter.

When the casket was ready, Bob, John, and I were called on to help move the casket from the altar to the dolly used to wheel the casket to the waiting hearse. We were joined by a couple male family members and directed by funeral home employees when to lift, and move, and release. We followed the dolly to the hearse so we could help move the casket into the car.

Having completed the first part of our task, we moved to our cars and followed the procession to the cemetery. When we arrived, you headed to meet Sarah and Jim's parents who were waiting for us to remove the casket from the hearse and carry it to the burial site.

Standing by the grave, we waited for the pastor to say some final words before his casket was lowered into the ground.

And, like a flash, it was over.

Jim was gone, but not forgotten. We knew that his influences and friendship would follow us throughout our lives until it was our turn to join him.

The rest of the day was truly a blur. We met at the Larkmans' house for food, but none of us felt like eating. And when we felt it was appropriate to leave, we said our goodbyes to Mr. and Mrs. Larkman and Sarah. We would have wanted Sarah to join us at the bar where we planned meeting up but knew she needed to stay with her parents, being the only child left.

We, of course, went to Cancun for Margaritas in honor of Jim. We knew he'd appreciate it. You, me, John, and Bob sat mostly in silence, chit-chatting about world news or music for a bit. We were all burned out by the day's events, and we knew it, so we just tried to enjoy each other's company until we had to leave, us for home, and John and Bob for Florida.

When we got home, we had a nightcap while I watched TV and you took a bath to wind down. We eventually crawled into bed, touching lightly as we normally did throughout the night. I knew the minute you fell asleep because I could hear the soft sounds of you breathing slowly. In and then out, and then in and then out, calming me until I could fall asleep.

This year was truly our best year, with all our travel and all the moments we had throughout the year. There were so many special moments we shared that I will always remember and cherish. But it will forever be burned into my mind as one of the worst because it was the year I lost Jim.

Diary: July 19

Crash and burn again . . .

Last night was my last date with Sonja. We dated only a couple times, but every time we went out, I thought of you. She's the third woman I've tried dating this month, trying to forget you.

It doesn't matter whom I'm with, I think of you. And the minute I do, the feelings come on again, the feelings of depression and loss . . . and they can see it in my eyes. They can see your loss in my eyes. And I definitely can't have the amount of fun with them I did with you.

In fact, no matter what I do or say, I can't feel anything for them. Besides friendship, that is.

Thing is, I know I can do this, I know I have it in my heart to move on.

Or am I just fooling myself?

CHAPTER
10

"What do you mean you don't want to date again?" June demanded.

"It's probably best if we don't," I responded, trying to tell her the reasoning behind my assumed madness. "Sure, we'd be fine for a week or two, then we'd start arguing and before you know it we'll be broken up again. It's like a continuous loop."

I paused for a minute and said, "It's better if we end it right here."

June looked at me for a minute, misty eyed and longing, and then nodded.

"You're probably right. It's best to leave as friends, huh?" she pondered.

"Yeah . . ." was all I could say.

It was always sad when you broke up with someone, but this was weird: breaking up before we ever went out. But it truly was for the best.

June and I had dated on and off for the last year. We'd go out for a few weeks, break up, realize we were lonely, date for a few weeks, and then break up again. Someone had to end the loop.

Plus, there was Judy.

About a month earlier, my friend Jim had started dating a girl named Hanna that he met through his sister Sarah. Best part about this new relationship, at least in my eyes, was that Sarah lived next door to another girl in her class.

"Dude, what are you doing after school?" Jim asked when we saw each other in the hall at school.

"Not much . . . why?"

"Because I may have found a girlfriend for you," he said, smiling like he stole something from me.

"Oh?" I said, intrigued.

"Yeah. Hanna has a next-door neighbor that just happens to be in her class. Her name is Judy. And I know she doesn't have a boyfriend."

Without hesitation I said, "Okay. I'm in."

Jim had made arrangements with Hanna for her to call when both she and Judy were home so we could stop by. Not sure if the girls had to *pretty themselves up* or they just wanted to talk about us while we weren't there. Either way, about an hour after we got to Jim's after school, Hanna called him, and we headed over.

When we got there, the girls were in the backyard on a swing set. Luck was on our side because Hanna's parents weren't home.

"Hi you," he said as he kissed her and proceeded to put his arms around her.

When they completed their *grappling*, I said hi to Hanna as well.

"Hi Mike!" Hanna said, pausing to look at Judy. "Mike, this is Judy."

"Hi Judy," I said to the beautiful girl sitting on the swing. And when I say beautiful, I'm probably understating how gorgeous the girl was. She had long brown hair that lifted just slightly with the light breeze that was blowing. Judy's eyes were a deep-sea blue and her body . . . her body . . . well, it was amazing. Even though she was only sixteen, she had the body of a twenty-year-old. Her breasts were superbly formed, her waist was skinny, and her butt was perfect.

If this worked out, I would owe Jim and Hanna big time.

"Hi Mike! It's nice to meet you!" Judy said as she tipped slightly forward and back on the swing.

Judy was smiling at me which, unless I was wrong, told me she was interested. I moved to sit on the swing next to her.

"We'll leave you two alone," Jim said as he and Hanna walked toward the house. It was obvious they were going to make use of the parentless home.

As we gently swung, keeping time with each other, Judy and I talked about school and our friendships and Jim and Hanna. Judy and Hanna had been friends since Hanna had moved in next to her the previous year. I, of course, bored her with our friendship and mutual love of blowing things up. This made her laugh. She had such a cute laugh.

"So, do you know Sarah, Jim's sister?"

"Yeah, but we're not really friends. She runs in a slightly different crowd than I do."

I laughed at this. "Oh yeah? How so?"

"Sarah and Hanna are both in band. I'm not. Plus, they're both kind of bookworms," Judy said, basically calling them geeks.

"Ahhh . . . I understand. Not my crowd either," I said. At this Judy smiled again. I guessed I said something right.

As we swung back and forth, we ran into each other occasionally. The more our conversation grew in depth, the more and more our swings connected. I guess you could call it a form of flirting, the way a person will touch a lover's arm or an elbow while conversing.

As our conversation lulled, the swinging died away, and we just sat in the swings discussing things all teens talk about. While doing this, I pushed against the ground, pushing my seat, so I could close the gap between us. I could see she was doing the same, both of us leaning against the chains separating us.

I finally worked up the courage to reach out and grab her seat's chain so I could pull her closer to me. When I did this, she lowered her hand to touch mine, our faces still seemed miles apart. Then it happened. Judy leaned in and kissed me. I pushed back as we turned our heads to taste each other. We both liked what we sampled, and she wanted more, as did I.

I stood, helping her rise out of the seat, and we embraced, holding each other, my hands on the small of her back, hers around my neck, all the while ignoring the time or location, the sights and sounds.

That was, until we heard a car pulling up the driveway.

It could only be Hanna's parents coming home from wherever they had been.

Just as the car reached the garage about twenty feet from us, we heard a noise from the bushes at the side of the house. Jim and Hanna had obviously heard the return of Hanna's parents and snuck out the front door and around the house so as to not rouse any suspicions.

When Hanna's parents approached, the four of us stood there as if nothing had taken place.

"Hi Mrs. Davidson . . . hi Mr. Davidson!" he said, obviously trying to lift the weight of guilt on his mind.

"Hi Jim," they both said in unison as they approached our group.

"How was school?" Mr. Davidson asked Hanna. As he did, Hanna turned slightly and ushered her parents toward the house. She looked back at us over her shoulder and mouthed *be right back* to him.

"So, you two hit it off," he stated, as his eyes moved down to our hand holding.

"I guess you could say that," Judy replied before I had a chance to respond. All I could do was nod.

When Hanna emerged from the house and rejoined our little group, we talked for a few minutes trying to figure out what to do. We eventually chose to walk someplace to get out from under the ever watching parental eyes, choosing a walk to the lake since it wasn't too far from their houses.

Judy and I let Jim and Hanna lead the way, us falling into step just slightly behind them so we could talk more and hold hands. When we reached the lake, Judy and I split off to walk along the beach as he and Hanna watched the waves while they kissed.

"I love the lake. It's perfect," Judy said as she admired the waves.

"It *is* perfect," I said as I held Judy's hand and looked into Judy's eye. She knew exactly what I meant. At this, we stopped and started kissing, feeling the warmth of the sun against our cheeks as the sun slowly set on the horizon.

When the sun was almost completely set, we broke our embrace knowing that was our queue to rejoin Jim and Hanna so we could walk home. Judy and I walked back along the beach, arm in arm, until we found the couple. As we approached, they stopped their necking, this time the two of them falling into step behind us as we walked toward the girls' homes.

The four of us stopped at the top of Hanna's street, just out of sight from their houses, so we could get a goodnight kiss. After, we walked the girls to their respective houses, said goodnight, and joined one another on Hanna's driveway. As we left the girls and walked to Jim's car, we were both smiling like idiots, idiots in love.

The next day, after school, I called Judy's house, having scored her number the previous evening. She answered, and we made arrangements to meet that night after dinner.

"I hear you have a motorcycle. Is that true?"

It was.

As soon as I turned eighteen, I begged my mom to cosign a loan for me so I could buy a new motorcycle. My friend Rob had bought one the year before from the local Suzuki dealer, a 500cc single stroke monster, and I was jealous. Rob had recommended the dealer, so, as part of my birthday present, we headed to the dealer. I found a 600cc crotch rocket and instantly fell in love. It was a beauty. All silver with a silver fairing on front and a banana seat with pegs for the back, ready for a passenger.

"I do," I replied.

"Can we go for a ride?"

"Will it be okay with your parents?"

"What they don't know . . ." she quipped.

"What?"

"I was kidding!" she said, but I could tell she wasn't. I could tell this girl was going to be trouble. "Meet me at the end of my street in ten minutes, okay?"

"Okay. See ya in a few," I reluctantly replied and hung up the phone. And, true to my word, I was at the end of her street ten minutes later.

As I sat there waiting for Judy, it dawned on me that even though the bike was passenger ready, I wasn't. When I bought the motorcycle, I only purchased one helmet figuring I'd be the only one on it. In order for us to ride, one of us would have to go without a helmet. I mentally kicked myself for having not thought of this in the past. Then again, the opportunity for me to give someone a ride really hadn't come up, so I tried to not kick myself too hard. While I sat there contemplating this situation, Judy came into view, and I totally lost my train of thought.

Judy had on a short, almost too tight, black t-shirt that barely touched the top of her blue jeans. As she walked — sauntered, really — the movement of her hips back and forth occasionally showed off her well-trimmed midriff. All thoughts of helmets left my mind, being replaced with thoughts of how I'd love to be kissing and caressing that area. She also wore a black leather jacket cut to the same length as her shirt, as to not obscure one's view of said midriff.

"Hi," she said casually as she stopped beside me. "Ready to go?"

"Ye-yes," I stuttered, trying to regain my composure. "Where would you like to go?"

"I don't know . . . you choose," Judy said as she threw her back leg over my bike.

I hated to spoil the moment, but in my mind I had no other choice.

"Here," I said as I handed her the helmet.

Judy took it, looked at it for a moment, and then looked up at me, "Do I have to wear it?"

"To be safe, yes."

After contemplating it for a minute, Judy looked at me, batted her eyelashes, and said, "But it will mess up my hair."

"So will forty-miles-an-hour winds. Please put it on."

She looked at me again, dropped her attitude, and put the helmet on. Score one for Mike.

"So, how does the valley sound?"

"Sounds great! I love the valley!" Judy said as she put her arms around me. And we were off.

Let me start by saying there's something magical about riding through the valley on a motorcycle. The feel of the cooler air on your face, the winding roads, the feel of driving through nature, the sound of the engine echoing off the trees. It's freeing and exciting. It's soothing and thought provoking. A thousand times better when there's a beautiful woman on the back tightly holding on to you. And Judy was holding me tight. She obviously loved the experience.

While in the valley, we didn't go overly fast, but just fast enough to get a thrill out of all the twists and turns. From what I could tell, Judy loved it. She was holding on just enough to keep her balance and squeezed me tight when we rounded the curves. After a few miles into the ride, I pulled the motorcycle into a parking lot so we could stretch our legs. I parked and locked the bike, and we both dismounted so we could walk around for a minute or two.

"Wow! That's fun!" Judy said as she stretched.

"Right? It's one of my favorite things . . . ever," I replied, and walked with her toward the trees and onto a paved walking path. As we walked, we held hands and bumped our shoulders into each other occasionally. Being a teenager *in like* is weird and wonderful.

When we reached a turn in the trail, we stopped at the side of the path and kissed for a few minutes. We stopped when we heard someone approaching and walked back toward the cycle. Once at the bike, we remounted and left to drop Judy off at home. Of course, I stopped at the end of her street and let her off the bike.

"Thank you for the ride," Judy said, and then gave me a goodnight kiss.

As she turned to leave, I grabbed her hand and asked, "Would you like to do something tomorrow night?"

"Sure!" Judy said, smiling. "What did you have in mind?"

"How about dinner and a movie?"

"Sounds good. Pick me up at 6:00 p.m.," she replied, smiled, and walked toward home. I couldn't help but stare at her butt as she walked away. The girl had an amazing body.

The next day was Friday, and I was ready for the weekend. I called Judy when I got home from school to make sure we were still good for 6:00 p.m. She said she was, and after talking about it for a few minutes, we picked a rom-com at the theater coupled with a fast dinner before.

"Want to pick me up on the motorcycle again?"

"Can do! See you in a bit," I said. I'm a sucker like that.

I agreed to pick her up at the end of the street like the previous night. Even though I thought it was shitty to not have met her parents yet, let alone pick her up like a true gentleman, I opted to please her. At the end of the day, it was her I was dating, not her parents, right?

As I arrived at the end of the street, I saw Judy approaching wearing the leather jacket from the night before, and a sun dress. Although she looked fantastic, we were riding on a motorcycle after all, and a sun dress is not the best choice, mostly because of all the wind and panty showing, let alone the potential for road rash. It wasn't a far ride though, so after mentioning this to her, and her ignoring said warning, we took off for the Bell.

The date night went well. Really well, I'd guess you'd say. I would. We ate tacos, and we saw the movie. Well, some of it at least. Judy insisted we sit in the back row so we could make out and fool around. And now I understood why she wanted to wear the sun dress.

Fifteen minutes into the movie, Judy placed her hand on my thigh and started rubbing, gently, slowly moving toward my groin. I quickly grabbed my jacket off the seat next to me and placed it on my lap.

"What are you doing?" I whispered, feeling a little than more embarrassed.

"You don't like it?" she sarcastically whispered back.

Judy took her *free* hand and grabbed my wrist. Lifting my arm, she lowered it onto her leg and used my hand to raise her skirt. Before I knew it, my fingers were touching her underwear. Knowing what she wanted, I did my best to please her.

"Can you at least put your jacket on your lap?" I asked softly, trying to remember how to speak. She did as I asked, reluctantly.

In a few minutes, we both completed our tasks and were kissing. By that point, I didn't care anymore who watched us.

Before the movie ended, I rose and walked to the restroom to clean myself up, holding my jacket casually over my arm draping it in front of my body. If you've ever tried this, you'll know it's nearly impossible to look cool. But I had no other option. When I returned to the movie, the credits were rolling and Judy was patiently waiting for me where I had left her. I sat down next to her waiting for the credits to finish.

"All cleaned up?" she gibed. At this I leaned in and kissed her hard, biting her lip a little.

"Yep," I said as I backed away to look into her eyes. "Ready to leave?"

We left the theater, and I drove her home. The whole time we were on the motorcycle, she rested her hand on my crotch, like she owned it. Which I guess, at this point, she kind of did. Or at least she owned the emotions attached to it. When we reached the bottom of her street, I stopped, as before. I kissed her goodnight, saying we'd talk the next day, and I watched her walk toward her house and up her driveway. It was about 10:00 p.m. when I arrived home and promptly went to bed.

The next day I woke with a smile on my face. The previous night had been something out of a dream. She was beautiful, she was witty, she was adventurous, and she was mine. I could not wait to see her again. I chose to wait until right before noon to call her, in case she slept in, so I could ask her if we could have a repeat performance of the previous evening. Well, I called her to see if she wanted to go for a motorcycle ride, *hoping* for a repeat performance of the previous evening, or maybe something more.

"I'm actually busy tonight Mike. Sorry."

"Oh? Something good, I hope?"

"I actually have a date with John, my boyfriend. He's home this weekend from OSU."

At this, I didn't know what to say, or how to continue, but I tried. "So . . . you have a boyfriend?"

"Yeah, I thought you knew." I didn't, of course. "He got home last night but was busy. I'm glad you weren't. I had a lot of fun! I love your bike!"

When I hung up the phone, I wasn't sure what to do. But then it came to me — Jim. I cleaned up quickly, hopped on my bike, and rode to his house. I was pretty sure he'd be there, and he was.

"Dude, she has a boyfriend," I said, hoping for some words of wisdom. Be careful what you wish for.

"So?"

"*So*! She has a *boyfriend*! She *has* a *boyfriend*! What don't you understand about that?"

Jim looked at me for a minute, and said, "So . . . what does it matter? He's away at school. You're here. She likes you. I say go for it!"

"Go for it?"

"Yeah, go for it," he restated. "Date her on the sly and, when her boy-friend fucks up, you have an *in*."

"I have an *in*? That's your answer?"

He just shrugged.

"Dude, I don't want an *in* . . . I want a *now*!"

"But you don't have a now," he declared. "You have a girl that likes you. And one that likes you a lot, apparently. Run with it. You never know where it'll take you."

I guess I couldn't argue with this logic. She was hot. She liked me. I was here. He was there. Could I be the part time booty call? I guess. I mean, there are a lot of guys that would *kill* to have a hot girl want them. I suppose I could continue this the way it was going and wait it out. That is, unless her boyfriend found out and kicked the shit out of me.

At this realization, this epiphany, I chose to *run with it*. Worst case I get my ass kicked. Best case . . . we'd see.

"So, are we good?" Jim asked, showing a little bit of empathy for my feelings.

"Yeah, I guess so," I said, changing the subject. "What's the plan for tonight?"

"John's coming over; we're playing D&D," he stated. "Want to join? We're doing a sleepover."

"Yeah, I guess," Okay, I really didn't want to play D&D, but I had nothing else planned that night, and I wanted to meet John.

John, the Dungeon Master, and Jim met at school one day when a group of guys were talking about D&D. John announced that he was a DM and would be more than happy to run D&D games for us. John was only a sophomore, so he couldn't drink, but he ran a great game. So I was told.

To me, D&D was a waste of time. Rolling dice and playing charac-
ters on paper was not my idea of a fun Saturday night. But hanging with
friends and drinking . . . now that was another story. I would have fun in
my own way.

Jim and I left a short while later on a beer run, selecting our favorite
cheapest beers. Quantity won over quality on a part time job paycheck. We
also made a run back to my house to grab some clothes so I could spend
the night at Jim's.

When we arrived back at Jim's, we set up the ping pong table in his
basement and collected chairs from around the house to place around the
table. When finished, we placed the night's game board on the table and
assessed our work. It was a job well done. It was also time for a beer.

The doorbell rang shortly into our first beer. Jim ran upstairs and a
minute later came down the steps with John. After introducing us, I questioned John about the D&D game. John spent some time with me, creating
a character and explaining how the play would go. It was interesting, but,
seriously, video games were much more interesting to me.

"Who all's coming tonight?"

"Well, the three of us of course. Rob, Hanna, Sarah, and Lisa."

"Who's Lisa?"

"Oh, yeah. You've never met her. Lisa is a friend of Sarah's from school."

"Oh, great. Another one of Sarah's friends. Will I survive?"

"Only time will tell, my friend," he said as we prepared to greet the
rest of the players.

A little while later, we heard Rob's motorcycle pull into the driveway,
followed eventually by a knock on the door. About fifteen minutes after
that Sarah, Hanna, and Lisa strolled in the door and headed downstairs.

"Hey Sarah. Hey Hanna. What's new?"

"Not much. You?" Sarah returned, being polite, as Hanna nodded and walked over to kiss Jim.

"Not much," I replied, staring at Lisa.

"Oh yeah, this is my friend Lisa." Sarah announced.

As I approached Lisa to say hi, I noticed one thing. Lisa was very unnoticeable. As to say, she was very plain. She wore no makeup unlike the other girls her age. Her long blonde hair was slightly unkempt, and her clothing was very drab. It's almost like she didn't want to be noticed. But there was a certain beauty about her. She had pretty blue eyes, she was skinny but well formed, and she had full lips, although uncolored.

"It's nice to meet you Lisa," I said, taking her hand for a slight shake.

"Hi" was all she said.

"Let's get started," John said as he walked to the head of the table and sat down.

We all followed suit. I, of course, somehow wound up at the seat next to Lisa. Yes, it was on purpose. Yeah, I have no shame. Well on this at least.

We played D&D until the wee hours of the morning, which is to say somewhere around 2:00 a.m. That's when Mrs. Larkman came downstairs to tell the under-aged girls to move their portion of the party upstairs to Sarah's bedroom.

Once Mrs. Larkman left, we said our goodnights to the ladies and I made sure to say goodnight to Lisa up close and personal. She smiled, and although she was very shy, I could tell that she liked me. Once they left, the boys cracked a final beer each and got ready for bed.

It was about a half an hour later when we heard someone walking down the stairs. We all thought it was Mrs. Larkman coming back down to yell at us for being too loud, but it turned out to be Sarah. She peeked her head around the corner, looking around until she saw me.

"Mike," she whispered and waved for me to follow her.

We climbed the stairs into the kitchen and stopped by the counter. After Sarah made a quick assessment of the surroundings, she whispered to me.

"Lisa likes you."

"Oh?" I said as I tried to act surprised.

"Yep. Are you interested in her?"

"I suppose. Why?" I asked, trying to be nonchalant.

"Because if you are, there's a few things you need to know about her."

To me, this was a little strange. Sarah was like a little sister to me, and how often are little sisters helpful? But if this would give me a leg up I was willing to listen.

"Go on."

"Well, she's very shy, to start. Also, she's never had a boyfriend before."

"Seriously?"

"Seriously. So I just want to make sure that, if you're interested, you take it slow with her."

"I promise," I said truthfully.

"Okay," Sarah said as she looked around once more. "I gotta get back in bed before Mom catches me."

After she left the kitchen, I went back downstairs, pretty full of myself, knowing that a girl liked me. Tonight had been a good night.

The next morning, which was only a couple hours later, Jim, John, Rob, and I headed out early for Jim's paper route. The route was easy with four people running from house to house, and we were done in no time. When we got back to his house, we crashed, hard, until almost noon. Then when we woke, we went downstairs for breakfast and found out the girls had already eaten and left for Hanna's house. I guessed I would have to see Lisa another day.

The opportunity actually came later that day, with some help from Jim and Hanna's mom.

After breakfast and some cleanup of the basement, Rob and John took off leaving Jim and me at the house by ourselves. We watched TV for a bit, went out to fiddle with his car and my motorcycle for a while, and then went back in to be a nuisance to his mom. Eventually, she couldn't take it anymore.

"Jim, why don't you two go pick up Sarah from Hannah's? She has homework tonight," Mrs. Larkman asked, which was more of a demand, to get rid of us.

"Sure thing Mom!" we both said in unison and walked to his car.

When we arrived at Hanna's, she and Sarah were saying their good-byes, and I could see Lisa was there as well. This could be my chance to ask Lisa out, I thought to myself, as he parked the car and we exited to see the girls.

"Hey. Mom wanted me to drive you home," he said to Sarah as he hugged and kissed Hanna.

I walked over to Lisa and said, "Hi!"

"Hi. How are you?" Lisa managed.

"Good! What are you up to?"

"Not much. I was just getting ready to walk home."

I thought about this for a moment, trying to figure out the logistics behind my next statement, which was "Can I walk you home?"

"Sure," she said without hesitation.

After talking it over with Jim, Lisa and I said our goodbyes to the group and started our journey to her house.

It was a nice evening, for Cleveland. Not warm, but not too cold, light-jacket weather. And while the sun was up, it was pleasant.

Lisa was shy, and reluctant to talk, so I made up for it. I told her about my family and school, about my dreams of becoming an architect someday, and about my friendships with Jim, Sarah, and the rest of our friends. I, of course, omitted any talk of June or Judy. I did not want to open those cans of worms.

By the time we got to Lisa's house, I had a good exchange going back and forth with her. She did, eventually, open up, and when I say open up, it was like flood gates. She told me about her mom and dad, her sister and brother.

Lisa was the middle child of the three and felt slighted a lot of the time, feeling she was inadequate. I guessed this is why she had never had a boyfriend.

I, of course, was willing and able to help her change that.

When we got to her house, we stopped for a moment in her drive-way, which I thought would be my signal to leave.

"Want to see my backyard?" Lisa asked, wincing at saying the only thing she could muster. "My parents are at bowling tonight. My sister and brother are probably watching TV so they won't care."

"Sure," I said, delighted I'd get to spend a few more minutes with her.

I followed her as we walked into her backyard and sat at a picnic table the family had near a grill. As the sun started to set and the evening air chilled, we sat closer together, thigh against thigh, talking about her family life. I eventually worked up the nerve to put my arm behind her, and she was receptive.

Since there was no sign of parental interruption, I made my move. I moved in close and kissed her tentatively on her lips to see how she would react. I could tell Lisa had never kissed a boy before because she didn't know how to respond. She just sat there with lips closed, accepting my kiss but no emotion on her side. Because she didn't pull away, I continued my actions.

I licked her lips to see if that would entice her to respond. After a couple gentle motions across her lips, she opened her mouth slightly and tested the touching of our tongues. Within a few seconds, we were deeply absorbed into each other's motions and actions.

That was about the time the back porch light went on.

We separated, fast, moving about a foot away from each other, and I quickly retracted my arm to my side. Lisa and I both turned toward the door and saw a boy, about a year or two younger than her, standing staring at us from the porch.

"John! What are you doing?" Lisa yelled at the boy.

"Mom and Dad won't like you back here alone with a boy!" John yelled back.

"I don't care! Get in the house and turn off the light . . . *now*!" Lisa yelled back while she moved to stand. John did as told, reluctantly. I stood along with Lisa, watching the door, while the lights went out. The backyard was dark and would take a moment to adjust.

"I should probably go," I said taking Lisa's hands to face her toward me.

"You don't have to. My mom and dad won't be home for a while."

"I know," I said, guessing. "But we both have school tomorrow, and I have some homework to finish."

This was a lie, of course. I didn't have any homework. Well, I did, but I had no real plans of completing it. I just figured it was time to go. I knew she liked me, and that was enough for one night. We had broken the ice by kissing, which was much more than I thought I'd have in one evening, and I wanted to leave on a high note.

From what I could see in the dim lighting, Lisa looked a little depressed.

"Can I call you after school tomorrow?" I asked to help her mood.

"I have band practice, then dinner. But you can call after that . . . is that ok?" Lisa asked shyly.

"Sure! About 7:00 p.m.?"

Lisa smiled and quickly nodded. I leaned in and gave her another kiss, and then turned to head back the way we came. All the while I held her hand, which was turning quite sweaty even with the colder night upon us.

My walk home took approximately thirty minutes, but I was fine with that. Mission accomplished. I had successfully located, hunted, and captured my prey, and I had the thrill of the kill in my heart. Yes, today was a good day.

As promised, the next day I called Lisa, and we set up a date for Friday night at Jim's house. As I understood it, this would be another D&D night with a sleepover involved. Again, I wasn't enamored with playing D&D, but I got more face time with Lisa. I checked with Jim, and he informed me it was basically the same crowd that had been at the previous game.

Friday night's gaming happened pretty much like the previous game. I showed up at Jim's to help set up, we drank, we welcomed everyone, and we played until people started falling asleep. During the game, I sat by Lisa and we held hands under the table when no one was watching. When we finally called it quits for the evening, Lisa got up and went over to Sarah for a minute and then meandered to the couch. I helped him out for a bit saying goodbye to people who were leaving, which was everyone except me, Lisa, Jim, Hanna, and Sarah. Then, seeing Lisa on the couch, I went over to sit with her.

"Aren't you guys headed upstairs?" I asked Lisa.

"No, Sarah said Hanna and I could sleep down here. She's going to grab some pillows and blankets from upstairs for us, then go up to bed."

At this piece of news, I excused myself from Lisa, got up, and walked over to him. "Dude, are you sleeping down here?"

"Yep. And you can too if you want to. I just found out Hanna's staying down here, so that's what I'm planning," he said with a smirk on his face. "You can head up to my room if you don't want to."

"Nah. Think I'll see if there's room on the couch," I said as I nodded toward where Lisa was placing covers, returning the smirk.

"Right on," Jim responded with a smile, giving me a mental high five for work well done.

He turned on a table lamp back in the corner and then turned off the overhead lighting, which made it cozy in the basement. Hanna had set up pillows and blankets under the ping pong table — a nest made for two — and a minute later, he joined Hanna under the table. Returning to Lisa, who was already laying down and covered, I asked if she had room for me under the covers.

"Of course," she said, as she raised the covers so I could crawl in with her.

When I got under the covers, the first thing I noticed was Lisa was very warm, almost to the point of sweating. This was intensified when I was under the covers with her. To top it off, we had all of our clothing on, and our bodies were touching. It was almost unbearable, except for the fact that we were together.

"Well, you got me here . . . now what?" I jokingly whispered into Lisa's ear as I put my arms around her.

With that she started kissing me. Lisa initiating and repeating the way we had started kissing the previous Sunday. As we became more caught up in our kissing, I pushed my leg between her legs to get better leverage. At first I thought she would stop me, but she didn't. It only drove her further into our embrace. I moved my hand up from her side so I could caress her breast from the outside of her shirt, wanting badly to slip my hand under the cloth, but I took it slow - there was no rush, after all.

Getting to know each other's bodies was abruptly halted a few minutes later when someone flipped on the overhead lights. I heard the sound of someone coming down the stairs from the kitchen and, assuming I knew who it was, separated from Lisa so we could both look toward the bottom of the landing.

My assumptions were verified when, lo and behold, Jim's mother rounded the corner.

"You ladies will get upstairs now," Mrs. Larkman stated in a calm but firm voice.

"And you two . . ." she continued, staring with burning eyes at us, "will get up to Jim's room and go to bed. Right now!"

Without hesitation, we walked around Mrs. Larkman, and climbed the stairs to his room. We could finish the cleanup in the morning.

The next morning, Jim and I rose early to deliver the papers and then headed back home to finish cleaning up the basement before breakfast.

Mrs. Larkman was kind enough to wait until after breakfast to reprimand us for our actions of the previous evening. And she didn't lay into us as bad as I thought she would, which was a blessing. But she did tell us that future D&D gaming would follow house rules, or there would be no future gaming. Although I didn't really need to, I nodded my head as enthusiastically as well. I was, after all, an *adopted* son.

Over the next two weeks, Lisa and I continued meeting and making out whenever we could. Sometimes at my house, sometimes at Jim's house, and even occasionally at her house, when her parents weren't home, that is. It wasn't that they didn't like me when they met me; it was just that they were very protective of their daughters. After getting to know this, it made

sense as to why Lisa had never kissed a boy before. The meek fail where the
bold survive, I guess.

And I could be bold.

It was somewhere around this three to four week mark that I realized, after being shut down several times, that Lisa didn't want to sleep with
me. We had discussed it several times, in several different ways, but she felt
that we needed to know each other a lot longer than we had.

As you may or may not know, this is the last thing any teenage boy
wants to hear. It's not like we want sex all the time. Well, mostly we do, but
there are quite a number of times that it's inconvenient. Like during a class,
or when you're out blowing stuff up. But when we wanted it, we wanted it.
And if you were fortunate enough to have a girlfriend of three weeks, you
kind of expected it. I know, I know, it sounds sexist — it kind of is. But I
was eighteen, and an eighteen-year-old's hormones beat on your brain like
a sledgehammer.

It was also somewhere around this time that I met Laura.

Laura was yet another friend of Hanna's. A girl she knew from math
class that just happened to be over one day when Jim and I went over to
Hanna's house for a visit after school. When we arrived at Hanna's house, we
were told by Hanna's mom that she and Laura were in the kitchen studying.
She let us in, and Jim led me toward the kitchen. As we entered the kitchen,
I saw the girls standing by the sink. And my jaw dropped.

Laura was, well, stunning, to say the least. That's really the only word
I can think of to describe her. She was just slightly shorter than me, with
blonde hair and green eyes, and one of the cutest faces I've ever seen. As
for her body, her breasts weren't too big, but they weren't too small either.
And her ass was just utter perfection. She was wearing corduroy pants that

fit like they were made just for her. They accented every inch they covered, hips to ankles. Not too tight, not too loose, and cupping her pear-shaped butt like they were painted on.

I wasn't sure if there was a ringing sound coming from somewhere or if it was all in my head, but somehow I had totally missed the introductions. The next thing I knew he was backhanding my arm and saying, "Mike, this is Laura!"

"Oh . . . uh . . . hi. It's nice to meet you," I muttered as I stuck out my hand to take hers. The moment we touched there was a spark.

As I looked into her beautiful green eyes, I could see she felt it too.

"Nice to meet you too . . . Mike," Laura said, forcing to get the words out.

Have you ever had that feeling when you've met someone? You know, like something in the universe just clicked? Like the stars and planets aligned in such a way that everything suddenly made sense? Well, that's what happened to me when I met Laura. It was as if something in the cosmos said, "Hey, you two were destined to be together." At least that's what I thought.

"Laura and I were just talking about heading to Taco Bell for dinner," Hanna said to Jim. "Would you two gentlemen like to take us?"

Jim and I looked at each other, and he replied, "We'd be delighted, ladies."

Before I knew it, Laura and I were loaded into the back seat of his car, and we were on our way to the Bell.

"Is it just me, or have we met before?" I asked Laura.

"I was thinking the same thing," she replied, and we started comparing notes.

Turned out we had met each other several times. Like, about a two or three dozen times, and we just didn't know it. Not only had both of our moms worked together, but our dads had worked together as well. About ten years previously, Laura's mother had worked part time for the restaurant that my mom worked at. For years, we had seen each other at Christmas parties and other restaurant events and just didn't know it. Also, my dad and her stepdad had worked at the same company, which meant we had seen each other at company picnics too.

We arrived at Taco Bell, ordered and received our food, and sat down in the dining area and ate. During which we talked with Jim and Hanna, telling them what we had discovered about each other.

"Wow, that's crazy!" Hanna said. "It's like the universe has been trying to put you two together for years!"

Hearing that out loud made me think. Maybe life had been trying to throw us together for years but we just didn't know it. It also helped that she was way hot. And if the universe was trying to throw us together, who was I to argue with it?

Just the thought of it that way made me bold. As we made our way back to the car, I asked, "So, would you like to go out sometime?"

"I actually just broke up with someone. I'm not sure if I'd be much fun."

"Oh, don't worry. I can be enough fun for both of us!" I said, which made her laugh.

"Okay," she chuckled. "But can we go out as friends?"

"Sure, we can take things slow if you want," I replied. She gave me a look of hesitation.

"Okay. We'll just be friends. I swear," I vowed, hoping I would eventually be able to break my vow.

"Would you like to come over Friday for dinner? I'm sure my mom and dad won't mind. You're practically family!" she said, laughing.

"Cool with me! What time?"

"Can you come over right after school?"

"Yep. Not a problem," I said, smiling. Yeah, I could make this work.

Jim drove us back to Hanna's, and we dropped the girls off. After he and Hanna had a brief make out session, we were off again back to Jim's house.

"So, you asked her out?" he asked.

"Yep. But she wants to go out as friends."

"Well, that's better than nothing, I guess."

"That was my thought. Plus, who knows, right?"

"Right," he said, and then paused. "But, what about Lisa?"

"Well, I was thinking about breaking up with her."

"Really? I mean, it's probably best if you're gonna see Laura . . . just wondering though."

"Eh. She doesn't want to go any farther."

He shrugged, accepting the response. And it was true: I was thinking about breaking up with her because it felt like she didn't want the relationship to go any farther. Why continue things with her if I had the prospect of something better? The universe thinks so, and I think so . . . so, there you go. As we pulled into Jim's driveway, my mind was set.

For the next few days, I avoided talking to Lisa. I was resolute in breaking up with her, but I didn't know how to do it. She was sweet and kind, and liked me a lot, so it was hard to break things off. But I knew I had to. The only thing that came to mind was delaying things until I could think of something.

In the meantime, I started talking to and, as promised, went over to Laura's house Friday after school. When I arrived, I rang the doorbell and was greeted by Laura a minute later. As she welcomed me into her home, I noticed she was the only one home. She explained that both of her parents worked, so she was used to coming home and being by herself after school. Her mom was usually home around 4:30 p.m., and they had dinner around 6:00 p.m., so that would give us some time to hang out.

Laura proceeded to show me her house, backyard, basement, etc., eventually ending up in her room. She put on some music — I believe it was *Cheap Trick* — and we sat on her bed and talked about growing up in Cleveland. She knew that my dad had passed away, so she mentioned that her dad also had passed away when she was young. So young, in fact, that she never really knew him. Her mom had met her stepdad when she was three, and he had helped raise her, so she considered him her dad.

We talked for about forty-five minutes before her mom got home. I was a little nervous being a stranger in her bedroom, but Laura told me she had let her mom know earlier that morning that I was coming over. When we heard her in the kitchen, we exited the bedroom and left to meet her.

As soon as I saw her, I recognized her. I remembered her name was Karen Harmon and had met her several times when I was younger before she left for another job.

"Hi Mrs. Harmon," I said, introducing myself. She remembered me right away and asked about my mom.

"She's fine. She still manages the office at the restaurant and manages to keep us in line," I joked. Yeah, when it comes to parents, I'm a charmer.

When her dad got home from work, we had dinner and sat around talking for a bit. He also remembered me, and my dad, and shared some stories from the job site that made us laugh. It was good hearing about my dad. It was usually a subject we avoided at home.

Before too long, Laura asked if we could be excused so we could hang out in her room. Mrs. Harmon gave us the go ahead, and we left the table. When we got into Laura's room, she shut the door and put on some music, *Journey* this time. We sat on the bed and just listened for a while, before she spoke up.

"Do you want to kiss me?"

I was taken aback by this. I mean, of course I did! How could I not? But didn't she just tell me the other day that she just got out of a relationship and only wanted to be friends? I wasn't sure if she changed her mind or just wanted to know if I wanted to. I was really confused. But I just nodded and waited to see where it took us.

Laura then leaned in and kissed me. And it was wonderful. We kissed a few times, lightly, only our lips touching. The minute I, we, started wanting more, Laura backed away and looked at me, her eyes happy, but a little distant.

"I hope that was okay."

"That was . . . um . . . nice," I uttered, not knowing what else to say or how to react. I couldn't just tell her it was wonderful. I had a feeling that if I did, she would bolt like a frightened horse and we'd never hang out again. But she wanted something. Some answer to a quiz where I had no instruction.

"Thank you," she said, and gave me another light kiss. Laura rose, turned, and offered me her hands. I could tell it was time to leave.

I walked home that night smiling, but puzzled, not knowing which end was up. Did the kiss mean she liked me? Did she want to date? I had no idea. All I could do was stay the course and see where it took me.

I woke early Saturday so I could help Jim with the paper route. It also gave me a chance to bounce these questions off him.

"Dude, she's playing with your feelings," he said point-blank.

"Really? I didn't get that impression."

"How could you not? She tells you she wants to be friends, and then kisses you? She's just playing with you."

I was offended. "I don't see it that way. I think she likes me."

"Just saying, man. She's got an agenda. I don't know what it is, but something just doesn't seem right," Jim said as he tossed a paper into a yard. In true poet fashion, he added, "Just watch your ass."

We continued the paper route, mostly silent, as we tossed papers here and there, running up and down different streets. All the while thinking about what he said. He was my best friend, after all, and I trusted him. But I had a feeling that there was more here than just her wanting to kiss me. When we finished, I chose to go home for breakfast and a shower, and to figure out my next move.

It was around 2:00 p.m. when I came to a decision: it was time to call Lisa and give her the bad news. I hated avoiding her, and the issue, but with a new prospect in my life, it was shitty to keep her in limbo. I decided to call her after dinner to let her know how I felt.

When dinner time rolled around, Jim stopped by to see if I wanted to hang out that evening and maybe hit the arcade. I figured it was about time I kicked his ass in Defender again, so I agreed and we hit the road. It was probably five minutes later that I realized I had forgotten to call Lisa. I shrugged to myself and figured it could wait one more day.

As promised, I trounced him a few times on Defender, letting him get close a few times but then eventually annihilating him. To be fair though, I let him kick my ass at Galaga, although each of the games was really close.

Around 10:00 p.m. the mall and arcade were closing, so we called it quits for the night. The 6:00 a.m. paper route would be here before we knew it, after all. As Jim drove me home and we approached my house, I noticed Hanna's car in the driveway.

"Dude, why is your girlfriend at my house?"

"I'm . . . not sure. I told her we were going out tonight. Maybe she was just stopping by to see if I was at your place yet?"

"Dude, that's way weird," I said, contemplating the situation. After a minute, I had it. "Hey. Do me a favor and drive up to the 7/11 so I can use the payphone." Jim looked at me confused but did as I asked.

The 7/11 was only about half a mile from my house. At the top of the street, practically, but using the phone there could make it sound like I was calling from anywhere. We pulled in, and as I headed for the phone, he headed inside to buy us Pepsi's. After a couple rings, the phone was answered by my mom.

"Hey Mom, just wanted to let you know that Jim and I are at Taco Bell in Westlake."

"Okay. How soon will you be home? You have some visitors here."

"Oh? Who's there?" I asked quizzically, trying to not let on that I knew.

"Hanna and Lisa are here waiting for you."

Crap.

Crap. Crap.

This was the point where I mentally kicked my ass for not having called Lisa. This was also the point where I needed an excuse to not go home. Yes, I was a chicken shit. I didn't want to face her and have her ball her eyes out at my house. I also didn't want to feel shittier than I was feeling for dumping her. I quickly thought of an excuse that might save my ass.

"Oh," I replied. "It may be a while before I'm home. Like, maybe in the morning. That was the other reason I was calling. To let you know that after Taco Bell, Jim and I were going to drive to Dave's house to pick him up so he can spend the night at Jim's."

Dave, a semi-distant friend of ours, had moved to Norwalk the previous year. Norwalk was a good forty-five minute drive one way, making for one very late night.

"Jim wanted the company, to stay awake, so I told him it was no problem. Cool?" I asked my mom.

"Okay honey. I'll let the girls know you won't be home for a while."

"Thanks Mom! Gotta run! Love you!" I said and hung up as her "I love you too" trailed off.

Yeah, that was really shitty of me to let my mom do the dirty work. But the alternative was tears. When Jim exited the store with our beverages, I explained to him what I had come up with.

"Dude. That's shitty," he said, echoing my thoughts. "Brilliant . . . but shitty."

"I couldn't agree more," I said, pondering. "So, now that I've put us in this mess, where do we go?"

"Let's drive to Norwalk and back. You're paying for the gas," he said, and we were off.

Two hours, one bag of donuts, and two Pepsi's each later, we were back at Jim's, just in time to deliver the papers. The paper driver had delivered the Sunday papers early, and we were wired on sugar, so it seemed the thing to do. After the papers were delivered and the sugar high evaporated, we crashed hard in his room. Sometime around noon, we awoke to a knocking on his door.

"Jim! Hanna's on the phone!" Sarah yelled through the door.

"Okay! I'll be down in a minute!" he barked back. Jim was *not* a morning person.

He left the room a minute later. I tried to fall back asleep for a bit knowing all I had to do was make it home sometime today. I was just about to slip into unconsciousness when he returned to the room.

"Dude, wake up. Hanna wants to talk to you," he said, holding the portable phone.

As I sat up, I was handed the phone. I looked at him curiously, but all he did was just shrugged his shoulders and released the phone into my grasp.

"Hi Hanna," I said experimentally into the phone. "What's up?"

"Lisa dumped you. That's what's up," Hanna said, sounding a little angry.

"Oh?"

"Yeah, *Oh*! Why haven't you called her lately?"

"Umm . . ." I started, trying to figure out the best response. I figured it was best to go the honest route. "because I was planning on breaking up with her, and I didn't know how."

"Well, problem solved!" Hanna barked, the anger in her voice growing stronger. "She asked me to take her over your house last night because you hadn't returned her calls."

"Yeah, I know. Dick move on my part. I just . . . didn't know what to say."

"Guess you don't have to worry about it now. She never wants to talk to you again."

This was a relief, a veritable weight off my shoulders, actually. I mean, it sucks that she never wanted to talk to me again. I was hoping to stay friends with her after the breakup. But I could understand her not wanting to be. I had treated her bad for the last couple weeks.

"Oh and, by the way Mike . . ." Hanna continued. "Lisa was planning on sleeping with you last night."

"Oh . . ." was all I uttered into the phone. "Okay. Sorry we weren't around last night."

"Save it. Let me talk to Jim," she said. I knew he was in for an earful now. I said goodbye to Hanna and handed back the phone.

This news, the realization that she really did like me, was a stab through the heart. I was way off base to think that she didn't. She had probably been waiting for the right moment. Man, did I fuck up.

Consigning myself to the fact that there was nothing else I could do about it, I got up, cleaned up, and left for home. It was almost a walk of shame. I had made Jim lie to his girlfriend, broken up with a girl that cared about me, and probably alienated Hanna — and I'm sure Sarah — in the process. The only thing I could do was grin and bear it.

After about twenty minutes of feeling sorry for myself, I realized I still had what I thought was a shot at happiness. Laura had some sort of feelings for me, and with my freed up schedule, I could concentrate my efforts into winning her over from friendship to relationship. As before, I let the winds of life take me toward a bigger and brighter future, or something like that.

An hour or so later, I called Laura to see what she was up to.

"Not much. I'm just working on homework. Mom and Dad are over a friend's house watching the baseball game. What are you up to?"

"Nothing, actually."

"Want to come over and visit?"

"Sure, if it's okay with your parents."

"No, they won't mind. You're like family."

Five minutes later, I was on my motorcycle riding over to her house.

This *visit* turned out to be very similar to the last *visit*. When I arrived at Laura's house, I was whisked away to her room, even though her parents weren't home. There she closed the door and put on some music. And, of course, she started to kiss me. The kissing was also followed by some mild petting, which I didn't mind in the least. Laura had an incredible body, and the most perfectly formed butt I have ever seen, let alone felt. We laid on Laura's bed talking, and occasionally making out, for about an hour before her parents arrived home.

When her parents' car turned into the driveway, we hurriedly finished what we were doing and sat up on her bed. Laura jumped up and opened the door halfway, I'm guessing so her parents wouldn't suspect we were up to no good. I also stood so I could adjust myself and say hi to her parents.

After greeting her parents, I was asked if I wanted to stay for dinner like last time. This time I declined, telling them I needed to get home and finish homework and excused myself from their home. Laura walked me out and gave me a kiss on my cheek before she turned to reenter the house. I smiled as I walked to my bike and started it, thinking that even though the morning started out horrible, it turned out to be a pretty fine day.

Laura and I kept this *relationship* — meeting after school at her house for make out sessions — for the next two weeks. And although she kept referring to me as her friend, I was glad to be that kind of friend. After all, I could turn this into something, right?

The thoughts of this came crashing down the following Thursday afternoon.

"Oh, hey. Just thought I'd tell you that I'm busy this weekend Mike," Laura said shortly after I answered the phone.

"Oh. Doing something good?"

"Yeah. Saturday night I'm going to a dance with Jake Mitchell. It was kind of last minute, so I'm going dress shopping with my mom tomorrow night."

Jake Mitchell was a senior in my school, in my class, and captain of the track team. He was a decent enough guy, always polite to me. I almost considered him a friend, almost.

"Really? I forgot there was a dance this weekend," I said, a little offended. "You didn't mention it before."

"You're not going?" Laura said quizzically. "I just assumed you knew about it. A lot of people I know are going. You should go. We could double!"

This, of course, was the last thing I wanted to do. To see her with another guy, especially all night long, would kill me, even if I was with another girl. And this certainly put a damper on any hopes I had of convincing her to be my girlfriend, at least short term.

"Eh, it's kind of late to look for a date. Plus, I really don't know anyone going. Jim and Hanna are playing D&D this Saturday, if I remember correctly."

"Okay. I hope you have a great weekend Mike! Wish me luck! Maybe I'll see you next week," Laura said as she ended the call.

As I hung up the phone, my thoughts turned toward what I would do that Saturday night. I was pretty sure Lisa was playing D&D with Jim and Hanna, and a few of our other friends. And, thanks to the badly ended relationship with Lisa, I'm sure the D&D group wouldn't be happy if I showed up to hang out and play. For the first Saturday night, I guessed I'd be hanging out at home with Mom and Dee. Unless they already had plans, which I would bet they did.

Well, there was always the arcade. And I had my motorcycle. I could probably find something to do, in lieu of being alone on a Saturday night.

Diary: August 19

I think I finally found someone that will put up with all my shit.

Her name is Beth, and she's from Ohio, not too far from where we lived, and she's been fantastic with my self-esteem. She, too, lost someone not too long ago. A breakup that crushed her, but she was able to move on.

Meeting Beth online was a thing of luck. She is so much like you, but so different. I know that doesn't make sense. Nothing about this makes sense. Nothing about my life in the last 11 months has made a whole lot of sense.

I have plans to meet her in the near future. Is that bad?

I keep asking myself if I'm healed enough to move on. Somedays I feel like it, somedays I don't. I can be somewhere feeling good about myself, and then a smell or sound or sight will trigger a thought of you, and the weight on my chest is back.

They say time heals all wounds. I pray this is true. I pray every night that I can keep this strength I've found.

I love you Amy. I will always love you.

CHAPTER

11

"You're going out again?" I asked Michelle as I walked into the bedroom and saw she was putting on her eyeliner.

"Gabby asked me to go to the club with her. Why is that a big deal?" she said without pausing.

"But you just saw your sister last night! I thought we could stay home and watch a movie?" I urged.

"Can we do it tomorrow night? Gabby really wants me to go tonight. She wants me to meet her new boyfriend."

"She has another new boyfriend? How many does that make this month?" I quipped.

"I know. There's been a few. But she says she's serious about this one," Michelle said as she zipped up her dress.

This had become the routine over the last two months. Now that her sister was back in town from her brief stay in California, Michelle went out with her almost every weekend. She could, of course, because with me home, there was someone to watch the kids. Not that they really needed watching.

"What time do you think you'll be home?"

"I'm not sure. It shouldn't be too late, but you know how Gabby is," she replied, hoping to appease me.

"Okay. Can I call you when I go to bed?"

"Of course! If I miss your call, I'll call you back as soon as I can. Okay sweetie?" She asked as she kissed me goodnight and headed down the steps.

I hoped it would be true this time. Once those two got together, the rest of the world just slipped away.

Not that Michelle didn't deserve nights out. She was a fantastic mother. Our two kids were bright and beautiful, full of smiles and self-esteem, at least as much as two teenagers could be. She spent a lot of her time on homework, housework, and the part time job she had, so she deserved nights out. Then again, because of her workload, that only left Friday and Saturday night for us to see each other. And, with her sister moving back to town, the time grew to be less and less.

Gabby arrived and entered our home, without knocking of course, and proceeded to rush her sister out the door.

"Come on! Alex is waiting in the car. I don't want to make him late!" Gabby said as she grabbed Michelle's coat and helped her put it on. I thought this was rather rude since I figured it was my job to help her on with said jacket.

"He's not coming in to say hi?" I asked, more than a little miffed.

"No. We've got reservations at the House of Blues downtown, and we're running late. The show starts at 7:00 p.m."

"Show?" I asked inquisitively.

"I say show, but it's really just an 80s band playing. It's no big deal, but our reservations are," Gabby said, looking toward Michelle. "So, can we go?"

A minute later, I was waving to the car as it exited the driveway and drove down the street. I closed the door and turned toward the living room trying to figure out what I would do that night. Both kids were tied up in what they were doing, so I resolved myself to making a sandwich and watching SyFy for the remainder of the night.

When midnight hit, I was growing tired so I tried calling Michelle's cell to check to see if she was having fun. After a few rings, I was sent to voicemail, so I left a message saying I was going to bed but that she should call if she had time. This never happened. While waiting for a return call, I fell asleep in my lounge chair, it was so comfy — and that's all she wrote.

It was around 2:00 a.m. when I was startled awake by the sound of keys jingling and being placed in the front door lock. A few seconds later, the door was pushed open and Michelle entered.

"Oh, hi honey," she said, seeing me in the lounge chair. "You didn't have to wait up for me."

"I wasn't, actually," I said amusingly as I yawned. "I was waiting for your phone call, and I fell asleep in my lounge chair."

At that Michelle walked over and kissed me on my forehead.

"Okay. I'm going to take a shower and head to bed," she said as she turned and walked toward the stairs.

"You want some company?" I asked her, smiling, hoping I could *get some.*

"If you don't mind, I just want to shower and go to bed. I'm kind of tired," she replied, and then asked, "Is that okay?"

"Yeah. I suppose," I said grudgingly as I climbed out of the lounge chair. "I'll see you in the bedroom."

Michelle smiled back at me as she climbed the stairs, truly looking tired. It must have been a long night with her sis. I couldn't begrudge her wanting to hit the bed. *It's been a long day*, I thought as I turned off the TV and lights downstairs. Two minutes later I was in bed. She followed five minutes later. When she was all tucked in bed, I rolled over and gave her a kiss goodnight, snuggling up next to her side. I was asleep a minute later.

Sundays were always hectic around the Samstag house. That was the day we cleaned, ran errands, did projects, and had family over for dinner. I usually woke early so I could get a jog in before the onset of these activities. The development we lived in didn't have much in the way of sidewalks, so I usually drove to the local gym. This Sunday was no different. My work brain woke me around 7:00 a.m., so I climbed out of bed, changed, and headed out.

After I finished at the gym, I stopped at the local bagel place and purchased a baker's dozen of various bagels and drove home. When I pulled into the driveway around 9:00 a.m., I could see a flurry of activity already taking place in the old homestead.

"Why do I have to vacuum? It's Brian's turn!" Heather was yelling at Michelle. "He always gets out of chores!"

"He's not getting out of chores, baby. He has a project due at school tomorrow" was the angered reply back. "Can't you just do what I ask for once?"

As I walked up the front steps onto the porch, I was buffeted with this and other spattering of words thrown back and forth between daughter and mother. I almost dreaded entering the house. As soon as I opened the door and Heather saw who I was, she started her rant with me.

"Dad! Brian's getting out of chores again!" were the words thrust upon me, now becoming the referee in this heated battle.

"Time out," I replied, holding up my free hand as I strode to the kitchen to unload myself of the bagel bag. Heather silenced her rant and followed me into the kitchen for bagels and sympathy.

After I had a chance to relax and handed her a bagel, I made my ruling. "You heard your mother. She asked you to vacuum. Just do it . . . I'll make sure your brother gets vacuum duties next week."

"And the following week?" Heather implored.

"And the following week," I answered, hoping this would appease her. It did, or the bagels did, I'm not sure which. Either way, we had peace once again in the Samstag household. And, as the lord and master, I didn't have to execute anyone today.

"Thank you," Michelle muttered as she entered the kitchen for her portion of the morning's treat. "I wish I could do that."

"You're welcome," I replied, and quipped. "And you could, you know. You don't always have to be the good mother."

"It's just seems easier for you," she continued. "I don't have that kind of sway with the kids."

"You just need to hold your ground . . . Hot Stove Rules," I said as I grabbed a bagel for myself and turned toward the toaster.

I've always thought the Hot Stove Rules were simple:

1. If you touch the stove, you will get burned. This means that if someone breaks a rule, the punishment, or talking to, should be immediate.

2. You were warned. Everyone from the time they're little knows what a hot stove can do: it'll burn you. So, it's important to make rules and stick to them.

3. The stove behaves the same every time. Cause = effect. The second touch of the stove is the same as the first.

4. The burn is impersonal. No matter who you are, man or woman, important or dreaded, the rule applies to you.

These were simple rules to follow, unless you can't stick to your guns. I first learned about them when I was in the army in leadership training. The course is taught to lead forces into battle. I ran into the same training when I took a management class in college. It's good to know some things are universally accepted.

"I know," Michelle said as she waited for the toaster to finish our snack. "It just doesn't work for me like it works for you."

I never had a good explanation for this. I'm sure she didn't have these kinds of problems as an assistant manager at the restaurant. But kids, her own kids, are different to a mom, I supposed.

After finishing my bagel and shower, I proceeded to help with the weekly chores around the house. Dusting, cleaning spots that couldn't be reached by the short people I lived with, moving furniture for better vacuuming, and the like.

Once completed, I booted up my laptop as I sat in front of the TV watching whatever was on. I checked my email and worked on bills for a bit until it was time to head to the store for the weekly shopping. I didn't need to go, and really hated shopping, but it was a way I could get out of the house for a bit and be alone — away from the kids — with Michelle.

Having been married for fifteen years, I looked forward to times like these. Times that we could spend together away from her family, my family, our family, and work, just the two of us accomplishing a common, combined effort.

When we arrived home, we put away the groceries, making sure to leave out the ingredients for that evening's meal. Once that was done, Michelle went to work making dinner, and I backed away slowly.

The kitchen was Michelle's home turf, and we all knew it. When she started cooking, you stayed out of her way until specifically asked to perform a task, such as peeling potatoes, stirring gravy, or setting the table. One could lose important limbs if in the wrong place or wrong mood at the wrong time.

Like clockwork, my mom arrived at 5:00 p.m. sharp, ready for dinner. She was our usual guest for Sunday night dinner since Dee had gotten divorced and moved to the east side of Cleveland. She was still single, of course, and we enjoyed getting her out of the house once a week to visit us and the grandkids.

"Meatloaf," I said, answering her question as to the delicacy for this evening's meal.

"Sounds great! Michelle always makes a great meal."

"Just the way her mom taught her," I responded in course.

Mom and I watched TV while we waited for Michelle to finish the side dishes. The kids finished setting the table and distributing the food around the table. And, when told, we made our way into the dining room to take our usual places.

As always, the food was delicious. After eating, I took our plates and other dirty dishes out to the kitchen so the kids could wash them while I entertained Mom, and Michelle relaxed.

Again, this was our normal routine.

When 8:00 p.m. rolled around, Mom announced she had to leave to get some *beauty sleep* prior to work the next day. We laughed and said our goodbyes as I escorted her out and to her car. As I opened the door for her and helped her into her car, she stopped me from closing the door right away.

"Mike, is everything okay with you and Michelle?"

"Yeah. Why do you ask?" I said without hesitation.

"I don't know. Just a feeling I have. Like something is off."

"I think it's your imagination Mom," I stated. "Things have never been better with us. The kids are doing well in school, work is going well, and I'm not traveling as much. Michelle has been making some killer money at work lately. S'all good."

"Okay honey. You know your world better than I do," she said, in true *mom* fashion. She closed her car door but rolled down the window. "But I'm always here for you if you need me."

"Duh! I know that!" I replied as I backed away from the car. "Now get going . . . and have a great week at work! Don't forget to call me when you get home!"

Mom nodded as she rolled up the window and placed the car in reverse. I stayed near the driveway as she finished backing up and put the car in drive. We waved to each other as she drove out of sight.

As I walked back into the house, I pondered her question. Had she seen something I hadn't? I don't like to think I'm a paranoid person, but she really had me freaked. I mean, when your mom, the woman that raised you and is supposed to be all knowing and all seeing, says something like that, maybe you should sit up and take notice.

The whole next day at work I kept thinking about what my mom said. So much so, I had to bounce it off Bill. He was, after all, my best work friend.

"What do you think?" I asked Bill as we sat at lunch.

"Well, it is a little weird how, all of a sudden, your sister-in-law moves back to town and your wife has to go out every weekend. Have you noticed anything unusual about Michelle lately?"

Come to think of it, I had. When she got home the other night, she didn't want to make love and insisted on taking a shower by herself. On one side, it was late at night and she had been dancing and drinking all night. On the other hand, she loved shower sex, whereas I hated it. So for her to turn it down felt weird. And there were many days where she would work all day and be too tired to take a shower before bed. Yet she goes out with her sister and has to take one when she got home. I just didn't know.

Why was I being so paranoid? Dammit Mom, why did you have to get into my head?

"Well, this isn't going to be solved here," Bill stated as he finished his meal. "But you might want to be a little more observant next time Michelle goes out."

I took Bill's advice with a grain of salt. I mean, the dude hadn't had a steady relationship in a while. Not like the fifteen-year one I had been in. Fifteen years of marriage might be blinding me, or it might be making me paranoid. The only way to know for sure was time.

The rest of the week was business as usual — work, home, sleep, work — with kids' homework and some weekly chores thrown in. Boring, but at least I wasn't on the road this week. And, as predicted, on Friday Michelle asked if it was okay if I watched the kids so she could go out with her sister.

"Yeah. I suppose. Not like I had any plans but spending the evening with you."

"I really appreciate it. I know I've been asking you a lot lately. Maybe we can have a quiet night at home tomorrow?" she queried, hoping it would satisfy me. It did.

"Okay. I'd like that. Where are you two going tonight?"

"I'm not sure. And it's three. Gabby mentioned that she and Matt wanted me to join them out."

I thought about this for a minute, and then asked, "Do you think we could double at some point? I mean, the kids *are* old enough to watch themselves. Worst case maybe I can ask my mom to watch them. In fact, I could call her up and see what she's doing tonight!"

"No, don't do that!" Michelle said nervously. "I don't want to impose on your mom on such short notice. You know how pissy she can get."

This was true. My mom, as she had gotten older, had resisted change. Then again, don't most older people?

"I suppose you're right. But can you check with Gabby about next weekend? I wouldn't mind going as a foursome."

"Will do!" she replied as she turned toward the stairs.

An hour or so later, Gabby arrived and, per her usual charming self, waited impatiently for her sister to get ready.

"Michelle! What's taking so long?" Gabby yelled up the stairs.

"I'm saying goodnight to the kids! Hold your horses!" came a shouted reply.

As we stood around, uncomfortably, I decided to pose the question. "So, where are you three off to tonight?"

"We're headed to Concoction downtown."

"I've heard about the club. Didn't it just open?"

"Yep," Gabby replied. "Last week. I can't wait to see it!"

"So, did Michelle mention I'd like it if we could double some time?"

"No . . . she didn't," Gabby responded tentatively. "Let me check with Matt to see when he's available."

"Sounds good," I said, as the footfalls of Michelle coming down the steps notified us she was ready.

I gave her a kiss goodnight as Gabby exited the house, and a moment later, she was gone as well.

To me, the entire conversation seemed off. Gabby had always been short with me from the time I first met her at sixteen, when I first started dating her sister. I knew there was a certain amount of resentment for taking her sister away from her.

I thought about it for a while and then made up my mind.

"Hey Mom!" I said as soon as she answered her phone. "Whatcha doing tonight?"

"Not much. I was just planning on watching some TV. What about you?"

"Well, I need to run some errands tonight. Would you mind coming over to watch the kids?"

"Sure. I don't see why not. What time should I be over?"

I asked her if 8:00 p.m. was okay and told her that I would be home no later than 11:00 p.m. She said that was perfectly fine and she would see me in a bit. Thus, my plan was set. I would head downtown to the new club and see what I could see.

Yeah, this was stalking, my own wife. But I consigned myself to the thought that she and Gabby weren't being totally honest with me. When you've been with someone for fifteen years, you get a feeling for their actions and replies, their wants and dislikes. So much so that you can almost read their minds and answer their questions before they ask them. And things in this case were not right.

When my mom arrived, I showed her the kids were actually alive — some days you just didn't know when they sequestered themselves in their rooms — and I hit the road to drive downtown to Concoction.

To say the place was packed was an understatement. As I drove by, there was a huge group waiting outside for entrance, and I questioned my decision to come down here. I mean, seriously, what was I thinking? What was I hoping to accomplish down here? What did I expect that I'd see? Three people drinking and having fun without me? I didn't know. I *did* know my Spidey sense was tingling, and the only way to satisfy the itch was to see what there was to be seen.

I found a parking spot on the street about two blocks away and walked toward the club. I had the hindsight enough to have changed my cloths before I left the house into a dark outfit. I also messed up my hair as to not look like my usual work self. I was, after all, ex-military and knew what camouflage was. If I didn't do anything dumb, I wouldn't be seen.

As I approached the club, it looked as if the crowd had thinned a bit, and it didn't take long for me to breach the entrance. I knew I had to be stealthy, not having been in this club before, so I stayed at the perimeter, against the walls, as much as I could. On the plus side, it wasn't difficult to stay hidden, owing to the density of the crowd. On the minus, there were maybe a thousand people in here, which would make seeing Michelle and Gabby nearly impossible.

What the hell was I thinking?

As I made my way around, I saw where the restrooms and bars were and figured if I could stay within sight of the main bar and girls' restroom, but still stay hidden, I could do this. A few minutes later, I found a decent, not perfect, spot close to the main bar. It was slightly hidden by a building column, so if I stayed between the column and the wall, I should be well hidden.

I stayed in this spot for probably fifteen or twenty minutes before I saw Gabby walking to the restroom. Gabby was known to have a historically weak bladder and, because of her small frame, couldn't hold her liquor. I figured she'd be pissing or puking before anyone else.

When Gabby exited the restroom, I made sure I followed her visually, keeping my distance, until I saw where she was going. She walked over to a small standing-room-only table set off to one side of the dance floor where three other people were standing. I could make out that one of them was Michelle, but I couldn't see who the other two were. All I could make out was that they were guys.

As Gabby reached the table, she made a beeline for one of the gents and kissed him on his cheek. I assumed this was her boyfriend Matt. She then turned and looked like she was conversing with the group for a moment, and then she and Matt headed to the dance floor. After they left, I could see Michelle talking to the guy standing who, I would say, was a little too close to my wife. I watched for a few minutes as they talked and laughed, and drank their drinks, seeming to just enjoy the club.

It hit me at this moment that I felt kind of stupid standing there, lurking in the shadows, watching two people talk. I mean, it was her night out with her sister, and who was I to be a voyeur on their fun? I thought I should probably leave and was ready to turn and go when I saw it. Something I never expected.

I saw Michelle kiss the guy.

This was not a simple peck on the cheek or a friendly gesture between two friends. This was a full on we're-dating-and-like-each-other kiss on the lips, heads-turned-want-to-get-physical, emotional kiss, a kiss two people share that have kissed before, numerous times.

For a moment I just stood there, watching. Not knowing what to do or how to proceed. Thoughts running through my head like gazelles. Should I go over and yank them apart? Should I break his face? Should I slap her? Should I cause a scene to embarrass them? Should I smash a bottle on his head and take back what was mine?

All these thoughts just bouncing around like ping pong balls while I stood there, stiff, angry, in disbelief, and yet calm. All these thoughts making me want to take action, but my body subconsciously holding back. That's when I made my move, toward the door.

Yeah, call me a pussy or whatever you want. As a man, this guy just severed a piece of my masculinity, threw it on the ground, and stepped on it. What the hell was I thinking? Well, I'll tell you. Violence never solves anything. It just creates more problems. I could, with my years of military experience, probably take this guy apart. But what would it solve? What would Michelle think? Would she consider me the hero?

Survey says no.

My body was the smart one here. It told me *you have kids at home along with a career, a house, and a car.* All could be taken away in moments with a rash decision, so I figured it would be best to leave these things to calmer emotions and quieter surroundings.

Before I knew it, I was back in my car and driving home.

"Did you get all your errands run honey?" my mom asked as I entered the house around 11:00 p.m.

"Yeah Mom," I replied, or think I replied. "Thanks for staying with the kids."

"My pleasure, sweetie. They never really came out of their rooms. Brian is playing video games, and Heather is on the phone with one of her friends."

My mom must have sensed something was wrong because she asked, "Is everything okay Mike? You look pale."

"Yeah, I'm fine. I just need some sleep I guess. It's been . . . a long day."

At that prompt, she grabbed her things and turned toward the door.

"Okay," she started, knowing something was off. She looked at me with what was probably the most serious face I've ever seen on her. "But if you need me for anything, I'm just a phone call away."

She approached me, hugged me hard, and kissed me on my cheek. I took this opportunity to ask her. "Any plans tomorrow night?"

"No. Why? Do you need me to watch the kids again?"

Was this lady psychic? Of course she was; she was my mom.

"Yeah . . . maybe. If you don't mind, that is? About 5:00 p.m. ok?"

"It would be my pleasure," she said as she left the doorway. "See you tomorrow at 5:00, honey."

A minute later, she was gone and on her way home. I made my way over to my lounge chair and sat for a minute, wondering where we go from here. I was numb all over as a thousand thoughts filled my head, but not one coherent. So there I stayed, for a bit, just waiting.

Brian and Heather had come downstairs in turn to say goodnight. I'm pretty sure I answered them and gave them kisses. And the TV was on, so at some point I had turned it on, or maybe my mom had, not sure who. It was late night comedy flashing skits of this and that, and I had no idea where one ended and the next began. Not laughing at one, there I sat, in the relative dark, thinking but not thinking.

It was around 2:00 a.m. when I heard the car approach and pull into the driveway. A car door opened and some chatter was uttered back and forth before the door closed and I heard footfalls on the porch. Then I heard the jingling of keys and the sound of a lock being turned.

I'm not sure when I had made the decision to not confront Michelle as soon as she walked in the door, but my mind was made up. Tomorrow would be better. When we were both rested and could talk like adults.

"Oh . . . hi," she said as she entered the house, closing and locking the door behind her. "What are you doing up?"

"I . . . I couldn't sleep" was all I could say back. This was true, I guess.

"Okay. I'm kind of cold. I'm going to take a shower. Want to join me?"

It took me a second or two to look up, kind of stunned and confused from the question. I looked at her with this expression on my face, I'm sure, as I uttered, "No thanks."

"Okay sweetie," she said as she turned and climbed the steps. About halfway up the steps, she stopped to look back at me. "Are you feeling okay? You're not getting sick, are you?"

"No," I uttered. "I'll be up in a little bit."

Michelle turned and continued her climb, and a minute or two later, I heard the shower start.

I sat there for a while longer, stunned. How was it possible for the woman you love to be kissing a guy in a club a few hours ago and now come home and ask me for intimate contact? Was this supposed to throw me off the track of her betrayal or did she really want to make love to me? Did he make her hot and horny and she felt she could use me to quench that thirst? Who could tell the thoughts of another? All I knew was I could not and would not get close to her tonight.

I waited probably an hour after the shower shut off before I shut down the lights, made sure the house was locked, and walked upstairs to our bedroom. I climbed into my side of the bed and slept on the edge as far as I could away from Michelle. It didn't take long to fall asleep, actually. My mind was spent.

In the morning, which was about three hours later, I woke before Michelle, changed into exercise gear, and went to the gym thinking maybe some metal music and burning of calories would help me sort out what I would say that day. And, as expected, it did. I was probably down to a hundred or so thoughts jumping around in my brain.

When I arrived home, Michelle was cooking breakfast for the family. This was something the kids would exit their rooms for. As I walked by, both were sitting at the table, Heather working on some sort of craft and Brian was playing a handheld video game.

"Hi Dad!" they both said as I waved.

"Good morning guys!" I replied as I waved in return and walked toward the stairs and a shower. As I passed her, I said hi but didn't kiss her like I normally did when greeting her.

When I came downstairs, Michelle was sitting at the table by herself reading a book. The kids, having devoured their food, had left for their exploits of the day. I figured this would be a good time to see when she was available to talk.

"Hey," I said in a soft voice as to not startle her while she read.

"Oh hey!" she said as she looked up from her book. "How was the gym?"

"Good," I responded and continued, "Hey, can we talk?"

She put down her book, marking the page she was reading. "Sure. What's up?"

"Can we have a date night tonight?"

She thought about it for a moment, and then said, "Sure. What were your thoughts?"

"I was thinking maybe just dinner out, if that's cool?"

"That's fine. Do you need me to ask Gabby to watch the kids?"

"No, I already talked to Mom. She'll be here around 5:00 p.m."

"Sounds good," she said, and asked, "Do you want some breakfast?"

"Not right now," I said, turning toward the living room. "I'm going to relax and watch some TV."

Soon it was 4:30 p.m.: time to spruce up for dinner. My mom arrived right at 5:00 p.m. as promised, we said goodbye to the kids, and hit the door.

"Where would you like to go?" I asked, jokingly adding, "Any place besides Taco Bell."

Michelle smiled and replied, "Mexican does sound good. What about El Toro? It just opened, and I heard it's good."

"Sounds good to me!" I said, put the car in drive, and drove to the mall.

Like the afternoon, I tried to keep calm and wait until we got to the restaurant to talk. You might be wondering why, at this point. Why didn't I just confront her right away? It's because calmer heads always prevail. I have learned over my many years of project management experience that anyone can jump the gun and let their emotions rule, but it usually turns out shitty. Work the problem; don't let the problem work you.

We arrived and were seated at a table for two. Nice and cozy, in the middle of the restaurant. After we ordered beers and looked over the menu, we had some small talk about the kids and our work weeks. Nothing major happened to either of us, which was good. Eventually the waiter came back, and we placed our food orders. I chose the seafood enchiladas, my usual choice at a Mexican restaurant. Michelle chose the fajitas, her typical as well.

When the meals arrived, we ate, and sat enjoying the surroundings. It was a nice place and was pretty packed being 6:00 p.m. on a Saturday. Perfect for what I had in mind. When the waiter came to pick up our plates, he asked if we wanted desert, which neither of us did considering the amount of food we just ingested.

"I will take another beer, though," I told the waiter. "Would you like one Michelle?"

She was surprised. "No . . . I'm alright. You don't want to get going?"

"After this beer," I replied and waited for the waiter to return with my Michelob Light.

I took a drink and started my inquest about the previous night. "So, did you have fun last night?"

Michelle looked at me, questioning my inquiry. "Yeah, it was alright. Concoction was fun. Gabby and Matt are cute together."

"So, was it just you guys last night?"

"Yeah . . . why do you ask?"

"I just wondered if there was anybody else that met you there."

"That seems like a weird question," she said, avoiding my question.

"Why? I just wondered if maybe you guys met up with another group of people. Gabby does know a lot of people."

"No. It was just us," she stated indignantly.

"So, there was no one else?"

"No, there was no one else!"

"You weren't there with another guy?"

"Why the hell would you ask *that* question? You don't trust me?" she asked, almost screaming at me.

"Calm down. We're in a restaurant," I said, pointing around the restaurant with my eyes.

In a lowered but angry voice she said, "I'm just hurt by the question. Don't you trust me?"

"Let's say I did, up until last night," I said back to her with a smirk on my face.

"What's that supposed to mean?" she said, raising her voice once again. I, again, pointed around the restaurant with my eyes.

You might be wondering, at this point, why I would bring Michelle to a crowded restaurant to question her about her activities. There were several reasons, actually, but the biggest was I was just so hurt I figured there was less of a chance I would lose my shit.

And you might be saying to yourself *But, dude, you love her. Why are you being such a dick*? Well, if you've never been in this situation, don't judge me. After fifteen years of marriage, she stepped in the shit, and it was time for me to call her on it. If she had been honest with me to say she had met someone I would have gone easy on her.

Yeah, dick mode activated.

"Concoction is a cool club. It sure was packed last night," I stated as I looked straight into her eyes. Her face went white.

"Yeah, Mom came over and watched the kids for a bit. Figured I'd see what the club was about," I said while gritting my teeth. "I saw . . . a lot."

Tears came to her eyes. I'm not sure if this was because she was actually emotionally affected by this realization, or if she knew I was a sucker for a sobbing woman. I was guessing the latter but still thinking it might be the former.

"Oh. What did you see?" she sniffled.

"I saw you making out with another guy."

She was about to say something, but I cut her off. "I mean, seriously Michelle! What were you thinking? Did you think I wouldn't find out?"

"I'm . . . I'm . . . sorry," she said as the tears started full on.

"Who is he?"

"He's a friend of Matt's."

I chose to broach the subject, even though I was afraid of what I might learn. "So, did you sleep—"

"No! I swear!" she blurted before I had a chance to ask my question. "I've only seen him a few times."

"And yet, you were making out with him . . . in a club . . . in a public place."

"I know," she said, sobbing. "I didn't mean for it to happen. It just . . . did."

I thought about this for a minute and said, "So, no more trips out with your sister?"

She looked at me for a minute, pondering the question, but eventually nodded in agreement.

"And I think we need to go to counseling . . . agreed?"

Again, she nodded. And, more so, I believed her.

"I'm going to run to the restroom, okay?" Michelle asked, and I nodded, knowing that our question and answer session was over. As soon as she got up and left, the waiter came over with our check. I handed him my credit card, not even looking at the bill, and he walked away to ring us up.

I must admit, the waiter was really cool about all this. I'm not sure if he'd seen all this before or been through it himself, but during the entire conversation, he stayed away until he noticed me looking for him. And, let's just say, he was well compensated for being so discreet.

A few minutes later she was back from the restroom, and we headed for home. I felt like a real asshole on the ride home, and I should have. I just embarrassed the woman I love in a public place. Some will say she deserved it and she got off easy, whereas some will say I was a total bastard. Well, both feelings were in me that night.

When we got home, we thanked my mom for watching the kids. And, with her smile, I knew she knew things were better, at least with me. Michelle, on the other hand, quickly said goodnight to her and went to bed.

Once my mom was gone and the Samstag house was secure, I too went toward the bedroom, making sure to tell the kids Mom and Dad were headed to bed and said goodnight.

When I entered the bedroom, she was there, on the edge of the bed, sitting waiting for me. As soon as she saw me, she started crying again. I did, truly, feel bad for her and everything she'd been through in the last few hours.

I closed the bedroom door, walked over to her, and hugged her. She continued to sob into my chest for a few minutes before I moved away to grab some tissues for her. After she dried her eyes and blew her nose, I hugged her again, not wanting to let go, never wanting to let her go again.

It was a little awkward, and a little rough, but we made love that night, twice. Angry sex. It was less kissing than we'd normally do. I didn't want to kiss her. I used the emotions of hurt and love to try to forget about all, just for a little while.

The next day we were back to our normal routine. The routine of marriage: homework, cleaning, work, paying bills, and family. Things that helped us hide what we were truly feeling, trying to bring consistency back into our lives.

The following week, we found a counselor and went for a few sessions until we both felt we didn't need to go anymore. Not because we were fixed by any stretch of the imagination. We were broken, and I think we both knew it. And we had been for a while. It just took one of us *slipping* to realize where we were, who we were, and what we really wanted.

We stayed together, for the kids, a couple years more. Not for love, but for routine. That is, until I met you, and realized there could be more to life than routine.

Diary: September 19

It's been one year since I lost you, Amy. One year. Where has the time gone?

All the memories and pain seem like glimpses through a window. I remember them. I learned from them.

I'm making this one short and sweet. I think I've said all I've had to say. And there's so much to do before tomorrow. People to contact and places to see. And one more trip to visit you.

I will see you soon, my love.

CHAPTER

12

I remember the day I lost you, the year I lost you.

It was the start of our eleventh year together, and I thought we were mostly happy. We had gone on a couple trips, saw a few concerts, and were generally having fun when we could. It was a good life, mostly.

Even though we were having fun, the year had been tough on you. You worked hard at your work, and I knew it. Work had offered you a well-deserved promotion, and I was very proud of you. Unfortunately, with the new job came new responsibilities and even harder work.

I, on the other hand, was actually working less. Work was steady, and I had three competent people working for me, which meant managing them was pretty simple. I was working my forty but had a lot of free time. You, well, not so much.

As your free time became less and my free time became more, I tried to resolve it by coming up with hobbies to fill my time.

First I tried working out. I already worked out a few days a week, but I ramped it up to an hour or two five to six days a week right after work. This too ate up a good deal of time, and less on money, but my body couldn't take the stress. I was always tired when you got home, and I often fell asleep in my lounge chair and missed the time you were home.

Next I tried movies, being somewhat a movie buff. But after a while, I realized seeing movies ate up way too much time. I also tried reading, but that was almost worse than working out, making my brain tired and forcing me to fall asleep early.

Not having come up with a good way to fill my time, I became despondent. In the past I always had you, Jim, or Bill to do things with, but with you being busy, Jim being gone, and Bill having moved away, I had no one to hang around with.

I then tried golf. There were several guys at work, including my boss, who golfed and often left work, when it was slow, to play. So I figured, why not join in? After all, playing golf with my boss could only lead to a better camaraderie and, dare I say, a raise.

Like anything else I do, I jumped in with both feet. I bought a cheap set of clubs and started out going to a driving range twice a week and playing nine holes once to twice a week. For a beginner I didn't do too badly, I guess. I quickly surpassed a few of the guys in the office that had been playing for a while, getting my games down to below fifty.

This was all well and good and usually ate up a good amount of time — and money — but there were rainy days and snowy days that got in the way a lot. This was Cleveland, after all, where we went from sunshine to rain to snow to sunshine in a four day time span.

Of course, during these inclement weather days, I was back to being bored. Until one day while traveling home on a rainy day, I passed by a new bar that had just opened, called Showcase. It was in the middle of a small shopping plaza surrounded by fast food places, cell phone stores, and the like. To me, with the surrounding stores, it seemed out of place. But it looked really cool from the outside, so I stopped to see what I could see.

As I walked in the door, I noticed something right away: it didn't have the feel of a normal bar. It was darkly illuminated, like a movie theater right before the start of the main feature and had several big screen televisions around the bar playing movies. It just happened that the current movie playing was *The Shining*, one of my all-time favorites.

"Hi! What can I get you?" came a call from the beautiful blonde bartender, who barely looked old enough to drink, let alone serve them.

"Just checking the place out," I replied, trying to figure out if I wanted to stay.

"Okay. My name is Steph. Let me know if I can help you," she said, and then moved down the bar to serve a patron.

Since it was raining, and a few hours before you got out of work, I stayed to have a drink. I sat down at one of the bar stools near the entrance and waited for Steph to finish serving a gentleman at the other end of the bar. He appeared to be the only other person in the place.

"So, you decided to stay?" Steph said as she approached. "What can I get you?"

"Do you have Angry Orchard?"

"Bottle or tap?" came the reply.

"Tap is fine," I said, not wanting to be a bother.

"Short or tall?" Steph asked as she stood in front of me.

"Short is fine. Not sure how long I'll be staying."

"Short it is," Steph said as she walked to the tap to pour my beer. As she walked back, I struck up a conversation.

"How long has this place been here? I haven't noticed it before."

"About six months," she said as she adjusted some glasses.

"Oh. I haven't seen it before. Do you get a lot of business?" I asked, noticeably looking around the place.

"Oh sure," Steph said as she placed her hands on the bar in front of me, highlighting her cleavage. "We're a lot busier at night. Days are kind of like this."

"Gotcha," I said as I sipped my beer. As she stood there, I could see why they hired her. She was quite stunning. Steph was well formed with beautiful green eyes and a killer smile. Frankly, I was surprised there weren't more patrons in here.

Steph left a few seconds later to head back down the bar, so I turned and started watching the movie. It was up to the part where Jack Nicholson was talking to the ghost bartender, trying to convince him to kill his wife.

About thirty minutes later, the gentleman sitting at the end of the bar got up, paid his tab, and left. This left me as the sole drinker in the establishment. But I was enjoying the movie and drink, so I didn't let it bother me.

A few minutes later, I heard a movement to my right which made me jump. I was so engrossed in the movie that I didn't see Steph come up and sit next to me on the patron side of the bar.

"Oh, sorry . . . didn't mean to startle you," Steph said, noticing my shock. "I hope it's okay if I sit here next to you. It can get a little lonely during the day here."

"No, I'm totally fine with it. I was just watching the movie a little too . . . intensely."

Steph laughed at this. "Oh, I understand. It's one of my favorites."

"Mine too. I'm a huge Stephen King fan."

"So am I!" said Steph, turning her chair toward mine. "I've read almost all his books."

"Cool! So have I," I retorted, turning my chair toward hers. "What's your favorite?"

"It would have to be *Pet Cemetery* . . . or *It*."

"Scary . . . mine too!" I said, laughing a little. "Great minds, I guess. By the way, I'm Mike."

I stuck out my hand and we shook, the way polite people do.

"It's nice to meet you Mike!" she said, smiling, and asked jokingly, "So what brings you in here this lovely day?"

"Well, mostly the rain. I was going to go golfing but . . . Cleveland," I jested.

"Ah . . . understandable."

"Well, that and waiting for my girlfriend to get out of work," I continued, mentioning our relationship so she wouldn't get the wrong impression.

"Oh, do you two have plans tonight?"

"No . . . not really," I answered. "Amy works later than I do most days, so I find ways to fill my time. The latest is golf."

"I see. Is that what you do for fun?"

"Eh. I do a lot of things for fun. This is just the latest hobby," I said, taking another drink. "What about you?"

"I don't have a lot of *hobby* time. My husband works second shift so we trade baby duty daily."

"Oh? How many kids do you have?"

"Just one," Steph replied.

I was actually relieved that Steph mentioned the husband and baby, probably for the same reason I mentioned you. Even though this girl was young enough to be my daughter, it didn't stop her from having *daddy issues* or wanting an older *sugar daddy*.

Steph and I continued our conversation for probably another hour, and then she moved to the other side of the bar when new customers came in. We discussed life, kids, spouses, movies, and a dozen other topics. And it was weird, because the conversation came easy. It was like I had known her my entire life.

Eventually, I received a text from you saying you were getting ready to leave work and asking what I was up to. And I told you where I was and that I would be leaving shortly to meet you at home.

"Well, I need to cash out Steph," I said as I pulled out my wallet. "It was nice meeting you."

As Steph took my credit card she said, "It was nice meeting you too Mike!"

She walked to the register, ran my card, and brought over the receipt to sign. Of course I gave her a healthy tip. She was "good people", as my mom put it, and "you always did good toward good people."

As I got ready to leave, Steph said, "Thanks! And don't be a stranger . . . good people are hard to find."

When I got home that night, I arrived a couple minutes before you, so I was able to grab you a frosted glass from the freezer along with your favorite ale. Having a beer waiting always made you happy when you walked in the door.

As we sat down to eat dinner, something you had picked us up from a local restaurant, we talked about our days. You told me of all the new procedures you were putting in place and how the president of the company liked what you had done. I, in turn, talked about my day and of meeting

Steph, making sure I mentioned her husband and child so you wouldn't get nervous I was doing something behind your back.

It was about three days later, on Friday, when rain struck again and I couldn't golf. Without anything better in mind to do and not wanting to go home yet, I chose to head back to Showcase. As before, Steph was working and the place was dead, so we had another nice conversation. The more we talked, the more I thought it strange that we had so much in common, even though there was a good twenty year age difference. Again, as soon as I got your text, I wrapped things up and got ready to go home to be with you.

As before, I told you about being screwed by Mother Nature and hanging at Showcase talking with Steph.

"Well it sounds like you had fun anyway," you said with a little anger in your voice.

"You don't mind me hanging there, do you?"

"I guess not," you replied and appeared to calm a little. "Guess I'm just not happy that you get to leave work earlier than me on a Friday."

I hugged and kissed you and asked, "But, on the plus side, it *is* Friday . . . what would you like to do tonight?"

"I'm a little tired. Can we just get pizza and watch movies?" you asked.

"Sure thing, my love," I replied as I picked up the phone to get the night, and pizza, under way.

That weekend came, and went, like they always did. We did go out dancing that Saturday night. And it was nice to see a smile on your face again. Sunday, we spent the early part of the day together and went out for a hike, but when the afternoon hit, you hopped on your computer to try to get a head start on some paperwork due the next day.

The next few weeks were like this. During the week, I was golfing or hanging at the bar with Steph, while you were working yourself to death. Every night you were coming home a little more drained and unhappy. I felt bad for you. I didn't know how to make your life easier except to keep my distance to allow you to work. It sounds bad to say it like that, but there was little I could do when you locked yourself away in your office.

As the weeks went by, my friendship with Steph grew. Sometimes she'd finish her shift early, and we'd hang out at her house with her husband Adam and her son until you got out of work. I knew you didn't like this much, but it's not like we were there alone. And somewhere along the way, Steph had become one of my best friends, even calling me her BFF.

Life is crazy like that sometimes. You never really know when or how but life steers you toward people sometimes. It had, after all, steered me toward you. And I felt like I was missing something in my life since Jim passed. Something Steph had brought back. A bond with someone you can share secrets with, besides your significant other.

And I figured if it was okay to have a best male friend, why not a best female friend?

Looking back on it, though, I believe this was when we started growing apart. Not sure if it was your job or my friendship with Steph, but we started wanting different things out of life.

"I think I want to use some of my vacation for Cape Cod this year," you told me as we were having dinner one night.

"But we just went last year. Why do you want to go again?"

"Because I need a break from work, and I miss the Cape."

"But I was hoping we could go somewhere else, like San Francisco or Los Angeles. You've never been to either one of those cities."

"I know, but what am I going to see there that I haven't seen in other big cities?"

"We won't know until we go."

"Can we do that later then? I really want to go to the Cape."

I thought about it for a few minutes, and then replied something I probably shouldn't have. "Is there anyone else you could go with? I really don't want to use my vacation time for the Cape again."

"Seriously?" you retorted angrily. "You really want me to go with someone else?"

"No," I replied, choosing my words more carefully. "I don't really want you to go with someone else. But we just went! Why can't we go somewhere else, and go to the Cape next year?"

At this you went into your office for a bit. I heard some shuffling of your papers, and then it got quiet and you came back out into the living room.

"What if I just planned a long weekend there? Maybe I can find a cottage that will rent just for the weekend. That way you wouldn't have to use so much vacation."

I waited a minute, considering it before I replied, "I suppose that would be okay. But can we plan a trip someplace else first?"

"I'll look," you said, although I didn't think that you would. Not because you wouldn't like a trip anyplace else, but because you were mad at me for not agreeing to Cape Cod right away.

"Thank you!" I said and came over to hug you. You hugged back, reluctantly, and I knew you were pissed.

I went to bed that night angry. Angry that you wouldn't really hug me back, angry that you wanted to go back to the Cape instead of going someplace new and exciting, angry that your job was putting so much pressure on you and messing with our lives, angry that your job and priorities meant more to you than I meant.

I've heard you should never go to sleep angry, but that's all I had at the moment.

As the alarm sounded the next morning and I started to wake, I could feel that I had calmed down. Maybe because I knew you'd enter the room in a minute to climb into bed next to me to kiss me, the start of our normal weekday routine. You did, kissing my shoulder and saying good morning — the only part of the morning I did like. After a minute or two, you rose and left the room, and I continued the routine.

I turned around on the bed, letting my legs dangle, and started my leg lifts. This helped to stretch out my back so my sciatic nerve didn't hurt. After one hundred of those, I got out of bed, turned on the bedroom light, and proceeded to make the bed. Once I topped off the bed with decorative pillows and stuffed animals, our children, I picked out my clothes for the day and laid them out on the bed.

Next, I went out to the kitchen so I could pour myself, and you, coffee in our to-go cups, making sure to crud up mine with sugar and cream. You took yours black, of course. After performing forty pushups, I shaved, showered, and trimmed like every other civilized man. Cologne and deodorant were then added so I did not offend, and I got dressed.

My total prep time was about an hour, a fact that I was very proud of. Compared to your two-and-half hour process, which I knew included secrets that are only talked about in dark alleys and women's lounges, it felt like the blink of an eye.

As I grabbed my laptop bag and coffee, I headed for the door making sure to stop by your bathroom to say goodbye and give you a kiss.

"Sweetie, I'm leaving," I announced as I poked my head into your sanctuary.

"Oh," you replied as if I startled you. "Okay . . . I'll be out in a minute."

I waited, and as promised you came out to kiss me.

As you released me from your hug, you said, "If I get a minute today, I'll look into the Cape trip. Is there any week you aren't available?"

"Nope. I'm wide open," I stated as I turned to leave, but added, "Sweetie, can you also look into where you'd want to go on the west coast?"

I could see a slight change in your face, as if you figured I would have forgotten the conversation from the night before, which of course I hadn't. I narrowed my eyes so you could see I knew what you were thinking.

"I'm serious. I would like to go to San Francisco or someplace like that. Can you please look?"

"Okay, I'll look," you said as you started back toward the bathroom. "Hope you have a good day! I love you!"

"I love you too!" I replied as I exited the apartment.

Somehow, in the back of my mind, I knew that you'd procrastinate on my wishes and research yours. It made me mad because I felt I was being brushed off again, making me feel like I didn't come first in your life. But what was I to do? You were important to me, and traveling was trivial. All I could do was hope you'd ease up and think about my request.

I was still pissed, though.

That night, after work, I sent Steph a text asking if she was working. She replied that she wasn't and I was welcome over if I wanted to stop by her house, so I did.

As I got there, I could see there was only one car in the driveway. I thought it odd but not out of the ordinary. Adam or Steph probably just ran to the store and would be right back. So I shut off my car, walked to the front door, and rang the bell. A minute later Steph answered the door.

"Hey, you made it! Come in!" she said, opening the door for me. I, of course, entered.

"Is Adam here?" I asked, broaching the subject.

"No, he's at his brother's house. He'll be home later."

"Is he cool with me being here? I don't want to cause any friction."

Steph looked at me like I was crazy for asking. "Of course! I just hung up with him. He said to say hi and hopefully he'd be home before you left. Care for a drink?"

Steph and I sat there and talked about life, while her son Ryan ran around like a maniac. He was two, almost three, after all. I think I had two drinks under my belt before you texted to tell me you were on your way home.

"Well, I better go . . . too bad Adam didn't make it home!"

"He'll be disappointed that he missed you!" Steph said as she showed me to the door. "He thinks you're a great guy."

"That's only because I am," I joked as I gave Steph a hug and headed home to you. I only wished you were as pleased to see me when I got there.

"So, you went over to her house and Adam wasn't there?" you asked, and then stated. "I'm not comfortable with this."

"Why not? She's just a friend . . . you know that, right?"

"But you were alone with her . . . in her house. Why did you think I'd be okay with that?"

"Well, she wasn't alone to start. Ryan her son was there," I said, feeling like I was on feeble ground. "And Adam was on his way home."

You thought about this for a minute, and then said, "I'm still not comfortable with this, any of this."

"Not sure why you're not comfortable! She's like my best friend!" I replied. You looked at me like I had just slapped you.

"I thought I was your best friend?" you said, and I knew I had misspoken.

"You *are* my best friend! I meant she's a *great* friend! She calls me her BFF," I said, trying to make things right. "Seriously . . . I don't mean to compare the two of you!"

You just glared at me for a minute and then turned and went to your office. I knew I had stepped on my dick by going over there without your permission. But I was an adult, after all. We were in a committed relationship, and I was really surprised you didn't trust me. Me! Someone you'd been with for almost twelve years! Someone you had lived with and made love to. Someone you had been there for during rough times. I truly felt let down.

I approached the office and popped my head through the doorway. "Listen . . . Amy. I'm sorry. I promise not to go back there again unless you say it's okay. Cool?"

You thought about it for a minute and replied, "I mean, I've never even met her. I think I need to meet her before you go back again. I *need* to feel comfortable about her."

"I understand. I'll see if there's someday the two of us can meet up with Steph and Adam. Cool?"

At that you stood up and came over to me for a hug, locking your leg around the back of mine. I truly was locked in forever.

The opportunity for you to meet Steph and Adam came about a week later. I had mentioned to Steph that you wanted to meet them, so Steph told me that she and Adam were having a family birthday party for Ryan the next weekend on Sunday and we were more than welcome to attend. And as it turned out, we didn't have any plans that day.

I do love it when a plan comes together by itself.

"Hey! Glad you could make it!" Steph said as she opened the door. "Come on in!"

As soon as we got in the doorway, Steph grabbed you and hugged you. That was her way. I saw you hug back provisionally. When Steph released you, she and I hugged, officially welcoming us to their house.

It was funny because I could tell right away you didn't like Steph. I'm not sure if it was the best friend thing, me going to her house when her husband wasn't home, or just something chemical. But there was definitely friction in the ether.

Steph showed us in and introduced us to her family and, of course, the birthday boy. You were never really a kid person, but in this case, you didn't let it show. I was happy that it seemed like you were accepting the hospitality and friendship being shown. Adam, who had been cooking out back, made his way in and said hi to both of us by shaking my hand and giving you a hug.

We stayed at Steph's for about an hour before I could tell you'd had enough. And not wanting to cause you any grief, I said my goodbyes and we drove home. The whole time we were driving home, you were stewing for no apparent reason at all. I was afraid to broach the subject, but I had to know. I chose to start by breaking the ice.

"So, did you have fun?" I asked, already knowing the answer.

"Not really."

"No? I thought the food was good. And there was cake . . . you had some cake."

I knew you knew I was trying to make you open up, but I also knew that you wouldn't be happy until you got whatever you were angry about off your chest.

"What's wrong?"

"You didn't tell me she was so pretty."

"Sorry . . . is that an issue?"

You just looked at me then and stated, "Yes . . . it's an issue. Of course it's an issue."

"Not sure I understand why it's an issue! I don't see her as pretty . . . I see her as a friend," I tried to say, but you didn't see it the way I saw it.

"Are you sure that's all you think about her?"

"Of *course* that's all I think about her! Why do you keep bringing this up?"

"Because I think you're attracted to her."

"What? How do you get *that* impression?" I scoffed.

"Because of the way you were fawning all over her," you said, turning away from me.

"I was by your side the entire time! What the fuck are you talking about?" I cried.

You then shot a look at me I'd never seen before — one of hurt and hate.

"Don't yell at me," you said, and then turned back toward the passenger window.

I calmed myself and replied, "I'm sorry for yelling. But, seriously, I didn't do anything. I was with you the entire time. I don't see how you think I'm attracted to her."

You sat there for a moment, and I could tell you were contemplating something. Without turning back toward me you said, "You need to stop seeing her."

"Honey, I'm not seeing her! I'm friends with her. There's a difference. A *huge* difference."

You were silent the rest of the way home. Then again, so was I. I was offended that you'd think there was something going on when you knew, you *knew*, I was in love with you. Yes, Steph and I had amiability with each other. We were friends, after all. But that was it. That was the extent in my eyes.

When we arrived home, you walked into your office to change into something more comfortable and I went to our bedroom to do the same.

Afterward, I headed to my lounge chair and turned on the TV to clear my head. About an hour later, you came out of your office and sat on the couch. You had calmed down some, and I knew you wanted to talk more, so I turned down the TV and faced you.

"What's up sweetie?"

"I . . . I just feel like you spend more time with Steph than you do with me."

"Honey . . . I'm here with you every night. I'm here with you every weekend. You are the one I love and want to spend my life with."

"Then why won't you end your friendship with Steph?"

"Because she's a friend . . . and I feel that's a shitty thing to do to a friend. I just don't understand your resentment of her."

You thought about it for a minute, and then said, "Because . . . it feels like you're having an affair with her."

At first I was floored and didn't know what to say. She thought I was having an affair? How the hell did she get that impression? So, I had spent time with her. So what? That's a far cry from having an affair. I thought about it for a minute and said my peace.

"I'm not having an affair. We are only friends . . . and I don't want to give her up as a friend. I've lost . . . I've lost too many people in my life to start kicking them to the curb."

At that you stood up and paced around the living room. I watched you for a bit, but then put my head in my hands and shook my head. I knew we were at an impasse and neither one of us was willing to concede.

"I think we should see a counselor," I heard you say, so I raised my head and looked at you, stunned.

"Really? You think this is so bad that we need to see a counselor?"

"I don't see any other way," you said. "Maybe someone impartial can help us sort this out."

"But, she's just a friend! Who has a husband and child! Why can't you understand my feelings?"

"But I can't help *my* feelings! Why can't you understand mine?"

I thought about it for a minute and agreed. "You're right . . . maybe we do need a counselor."

After all, maybe a counselor would help you understand that I wasn't attracted to Steph, that I wasn't attracted to anyone except you! And maybe a counselor would help me understand why you felt this way. To me, the whole thing was crazy. But if it would help reconcile this, I was willing.

The next day you found a counselor not too far from our place and asked if the following Tuesday was okay with me. All I could think was the sooner we got this resolved, the better.

Our first session was pretty much just getting used to the counselor. Her name was Dorothy, and she had been counseling married couples for ten years. We started out by just talking about our lives growing up and how long we had been together. I think we were both a little hesitant about opening up to a stranger, but at least it was a start. When the session finished, we made an appointment to come back the next Tuesday.

As part of trying to make things work, I made the decision not to hang out with Steph. I felt bad for putting our friendship on hold, but after talking to Steph about it, she understood. She told me she really did like you and hoped we could work things out.

You and I spent the weekend together, going for a hike Saturday morning and dinner Saturday night. I made reservations at your favorite steakhouse where we drank wine, laughed, and had a great time together. That night when we got home, we made love and held each other until we fell asleep, just two people in love.

The following Tuesday session with Dorothy we opened the flood gates. We did discuss what we thought the issues were with the relationship, and I was kind of surprised myself by bringing up your work and how I felt you didn't have time for me. I think this surprised and offended you. Work to you was work, a necessity in life. To me, it was always just a means to an end. Even though I had a good career, at the end of the day, it was just a paycheck.

While we talked, I got the impression that Dorothy was on your side of the Steph issue, asking me several times why I needed to keep the friendship with her.

"In our lives I believe we meet only so many friends that are true friends . . . friends that you click with, and have fun with," I said, and added, "Even though I've only known Steph for a short while, she is one of those friends to me."

"But isn't Amy more important to you than Steph?" Dorothy asked.

"Of course she's more important! I love her with all my heart. But Steph is just a friend. A good friend. And I don't think I should have to drop her as a friend because Amy is jealous of her. If she were a guy, this wouldn't be an issue, would it?"

You didn't respond to this, and I knew you felt that was true. If Steph were a guy, we wouldn't be sitting here. The more I thought about that fact, the more upset I got.

"I was raised by my mom and sister and have always had both male and female friends. Why can't you just get over your jealousy and let me have a friend?" I demanded.

"Why can't you understand that I don't feel good about your relationship with her?"

"Mike, can you see where Amy is coming from?"

"Can't Amy see where I'm coming from?" I retorted.

At this point I was at my wits' end. I was pissed that Dorothy seemed to be taking your side and not mine. I was pissed that *you* couldn't just trust me. I was pissed that in order to make this work, I would have to give up another friend in my life like I did years ago with Heather.

"Mike, do you want to add anything else?" Dorothy inquired.

"No . . . no, I'm done," I said, with a much deeper meaning. These sessions would get us nowhere if I didn't have someone in my corner of this debate, someone that would listen to, and believe, my side of the story.

"Okay, would you like to schedule for next Tuesday?" You and I both agreed, and we left for home.

When we got home, I was exhausted. I turned on the TV and sat down in the lounge chair while you changed out of your work clothes. When you entered the living room, I made up my mind to tell you how I felt.

"Sweetie, I don't want to go back to her again."

You looked at me astonished and asked, "What? Why?"

"I feel that Dorothy is listening to your side, and not to mine! I feel like both of you are ganging up on me in there."

I could see you were pissed at this statement. "So, you just want to stop going?"

"I just don't feel like we're getting anywhere! I've never given you any reason to doubt my loyalty to you, but I feel that you do," I said, and then stated, "I don't want to lose Steph as a friend."

I could see your anger well up, so much so you left the room and went into your office. I could hear different sounds from the office as if you were throwing stuff around, and I hoped you weren't hurting yourself. I was about to get up to check when you came back into the living room.

"I think you should move out," you announced, and I could see tears rolling down your cheeks.

I was stunned. I really didn't think we were at a point where you wanted to get rid of me, but I guess I was wrong.

"Oh . . ." I uttered. "But, don't you love me?"

"Yes I do, but you obviously think more about Steph than you do me, so I think you should leave."

"It's not true . . . but if that's what will make you happy, I'll move out."

At this I stood up and approached you to hug you. You had your arms crossed but I hugged you anyway and said, "I love you Amy."

"I love you too," you said, uncrossing your arms to hug me back. But I could tell your mind was made up.

When we broke our embrace, you left the room for your office, and I sat down and cried. What had we just done? How would we live our lives without one another? Why couldn't we just be?

So, that was it. I spent the next week looking for apartments, thinking how stupid this all was. How stupid we were being.

Also, during that week, I never stopped telling you I loved you and how I wanted to always love you and always be with you. How I always wanted to be there to make the bed for you and make coffee for you and tuck you in at night. I truly never wanted us to be apart.

"How am I going to live without you?" you asked when I was tucking you in on the last night we were together.

"You don't have to," I replied as I hugged and kissed you before leaving the room.

That night I sat in the dark for a while, contemplating the situation. Thinking about how much I loved our life together. How you were the love of my life and I didn't want to live without you. I crawled into bed next to you, feeling your warmth, thinking these thoughts while I fell asleep.

The next morning I woke, and that's all I thought about: how we were — I was — letting something this special and amazing end. I was in a daze and moving slow. So slow you actually beat me out the door.

As you left, I hugged and kissed you, and told you I loved you.

"I love you too! Now hurry up or you'll be late for work!" you jested as I shut and locked the door behind you.

Instead of getting ready though, I moved to my lounge chair to think, and it didn't take me long to make up my mind. I picked up my cell phone and dialed your number.

When you answered, I said, "Amy, I was wrong. I don't want to move out . . . I don't want to lose you! I'm sorry for everything. I will end my friendship with Steph, if that's what it takes to keep you. Can we . . . can we give it another shot?"

I could hear you tear up on the other end of the phone as you said, "I would like that. I don't want to lose you either."

"I love you Amy, with all my heart."

"I lov—" you started, but then there was a huge bang and a second later the line went dead. I was used to calls dropping in and out, but this felt different.

I waited a few seconds, waiting for the line to reset, and I tried dialing your number again. The phone rang a few times, but then went to voice-mail, which I thought was weird. I don't ever remember having this kind of problem with your drive to work before, but maybe there was a problem with the cell tower. Maybe the bang was the cell tower having a power surge. I decided to not leave a voicemail and try one more time before I hit the road for work.

After about a minute this time, I tried again, and I hoped the delay would either allow you time to call back or you'd switch cell towers and I could get through. This time, however, it didn't ring at all. It simply went straight to voicemail. Not wanting to delay any longer, I grabbed my bag and left for work.

It was probably about fifteen or twenty minutes after I arrived at work when I got the call.

"This is Mike," I answered with my standard greeting.

"Is this Michael Samstag?" came a male voice from the other end of the line.

"Yes. Can I help you?"

"Michael, this is Officer Carlin from the Bath police department," replied the caller, and it took me a moment to acknowledge what was being said. "There's been an accident involving Amy Ferris. She listed you as her emergency contact, is that correct?"

"Yea . . . yes," I replied, bewildered. "Is . . . is she okay?"

"Mr. Samstag, Amy has been admitted to Akron General . . . do you know where that is?" the officer asked.

"No . . . I'm not sure . . . but I'll find it. Is she okay?" I inquired again.

There was a pause, and then the officer replied, "All I know is she was admitted to the hospital a few minutes ago, and they require you down there Mr. Samstag."

"Yes sir. I'm on my way" was all I could think to say before I hung up. I felt like I was in a fog, knowing I needed to move, but my brain wouldn't let me body break away.

Move it! I told myself and I snapped out of it. I told my boss I was leaving, and I hit the road after checking the location on my GPS.

I tried not to drive like a madman, using the cruise control as much as I could to make sure I wasn't breaking speed limits. I arrived at the hospital about thirty minutes later and ran straight to Emergency.

As I walked through the door, my legs felt like gelatin. But my brain kept telling my body to move. I approached the receptionist's desk and got her attention.

"I'm Mike Samstag. Here to see Amy Ferris?"

"Is she a patient sir?"

"I'm not sure. The police said I should come here."

The receptionist looked at her computer screen as she entered what I assumed was your name and then picked up the phone to contact someone.

When she hung up, she addressed me, "Mr. Samstag, can you come in the doors to your right?"

I nodded and entered the back room, where I was directed to a small waiting room. Obviously I was freaking out. I had no words, nothing I could ask or say that would get answered, and I knew that. So, I waited. After sitting for a few minutes, a man entered the room, closed the door, and sat down next to me.

"Mr. Samstag, I'm Ben Foster. I'm a social worker here at Akron General," he said as he folded his hands in his lap.

"Is Amy okay? Where is she?" I asked as I turned in my chair to face him.

"Mr. Samstag. Amy was involved in a severe car accident," he said. All I could do was nod.

"Amy had multiple fractures along with some damage to her spinal cord and brain," he continued, as my entire body went limp.

"When the EMTs arrived, Amy had stopped breathing, so they tried resuscitating her on site and in the ambulance, but the extent of the damage was too great."

He paused, unfolded his hands, and reached over to take mine trying to comfort me. "I'm sorry to be the bearer of this news."

"So . . . she's gone?" I asked, saying it the best way I could think.

"Yes sir," the social worker said, and then added, "I can only tell you she didn't suffer. I hope that you can find some comfort in that."

I didn't believe it. I couldn't believe it. I was just told that I would never see you again, that I'd never hear your voice or see you smile. I would never see *you* again.

I stayed at the hospital a little while longer while Mr. Foster tried to console me. He went on to say that someone had contacted your family with the news. It's too painful to go into everything else that happened while I was there, and it really doesn't matter.

When all was said and done, I made my way back to my car and sat for a bit. I didn't know where to go or what to do. I didn't want to go home to the empty house without you. I couldn't go back to work to be questioned and sympathized by my fellow employees. I just sat there until the tears came and went. And then, I moved on.

So that's it, my love. That is how I lost you.

As we discussed, I picked this spot here on Cape Cod for you because it was your favorite spot, our favorite spot, in view of the dunes and lighthouses, in view of the ocean and sunrise. *You're* the most beautiful spot on Earth. I hope you're happy here. You get to *live* here year-round now, like you always wanted, alive with every morning sun shining on the sea, alive with every moon sparkling in the midnight surf. Because, my love, you will always be alive in my heart.

And although I can't come here every month like I've have been, I do promise to keep coming here in the Fall - your favorite season - to visit and reminisce our times, both good and bad, and to celebrate your life. You deserve it. You gave me so much — so much.

Okay, enough tears. I'm leaving now, for the year this time. The colder winds are starting to blow in and almost all the leaves have left the trees. It won't be long now before the first snow falls and winter sets in.

While I'm away, please remember, like I remember, that I will always love you.

Diary: September 20

I think this will be my last entry in this diary.

I'm on the plane now, moving back home to Ohio. Back to be with family and friends. Back to the people who love me and care about me.

It was great living in the Cape like Amy and I always said we would. I will always love and cherish it, but I feel it's time to move on.

It was one year ago yesterday that my therapist suggested I start writing down my feelings. How I felt about Amy's death. It hasn't been easy at times, that's for sure. There were more than a few times along the way when I thought it would be better off to join her.

All in all, though, writing down my emotions did me a lot of good. It certainly improved my writing skills. See, I don't think I would have joked about this a year ago, or even six months ago.

More importantly, it helped remind me of her daily. All the fond memories. All our hopes and dreams. All that was good and pure in our relationship. In how special our love was . . . .. how special it still is.

And, not to be too religious, but I thank God every day for putting her on this Earth and bringing us together.

I also thank God that I found Beth. She has been good for me in so many ways. She's helped me realize I don't have to be alone, or be in sorrow, or to stop loving Amy to love her.

Amy was — is — the love of my life. But it doesn't mean I have to love only her. After all, we are all boats on an ocean, trying to keep a course through sun and storm, trying not to sink as we reach our final destination.

At this destination, I believe I will see Amy again, someday, in some sort of afterlife.

This I believe with my whole heart. And this belief will hold me, I think, as it holds everyone.

And I know, someday, when I join her at journey's end, that is when I'll truly be fine again.